Praise for Jeremy Page's

'Stunningly good. Captures the la
water-colourist's touch. His ear for Norfolk cadence is acute.
Rose Tremain

'Jeremy Page writes with feeling and intimacy. Whether he is describing wind, storm, mountain light or the rotten tang of estuarine mud, the charge of a stallion or the settling of a butterfly, his touch is poetic and sure.'
Helen Dunmore, *The Guardian*

'It was always on the cards that the best British shot at magic realism would emerge from the hallucinatory flatlands of East Anglia. Page's electrifying saga of family dysfunction glides from the bleakness of the Fens to the vast and ecstatic marshes of north Norfolk. You can smell every barn and barnacle.'
Richard Mabey, *The Week*

'A powerful new voice. Funny, flavoursome ... Page brilliantly evokes Norfolk's bleakness, the harsh round of the seasons.'
The Independent

'What Page has created out of sea and madness and blood is truly rich and strange, gorgeous in detailing and heartbreaking in its message. A book to savour.'
The Chicago Tribune

'Page is a pensive, sensitive writer ... seek it out; it won't lead you astray.'
The Washington Post

pale winter light

strange stories
by Jeremy Page

Jeremy Page

propolis

For Andrew,
because you saw it too

First published in 2025

by Propolis Books
The Book Hive,
53 London Street,
Norwich, NR2 1HL

Cover by Niki Medlik at **studio medlikova**
(original photograph by Jeremy Page)

Text design and typesetting by Ruth Rudd

A CIP record for this book
is available from the British Library

9781916905191

All photographs by Jeremy Page

Contents

Sight Unseen

The auction catalogue described the box as '*Sight Unseen: Various medical journals and equipment.*' He could see it on a shelf along the back wall of the warehouse – a large plastic crate with the lot number glued to the side. It was a cold, blustery November Tuesday, and hardly anyone had turned up. When it came to the sale there was no interest in the room and nothing on the internet. He bought it for the reserve price of £15 and, after the sale, got one of the porters to help him load it into the back of his car.

On the journey back home, he pulled into one of the deserted picnic sites on the heath, so he could take a look. Inside the crate was a collection of A4 leather-bound journals, some spotted with mould, and several folders of typewritten sheets tied with faded ribbon. Everything looked old, distinctly academic. On some of the official papers he saw one of the Cambridge colleges listed as an affiliate institution. Embossed on each of the journals was a typewritten name: Dr Henry Borg MD, MRCPsych. Even in the open air the crate smelt dusty, with a chemical scent he couldn't quite place. He flicked through some pages and saw they were filled with entries made in small scratchy handwriting. He read a title:

Tests of psychoactive agents and recorded effects on sensory perceptual neural structures. Challenge and sample results.

Beneath the journals was an assortment of glass equipment rolled in newspaper, a range of jars, and a few tin containers. He unwrapped one of the newspaper packages and discovered a laboratory condenser tube, cracked in several places. He wrapped it up again, noticing a tiny bead of blood where a shard had quickly cut him on the side of his thumb. No matter, he thought, suspecting not much of this equipment would make sense, but thrilled nonetheless by his purchase. He'd been lucky.

Arriving back at the house, he made the decision to hide the crate in his workshop in the garden. As he carried it past the veg patch he congratulated himself for being so sensible. Sylvie was a de-clutterer. She prided herself on living in simple, tidy spaces, organising cupboards so the taller objects were placed at the back. She had a dim view of someone else's discarded possessions, and buying an unseen lot at a county auction was the kind of thing she thought he didn't do anymore.

The workshop was at the far side of the garden. It was a rough building, converted from an old shed, the windows had a permanent film of cobwebs in the corners. Now it was cold, he tended to have an oil-fired radiator on all day, hot to touch, although the room was still too chilly for his feet and hands. But it was his space, and that counted for something. From the window he looked along the line of a hedge that separated his garden from the field, towards a row of willows by the stream, and the woodpile where he stacked logs. There, in the pale winter light, he noticed the fox was already in its preferred spot, curled up on top of the wood. The fox's head was tucked up neatly beneath a hind leg, a greasy sheen glowed across the tips of its fur. He sometimes thought he and the fox had many things in common; naturally solitary, passing their time in the garden, aware of each other, but always keeping a respectful distance.

That night, after Sylvie had gone to bed, he slipped out to the workshop and began to go through the crate more systematically. The journals contained notes forming an apparently unpublished thesis investigating psychoactive substances on neural pathways, particularly relating to the cerebrum, the parietal lobes, the limbic lobe, and with a specific study of the amygdala. The written language was academic, dense and baffling. Several experiments were listed, some of them crossed out in a rapid scribble of pen marks, suggesting great frustration, and perhaps a reason why the job lot had ended up in the auction house. It tended to be house clearances or bereavements if it was all bundled up in crates. Unwrapping the remainder of the newspaper packages, he found a largely useless collection of lab equipment. Clamps, rubber piping, and filthy-looking test tubes, many of them broken, and some with a residue of powder almost etched into the glass. The newspaper was dated from twenty years ago. Turning to the collection of jars he found a range of finely ground substances, mostly grey or dark brown, neatly labelled with Latin names or reference numbers.

One of the large tins from the bottom of the crate was heavier than the others, it tipped in his hand with the motion of a liquid. Unscrewing the lid he found the tin was cork-lined, containing a glass jar. He carefully slid the jar into his hand, and immediately saw the unmistakable shape of a brain, submerged in a cloudy grey-green liquid. He placed the jar carefully on his workbench, and watched as the brain floated softly to the bottom of the fluid, noticing the tightly wound patterns of curves and ridges. Where the brain touched the glass it appeared creamy white, but the rest of it was difficult to see, as it vanished into a murky shadow.

A couple of hours later he crept into bed alongside his wife, making careful movements so he didn't wake her. She'd only ask him what time it was, and he'd have no explanation for being up so late. He listened to her breathing, which didn't change its calm rhythm. His mind was spinning with the extraordinary discovery of the brain, and the weight of a secret that was exciting and startling. He'd bought a brain! A part of someone's body. It felt transgressive and barely legal and possibly something he needed to report. The brain was clearly human. He turned to his side, the usual route he took towards sleep, and knew that at some point tomorrow he'd be examining those journals and looking at the powders. He wouldn't be able to stop himself, he could think of nothing else. Outside, he heard the fox as it barked and yelped, pacing its territory through the night. Yes, you know about my secret life in the workshop, don't you, he thought, admiring the fox's independent spirit and reliable discretion. Hours spent in the workshop existed alongside the other parts of his life, but there was a recognisable division between them. Investigating a mystery, living a double life, he was gripped by it.

He and Sylvie had breakfast together although, as usual, she didn't sit down. He quietly stirred his coffee, making a point of taking his time, waiting until all the sugar was dissolved, while she hurriedly spread marmalade on her toast by the sink.

She kept looking at her watch, and was already wearing her comfortable shoes. A day of standing up, ahead of her.

'What's the plan?' she asked, while she scrolled through the emails on her mobile.

'Oh, today? Well – I have to sort out the workshop. And the veg patch.'

'Leaves need raking. And put a wash on, will you? Colours.'

'No problem.' She had a habit of filling his day, making sure he had a list to get through. It was fair enough. When he had nothing to do, he got a little cranky.

'You'll be OK?' she asked.

He smiled, blandly reassuring her, but it felt false to him. He tried not to think about the brain in the jar, his glorious secret, in case she somehow picked up on it.

'Keep busy,' she added.

'Always.'

She paused, taking stock of him, giving a semi-professional look that she often used with her clients. 'Are you going to change out of your dressing gown?'

'Sylvie – I'm not going to mope around all day.'

'Good.' She smiled, partly satisfied. He was two months into the sabbatical his work called *garden leave*. It was a gentle term, misleading and inaccurate, for the fact that he'd not been coping. He'd made mistakes, lost his temper too often, been taken aside several times before they decided he needed time off. 'Sorry I have to go,' she added. 'I've got patients all day.'

'So when are you back?'

'Five?' She looked at her watch again. It couldn't have changed much since she last checked. 'Maybe earlier if I can shunt appointments around.'

He took a sip of his coffee. He didn't fancy eating anything.

'Right,' she said, already sounding weary about the day ahead. 'I'll be off.'

He stood, kissed her on the cheek, then took her plate to the sink, demonstrating the kind of order the house would have today. She looked bothered, as though she was going to say more, but stopped herself. Then she said: 'Just remember, you're very special, and you should use this time well.'

She had the habit of coming back to the house because she'd forgotten something, so he waited a full fifteen minutes after her car had left before going to the workshop, still wearing his dressing gown. He arranged the journals into a neat stack on the desk, then began to go through them. He quickly got a gist of what they were about. Most of the entries related to various psychotropic substances, largely extracted from psilocybin-bearing fungi, and their possible effects on the brain. Various preparations and mixes were outlined alongside a series of experiments and procedures. A book of invoices and receipts suggested some of these fungi samples had been sourced from across Europe: in Italy, Slovakia and Poland, as well as across the British Isles. A detailed method was described where the fungi – arriving in dried form – was rigorously identified, before being stored in the dark at no higher than twenty degrees centigrade. When ready, they were ground by a mortar and pestle, then mixed with acetic acid in methanol. The liquid was shaken by a vortex of thirteen times gravity for an hour, before test tubes were spun in a centrifuge for ten minutes at eight hundred and fifty seven times gravity. The resulting suspensions were filtered using Eppendorf tubes, the remaining pellets were remixed with ethanol, ultra-filtered, then left as a powder. Some had been purged with nitrogen before being sealed in the jars.

By late morning he was fairly confident with many of the scientific terms, and had identified some of the specimens by their individual reference numbers, lining them up on his workbench alongside the brain in its jar. The powders looked unremarkable.

He lifted the brain and studied it closely, holding it up to the light coming in through the window. It floated softly from side to side as he tilted the jar, giving the brain an uncanny motion, as if someone was facing him, head on one side to be confrontational. With his finger, he touched where a label had been stuck to the base of the glass. He held the jar up and read the words: *This belongs to Dr Henry Borg.*

What did? he wondered. The jar? Or was it in fact the doctor's brain? He pushed the thought from his mind.

He Googled the doctor's name, but found nothing.

He stirred five grams of *liberty cap* extract into a cup of warm water. It smelt vegetative and darkly fungal, with a putty-grey scum that rose to the surface. Deliberately placing the drink next to the brain, he took an extra moment to consider. The garden was dull and featureless through the window. Recklessness was a thing of his youth, but he still remembered its allure at moments like this, when he had no one to ameliorate his more radical impulses. He took an explorative sip and sat back in his chair. It was stale and yeasty on his tongue, with a bitter aftertaste. He leant further back, relaxed, listening to his breathing and staring out through the window across the veg patch. He noticed no discernable effect, no change to his heartbeat. Guessing the powder was way too old to be potent he tried more, downing most of the drink and grimacing with the bitter taste. Perhaps some of the other powders might have had a longer shelf life he thought, deciding to unscrew other lids to take a careful sniff. Most had the same woody, fungal scent, and some had become solid and caulked in the base of the jars. This was disappointing, he thought, as he stared out into the gloomy garden, wondering whether he'd have to source these substances and try the complicated process of preparing them himself. Perhaps it was all a big waste of time.

After ten minutes he realised the things he'd been looking at through the window had changed. The woodpile, beneath the dropping branches of the willows, was levitating several feet off the ground. He stared, amazed. The logs were untangling with the fleshy aspect of discarded limbs. It was disturbing and fascinating and totally absorbing. Closer to the window he noticed the dense leaves of kale in the veg patch were beginning to inflate, with a partial breath. He watched them in a half-panic, as each stem became a dark brawny lung. Twelve stout shapes out there, breathing in and out, in synchronised motion. He pulled the blind down and quickly tidied up the bench, trying to concentrate on establishing an order, before leaving the workshop to return to the house. He refused to look back at the garden, afraid the bushes would be shuffling towards him. Take it easy, he thought. Deep breaths. But inside doing the laundry, putting the clothes in to wash, he realised the washing machine had a surprisingly doughy, wondrous appearance. It sat heavily on the floor, sad faced and resigned: a tragic and lonely machine. He lay his hand on it, full of compassion. However, itching for his attention was the cordless drill lying nearby, and it now seemed filled with a sparky sense of happy self-belief. Like a puppy, wanting to show off its tail. How strange. And then he had a need to run his hand along the wallpaper, and as he did the entire wall felt pliable and uncertain, holding back a secretive world he'd never quite noticed before.

At dinner with Sylvie he began to feel less peculiar. The patterns on his plate gradually stopped inching around the rim, like slowly turning wheels, the pasta he'd made had stopped wriggling, and was now thankfully resembling linguine. Luckily, Sylvie was preoccupied by her long day crossing and recrossing the county, trying to fit in all her physiotherapy appointments. The clients either had nothing to say or wouldn't stop talking. It was a familiar complaint. She was particularly annoyed about an old man called Mr Jelf, who'd kept her waiting in her car for a full half hour, before arriving back at the house without apologising. He listened to his wife, sympathetic, but couldn't stop thinking about the experiment he'd done, and the revelatory perspective it had given him. The house had seemed a wondrous living entity, full of surprises. Textures had grown significant, suggesting subtle comparisons between things he'd never associated before, as though a veil had been partially lifted. There was something, tantalisingly beyond reach, but only just, that he needed to understand.

He waited until Sylvie went to bed, before going back to the workshop. Turning to one of the experiments, he followed the complicated preparation of mixing a ratio of two separate powders into an infusion: *Psilocybe cyanescens (concentrate)* and *Gymnopilus junonius*, which also had *Laughing Jim* handwritten in brackets on the label.

After drinking it, he decided to follow a further part of the experiment, where it suggested the patient gazed at specific images – in this case several black and white photographs tucked into the journal: a dog with bared teeth, biting through a wooden partition; a picture of an old woman walking down a country road, head bowed, eyes glinting up; black ants, crawling across a tabletop. The infusion tasted terrible. He nearly gagged. Knocking it back, he decided to follow it with a bit of the liberty cap, too, because he felt it was something he could at least trust.

Within a few minutes his vision started to pitch from side to side. Nausea rose in him, and he was forced to hold onto the desk as firmly as he could. But even while he was doing this, he couldn't stop himself looking up at the ceiling, where a spill of light was beginning to stream down towards him. Tendrils of sparkling colours extended, dripping softly, as fine as thread. He looked in wonder as the patterns settled across the desk and down his arms, shimmering with a living quality he didn't want to disturb. The reds and yellows were sleeping, they shouldn't be roused, because beneath them he sensed a layer that was dangerous and mistrustful. He stretched his fingers into the light, guiding the colours this way and that, watching them react to his skin with a quivering glimmer. Then, as he moved his arms, the drips of light began to shed their vibrancy, and he saw his hands had turned grey and lifeless as the hidden layer rose up around him like a thick liquid shadow. He looked up towards the roof, anxious, but the stream of colour had already sealed itself off. In its place was a dark rent in the wood that he thought he could climb through if it grew any darker.

He stood, abrupt and unsteady, wanting to get away from the unease that was now coming for him, but all he saw was the brain, stuck inside the jar, and now it was drifting in the liquid with a subtle trembling motion, pressing anxiously against the side of the glass. He watched in horror as a deep rooted pulse shot through the flesh, followed by another. A sporadic heartbeat.

He reeled back, swaying, then ran to the house that now appeared larger and darker than he remembered. Inside, he discovered new dimensions to the shadows – a depth to the corridor that he'd never noticed before, and a staircase where each step felt spongy, with a pattern of wood grain that swirled into miniature eyes, collecting around his feet. The house was alien and tinged with ugly menace. He took a deep breath and entered his bedroom. He approached the bed, where the duvet was now crawling with life. Patterns overlapped and readjusted as he came closer. Watchful and sinister. And Sylvie, turned away from him, but with hair that was like twists of sharp wire, and the nape of her neck now dry and scaly-skinned.

After a sleep that was thick and dreamless, he woke full of purpose. The brain must go. Last night had been a terrible mistake. He'd been irresponsible. And the sight of that grey flesh pulsing with life kept returning to him, unwanted and without any loss of just how terrifying it had been. But how to get rid of it? It was, after all, part of a body. Did it have to be taken to a police station, or a hospital? It couldn't go in the landfill, surely. No. He drank a strong black coffee, deciding.

After Sylvie went into her home office, he knew what he should do. In the workshop, he began by reading the experiment again and, when he turned the page, he saw with dismay that the experiment had continued before coming to an abrupt halt, with a rapid scrawl of pen lines obliterating the last few sentences.

Without pausing, in case he reconsidered, he picked up the brain jar and took it to the far end of the veg patch, to an area of scrubby dirt where no one went, where nothing in particular ever grew. He dug a hole with a trowel as deep as he could before hitting a tangle of roots, checked Sylvie wasn't anywhere near, then opened the jar. A pungent smell of formaldehyde rose up, and through the liquid he could see the top of the brain bobbing against the surface. He tipped the jar to one side and the brain slipped out with a sickening gush, filling the hole like it was the shapeless, congealed fat of a Sunday roast.

That's it, he thought, quickly packing the soil into the hole, feeling instant relief as he returned to the house. He scrubbed his hands clean, changed his shirt, and knocked politely on the door to Sylvie's home office.

'Hi,' he said. 'You busy?'

'It's manageable.'

'I thought I might take you out. Let's go out for coffee?'

'I'm working today.'

'I know. But it's not that crazy. Is it?'

He grinned, trying not to think about what he'd just done, which was *really* crazy: digging a hole with a trowel and burying a human brain in the garden.

'What's so funny?' she asked.

A squishy brain, in the soil!

'Like we used to?' he said.

She sat back in her chair, taking off the headset she used for online calls. She looked at him with curiosity, an expression that lingered, and he felt unable to hide any of his many secrets.

'You're lucky,' she said, 'it turns out I've had a cancellation.'

They had afternoon tea and cake at a café they hadn't visited in several years, and he asked her patiently about the trials with her job, trying not to picture how, just a couple of hours ago, he'd been pressing his foot on the freshly turned soil, wondering whether part of the man's brain might squirt out around his boot. He felt indecent, marvellously shifty, almost murderous. He wanted to make mad boasts about just how weird his last couple of days had been. Multicoloured lights dripping down through gaps in the ceiling, and a pulse of life shooting through the preserved flesh of a brain. Sheer relief to be beyond it made him over-talk, and Sylvie seemed perplexed by the sudden shift in his mood. She looked at him with a hint of suspicion. When she went to the toilet, he took a moment to collect himself, then stirred half a teaspoon of liberty cap powder into his afternoon blend to calm himself down. Why not, he thought, feeling a kinship towards the mixture, remembering the enjoyable sight of the woodpile beginning to levitate under the shadows of the willows.

They spent the evening watching TV, side by side on the sofa. He was relaxed, glad he'd dabbled with the medical equipment, but equally glad he'd discovered his own limit with illicit substances. It was important to know what you would and wouldn't do in life. He was in control, mostly, although he couldn't quite follow what he was watching on TV, and at one point one of the actors seemed to turn towards him, extending a long snakelike arm that pierced the screen and began to emerge a few inches into the room. *Wow*, he said, jolting with fear, and immediately realised Sylvie was looking at him with concern.

'Are you OK?' she asked. 'You fell asleep.'

*

Next morning, he went onto the auction house's website and filled in an online form. *Miscellaneous scientific equipment, some in good order*, he wrote. *No reserve.* He clicked submit, then went to the workshop to pack up the crate, glad he'd made this decision, but slightly bothered by the fact he might be passing on these alarming concoctions to someone else. Nonetheless, he wrapped the jars and the unbroken glassware, then placed them carefully with the journals laid on top. He could at least be neat about it. When it was all ready he wandered out into the garden and did some light weeding in the veg patch, relieved that the fat leaves of dark green kale were no longer the half-animated lungs he'd seen the other night. The birds were singing; the air was fresh. This would do him good. Activity, at his own pace. Garden leave. Embrace it. But as he worked his way to the end of the row, he abruptly stopped, suddenly hot with panic: the ground where he'd buried the brain had been disturbed. Something had dug into the freshly packed soil. He rushed over and saw the unmistakable signs that the fox had scratched out the hole. The brain was gone.

Almost as if he'd conjured it, he saw the fox emerge from behind the woodpile, low slung, moving uncertainly, with its head hanging slightly to one side. He watched it, anxious, as the animal leant against the logs, a slight tremble in its hind legs. Its mouth was moving as if something was stuck there, between its teeth. The fox appeared to take a deep breath, then raised its neck and did something it had never done before: it looked directly at him.

He stayed in the house all day, but at several points he found himself hiding by the windows, each time spying on the fox as it paced uncertainly round the perimeter of the garden. It knew it was being watched, and kept staring at him with an unflinching focus. Sometimes a twitch of muscle flicked across its side, or it broke away from its stare to drag its nose through the grass, before shaking its head. He'd never seen the fox behave like this before.

Feeling under siege, he went to bed early, claiming to have a migraine. He lay in bed, listening to the fox making a high-pitched yelping as it continued to pace around the garden. He breathed deeply, trying to calm himself. Sylvie was going away for the weekend to visit her parents, and he was afraid to be left here, alone. He would pull the curtains closed, he decided. Limit his time outside, keep a broom handle with him in case the fox became aggressive. Four more months and he'd have to go back to work. He didn't think he'd manage it. He continued to breathe deeply, counting, trying to empty his mind. Sometime in the middle of the night he heard the fox screaming, loud and intense, below his bedroom window. He wasn't entirely sure whether he was awake or not, or whether this was happening in some confusing part of a dream he was now having, but he walked silently towards the window as the fox continued to scream up from below. But when he pulled the curtain to one side and looked down at the garden, he didn't see the fox. Instead, in the middle of the darkly shadowed lawn he saw the shape of a man, yelping with pain, clutching his head with both hands.

In the morning he dropped Sylvie at the train station, then walked quickly back to the car trying to focus on one thing at a time. She'd been breezy, trying to raise his mood, but knew something was wrong with him. It's only one night, she said, as if she knew there was a limit to how much time he could spend on his own. She was probably right. Things have to change, he said, out loud, clipping in the safety belt, knowing what he now had to do. Twenty minutes later he was at the agricultural supply shop on the industrial estate, where he picked up a heavy-duty wire snare. *Medium mammal* was written on the label alongside silhouettes of a badger, hare and fox. Back at the house he quickly began to set the trap near the wood pile, making a noose of the wire about eight inches off the ground, connected to a peg that he hammered deep into the soil. The snare was set over a faint track he saw in the foliage, and he bent some of the plants towards it, to encourage the fox along its path. He wore a pair of marigold gloves to mask any scent. At lunchtime, from his workshop window, he saw the fox trotting through that area of the garden, shaking its head rapidly, pausing to scratch at an area behind one of its ears. The fox looked ill. Agitated and alert. Easily a match for any rudimentary attempt to catch it. He pulled the blind down and went in to the house, locking the door behind him, deciding to lie on the sofa to try and shift the headache that was growing. A sense of unresolved issues began to rise. Problems. An unsettled future. Time that was shapeless and lacking the certainty that he'd once known. He held the palms of his hands over his eyes, unable to trust himself anymore, and listened with a new sense of alarm as he heard the fox, now suddenly yelping in pain.

When he approached the woodpile, he saw the fox flattened to the ground, with the snare buried deep into the fur behind its head. The animal looked wildly at him, instinctive and motionless. Its eye was bloodshot, rimmed with white, staring at him with intent. As he stepped closer the animal launched into the air, but was jolted back by the wire. It fell on the ground, twisted and awkward. Panting rapidly, it snarled, viciously curling its lip to expose a row of sharp teeth. This close, the fox looked strong, mad, unpredictable. Quickly, he went up to the loft and pulled out one of the old sleeping bags from among the camping equipment. He bent a piece of hardboard into the back of the car, making a makeshift partition, then put on his heaviest pair of gardening gloves.

He went at the fox quickly, smothering it with the unzipped sleeping bag. The animal immediately thrashed beneath him, with wild ferocity. The nylon ripped as the claws tore into it. He tried to get his knee across the shape of the fox, but it was quickly writhing into new positions, snapping at the fabric. He touched the harsh shape of the wire snare and began to work it loose, hearing himself crying out with the sheer panic of what he was doing as, in his hands, the material of the sleeping bag kept slipping, impossible to grip. Then the fox stopped moving as it re-gathered strength. The snare pulled free, in his hands. He took the chance, scooping up the bag and the animal and rushing to the open back of the car. He threw the bundle in and slammed the hatch down as the fox threw itself at the glass, suddenly free. It snarled against the window, baring pointed teeth and flashing wild white eyes, misting the glass, then hurled itself around the boot space, leaping up at the hardboard partition.

Sweating, hot, shaking with effort, he got into the car and

immediately turned the ignition. The fox threw itself at the hardboard again, getting a long dirty paw through one of the gaps down the side. Should have spent more time with that, he realised, angry that he'd rushed the preparation. The fox smelt terrible. Musty and hormonal. He drove as fast as he could, choosing the quieter country lanes where he wouldn't encounter anyone, as the fox started to bite through the top of the hardboard. He turned the rear-view mirror to see what was going on, and saw its teeth nibbling away at the wood with manic energy. Oh god, what an awful week, he thought. Across the dashboard and springing up at the windscreen were several fleas. He immediately felt itchy and afraid. He had decided on a forest ten miles away but knew he'd never get that far. The fox would be through the hardboard in a matter of minutes. Instead, he saw a copse appearing beyond one of the fields, and he turned off onto a grassy lane, approaching it. Bumping the car fast along the track he skidded to a halt at the edge of the wood, where the grass was long and muddy, and almost fell out of the door in his rush to escape. He slammed it shut and crawled away a few feet as the fox vanished beneath the level of the rear window.

He waited, gathering his breath, too far into a plan to do anything other than go through with it. The car would have to be hosed down, somehow. His whole day was going to be taken up with this thing.

Approaching the vehicle, he unclicked the boot, and stepped back as the hatchback rose quietly into the air. The fox was huddled into one of the corners, looking small and afraid. He stepped back a few paces, taking his time, curiously calm. The fox shifted, sniffed the air, then sat up. It looked directly at him, defiant and focused.

'Get out,' he said. 'Go on you bastard. Get out.'

The fox didn't move. It lay down, staring at him with an expression that felt as if a judgement was being made. It's just a fox, he reminded himself, but knew that the fox had changed. Infected. Altered. Something terrible and unknowable had happened. The fox had become something else.

'Please. Get out,' he said.

The fox shook a little, and again he saw a muscle twitching deep in its flank. Then, slowly, it inched forward, watching him with a human comprehension in its eyes: malice and intention. It maintained its glare, before slipping out of the boot onto the ground, and trotting quietly into a patch of long grass.

He waited, breathless, before suddenly rushing to the car, pulling the sleeping bag out and dumping it near the hedge, slamming the boot shut and jumping into the driver's seat. He turned the car around and drove quietly back down the track, looking in the rear view mirror at the wood as it receded. At the junction with the road he stopped, and saw the unmistakable shape of the fox beginning to trot along the path, its head slung low. He turned onto the road and accelerated, but after a few hundred yards he slowed down and stopped once more. Looking into the mirror he saw the fox turn onto the road, coming in his direction.

'Go away,' he said, under his breath, as the fox trotted closer. He drove forward, approaching a junction were he made a right turn. A little way beyond the junction he came to a halt again. He knew what was going to happen. A few seconds later the fox turned onto the same road, neither faster nor slower than it had been. It trotted towards him, relentless, following, coming home.

Twin

Rae stood in the corner of the day room, reeling with the news. She started to breathe slower, calming herself, while she looked at a handwritten menu of the lunch the residents would be eating. Lamb stew. Seasonal vegetables. Apple crumble and custard. She took her time, waiting until she felt steadier, then stepped towards the window. The care home had plenty of these non-spaces where someone could just stand and be upset. It was as if they'd been purposefully designed for just that. Outside, there were planters filled with herbs and scented flowers, raised so they could be touched from the height of a wheelchair. She paused. This revelation would take time for her to process.

She was at the school by mid-morning, ready for her timetable of music lessons. Sitting quietly by the piano, she listened as one of the kids laboured their way up and down the keys, practicing the scales. The child played slowly, meticulously, and sat bolt upright on the little stool. At the end of the exercise Rae said, 'once more,' then immediately felt sympathy for the child, who was trying so hard to do it properly. As the practice continued, Rae reflected about what her father had told her that morning. Sitting in his favourite easy chair in the care home, he'd chosen his time to make his announcement, then watched her calmly for her reaction.

She'd not liked the intensity of his gaze. 'Why are you telling me this now?' she'd asked, instantly on the verge of tears.

'You have a right to know.'

'But why now?'

'I'm old.'

She knew that he'd clam up if she cried, it was one of his things. Moments of openness, then whole weeks of being distant. 'And did you consider that I might not want to know this?' she blurted out.

He nodded, quietly, then looked away from her. And that was when she'd burst out of the room, too upset to continue.

The girl was sitting quietly at the piano, her hands resting on her lap, politely.

'That's lovely, Eve,' Rae said. 'Shall we try the first piece?'

As the girl began to play the tune, haltingly, Rae realised that, this morning, her life had changed in an instant. Stark, and irreversible. Her father had told her that when she was born, thirty-five years ago, she had in fact been one of two children. But only Rae had survived.

Over lunch, which was a sandwich in the small park where the kids did their summer term sports day, she couldn't stop thinking about all the questions she needed to ask. Waves of panic and upset kept rising in her, making it difficult for her to swallow her food, and uppermost in her mind was why her own mother had never revealed the truth about her birth. Yet this loss, this huge absence, must have been something she'd known every day of her life. She sensed a headache growing, so reached into her bag and found a couple of paracetamol. Not just the usual headache this time, but a persistent stab of pain above the eyes. Was her father telling her this because he was the only parent left, and had made the decision himself, or had this been an arrangement her parents had agreed together? A tacit arrangement that, one day, whoever remained, would have the duty to tell Rae the truth?

She decided it was best to stay busy, so she walked back to the school and prepared the room for the afternoon's music classes. The school concert was in two days time, and the lessons were all geared around the upcoming performance. She found herself fiddling with the equipment, adjusting the music stands, getting the scores in order, but knew she was deliberately trying to distract herself. Her mood lifted for the first few lessons, but at three o'clock, just as she was about to finish, she remembered her last lesson was with Joel and Jed. Twins.

For the first time she realised that she was once one of a pair of twins herself, and as the boys came in, with Joel walking immediately to the piano while his brother opened up his guitar case, she looked at them with poorly disguised fascination. They seemed to communicate intuitively, not looking at each other, but at all times knowing instinctively what the other was doing. Today, Jed adjusted his hold on the guitar, then rested his thumb on the E string at exactly the same moment that Joel arranged his hands on the keyboard, his index finger raised above the opening key.

'Are you ready?' Rae asked, and both boys nodded without enthusiasm. Joel and Jed were identical twins, and sometimes Rae was only certain which one was which when they sat at their instruments. In fact, in the first few weeks of lessons they had once played a trick on her, with Jed sitting at the piano as Joel strolled in with the guitar. She hadn't noticed, which made the boys laugh, satisfied with their prank, laying down the possibility that they could repeat it any time they liked. She'd recovered by telling them she would've noticed once they started playing the instruments, but the die had been cast. They had the upper hand on her.

Oddly, Joel and Jed performed badly together. Joel would thump the rhythm on the piano, pushing the tempo, bullying his brother to keep up, and Jed would react by abruptly stopping, making a fuss of composing his fingers on the frets, suggesting he was wanting to get it right. It was a constant battle between them.

Today, the piece kept breaking down, so Rae decided to stop them.

'How are you, boys? How's your week been?' she asked. They turned to her in unison. It was almost comic synchronisation.

'Don't know,' Jed said. 'Same as always.'

'Yeah,' Joel added. Joel's name was always listed first, and she assumed he was the slightly older twin, but it was Jed who always spoke first.

'That was an odd question to ask, Miss,' Jed added. Both boys looked at her, unblinking, pale eyed. Rae began to blush, faced with a scrutiny that seemed to latch onto something that she was showing.

'Just making conversation,' she replied, fiddling with her reading glasses to divert attention. 'From the top then, shall we?'

Tom was due to come over that evening, so when Rae got back to her flat she spent an hour tidying up. Continuing the process of keeping busy. It made her energised and capable. She cleared the kitchen, wiped the counter tops, plumped up the cushions on the sofa, then gathered her laundry and shoved it in the airing cupboard. Jobs done, she laid out a choice of takeaway menus on the table, like a fan, with her preferred sushi place on top, then sat on the sofa to go through emails. She didn't know that much about Tom, yet. He was a PE teacher at one of the primaries she used to teach at and, if she was being truly honest, was probably working his way through all the single female staff, although he'd never admit that, and was also too likeable to have a bad reputation stick to him. He was probably a curry guy, she thought. She answered some emails about payments for lessons and booking exam dates then, mid-sentence, she suddenly stopped typing. In the corner of her eye she saw – on the sofa – one of the cushions flattening, forming a shallow dished shape as if a weight was sitting there. She held her breath, fixing her attention on the laptop in front of her until all the movement stopped. A definite impression in the cushion, near her on the sofa. If she reached out her hand she would be able to touch that place. Gradually, she turned towards it and saw she was mistaken. The cushion was plumped and full, just as she'd left it.

Still, she felt an odd sensation that she'd not been entirely alone. And as she considered it, she realised that something had always walked alongside her. She was so used to this awareness that it hadn't been properly noticed for years. When she sat at a table, any table, she always wanted to keep an empty space by her side. If she glanced at a nearby seat on a bus or a train, she felt it had a loaded quality. A space that shouldn't be disturbed. Sometimes, at night, she had a feeling that her breath was just half a breath. That when she exhaled there was something incomplete and expectant in the moment that followed. She thought further. There had been an occasion recently, when Tom had made her laugh, and at that moment her happiness had had an extra resonance, almost like an echo. Yes, that had been strange. And the time last week when she touched a pan that had just come out of the oven: when she'd run her hand under cold water, she'd known the pain was not only hers to have.

Rae noticed her fingers trembling as she considered the implication of what all this might mean. She tried to push the thoughts away. Be rational, she said, out loud. You've had a big day. You've had a shock. There's no need to react like this. But then she thought about the stabbing headache she'd had in the park at lunchtime, and knew that it had been strange, too. There had been times, countless times, when she'd experienced a peculiar ache in some part of her body and known that it would quickly vanish, because it had no proper source. And she knew other people, the vast majority of other people, had no understanding of this.

When Tom arrived she decided not to tell him anything. She didn't want to recount what her father had revealed to her that morning, or admit her daily awareness that she, in fact, never felt entirely alone. They ordered a curry. When they ate, she smiled sweetly and privately at the spare seat that was also tucked in on the other side of the table. Hello, she thought, to herself. Tom didn't notice. He had his own issues. On the rebound, for a starter, she knew that, and probably already slightly struggling that he was seeing a music teacher ten years older than he was. It didn't sound very appealing when she thought about it. Even though, when Tom wasn't wearing his tracksuit, he dressed a bit like a middle-aged guy, himself. It was odd. Still, he wolfed down the curry, then said he'd like to stay over, which wasn't something she'd expected.

In the middle of the night she woke, startled, pulling herself out of a dream where a voice had spoken quietly, but urgently, in her ear. She held her breath, chasing images that eluded her, half-formed, leaving only a fleeting trace. In the dream she'd been surrounded by a sense of comfort and love, but it had quickly been replaced by a vague threat, of something that was near and beyond her understanding. She listened to the sounds of the room. Tom, deeply asleep, snoring. His big shoulders and strong legs, a strange presence in her bed. From the kitchen, the quiet whirring of the fridge. In the street outside, the sound of cars occasionally passing at the junction. It sounded like it was very early, and had been raining. Nothing else. She turned onto her side, listening to her own breath, glad that Tom had stayed, and wondering whether he'd want a full English for breakfast.

Before her alarm went off, she was aware of commotion in the room, and woke to see Tom sitting on the edge of the bed, facing away from her. He seemed agitated. She reached out and gently touched her finger against his bare leg.

'What the hell's going on?' he said, angrily.

She propped herself on an elbow.

'Tom?' she whispered.

He turned towards her and she gasped with shock. His face was covered with scratches. Deep, red scratches across his cheeks and forehead.

'Oh god, Tom – what's happened?'

He stared at her, grasping to make sense of it. And not hiding a look of accusation.

'Heh – that's nothing to do with me –' she said.

'– how can I go to work like this?'

'How did it happen?'

'You tell me.'

She sat up, gathering the duvet up to her neck.

'I don't understand, Tom. I really don't,' she said. The scratches were sore and livid. She knew she was about to cry and wished she had a plausible explanation. She wanted to return to a moment from the night before, when he'd kissed her on the sofa and suggested they go to the bedroom.

Tom started to put on his clothes, and she knew he was already making mental checks not to leave any of his stuff in the flat. She thought about saying *don't go*, but knew it would sound like a cliché, and weak. Instead, she watched him gather his things, wondering how he'd say it: how he'd break up with her.

When he'd fully dressed, he slipped his mobile into his jeans pocket, then sat on the end of the bed with his back to her. He wound his charger cable up, slowly and precisely before, surprisingly, placing his hand on her ankle. He gave her foot a gentle squeeze, affectionately, before abruptly getting up and leaving the room.

She went after him, not knowing what to say, but knowing it shouldn't end like this. He was already by the front door, putting on his trainers. She crouched by him and gently kissed his cheek, trying to avoid touching one of the scratches. It looked painful, and a tiny bead of blood had dried where the skin had torn. Slowly, without saying anything, she led him into the bathroom, then guided him to sit on the seat of the toilet. She opened up her first aid bag and found a tube of antiseptic cream.

'Let me do this,' she said, quiet and insistent.

He let her, resigned to it. Perching against the rim of the bath, she put a tiny bit of the cream on a corner of lint, then began to dab the wounds, aware of his sad eyed expression that looked through her, beyond her.

'I'll say I fell off my bike,' he said.

After he left, Rae rushed to the kitchen window, and saw Tom unchaining his bike from the railings in the courtyard. He swung his leg over the saddle and powered off down the street, not looking back once.

She cancelled a morning lesson, claiming to have a migraine, and with her diary free she considered going to see her father again, to ask more questions. But a whirlpool of upset, confusion and its aftermath surrounded her. She wanted time to work things through. Her father's silences and inability to engage with emotion was the last thing she needed. Instead, she took a long shower, hanging her head in the flow and letting the water run as hot as she could take it. Tom would be halfway to work by now, she thought. He was probably picking up a bacon roll from a café. Preparing his story about what had happened to his face. And making a decision about what to say if she called him. Or what not to say. Would he even answer?

She felt miserable. Hanging her head in the shower seemed a good place to cry, she thought. There'd been too many men over the last couple of years. Each new relationship began to encounter a residual echo of a previous failure, and each one of them had managed to find their own route to get away from her. She wondered what it was that signalled an alarm to all these different men, however carefully she tried to make fresh starts. Men must be instinctive, after all, she thought. They certainly acted in similar ways. Tom wasn't the first to have chained his bike to that particular railing. Men liked to think they were unique, but their behaviour was uncannily similar. They all chose the same railing, pointing their bikes towards the open road rather than towards her door. They always checked their mobiles before walking across the courtyard, loose limbed, expectant, preening, before pressing her buzzer.

When she stepped out from the shower the air in the bathroom was full of steam. She approached the mirror, about to wipe it clear with the palm of her hand. But she stopped herself, cautious of what she might see in it. It was suddenly apparent that she didn't want to see a reflection of the space that surrounded her.

Throughout her flat, she decided to cover the mirrors, hanging thin pieces of material over the glass so she wouldn't be able to see herself, or anything else. It seemed an improvement, and for once the flat felt entirely hers. A neutral space. She sat on the sofa and thought about the strange moment with the cushion, and almost chided herself for being so ridiculously over-sensitive. She picked up the cushion and examined it, turning it over in her hands. Normal. Without significance. What more could be said? She chucked it back where it belonged and applied the same attitude to the chair tucked in at the side of the kitchen table. She'd actually said hello to it, to its sense of presence, yesterday. How irrational was that?

She knew it was a mistake to have cancelled her morning lesson. Yesterday was a day of unravelling and hurt, it was no wonder she'd been so acutely aware of a presence alongside her. She'd been unsettled and lonely. It was natural to reach out for some semblance of company. But today could be different. It could be about repair and reassurance. She phoned the woman who'd signed up for piano tutorials and said she could do the session after all, later in the afternoon. It was good to populate the diary again. It gave shape to the day.

At three o'clock she drove to give her lesson. It was a large house with a beautiful garden. The woman she taught was married to a highly paid lawyer. The kitchen always smelt good, with a mix of fresh cut flowers and roasted coffee. Some people's lives just had that air about them – effortlessly arranged, settled, with an untroubled path rolling out before them. Rae gathered her things and started to walk up to the house, crossing the lawn towards the front door. A large tree overhung her, underneath it the grass was still wet from the overnight rain. As she passed, she noticed, in the side of her vision, a line of footprints appearing. Gentle imprints, in the damp grass, emerging almost in step with hers. Rae stopped, dry-mouthed and acutely aware. From the corner of her eye she saw a final footprint pressing slowly into the grass, as if someone was trying to move without being seen. Rae slowly turned towards them. She immediately saw the grass was entirely untouched. Each blade, fresh and undisturbed, glistening with the rain.

The lesson wasn't as she'd expected it. The lawyer's wife sat awkwardly on the piano stool, bashing out Chopin with no feeling, and broke away from playing when she received a text on her mobile. She read the text, looked at Rae without apology, then suggested they have a cup of tea together. Moving next door to the beautifully designed kitchen, with its modern extension overlooking a back garden that was as equally large and manicured, the lawyer's wife suggested they shouldn't have any more lessons. Rae was caught totally by surprise.

'Have you decided not to learn anymore?' Rae asked.

'It's not that,' the woman said, with a tight smile. Rae waited, confused. It surely wasn't an issue of money. The woman continued: 'I don't think you're the right teacher for me.'

Rae didn't know how to react. The woman regarded her with an air of sympathy. It was patronising.

'You're a bit unreliable, Rae. Like this morning, saying you had a migraine, then calling me up again to say it had gone. It's not the way to do things.'

'I did have a migraine.'

'I'm not doubting that. But I have a packed diary, too. I can't just change things around. It's not the first time it's happened.'

Rae nodded, feeling told off by a woman whose life was more organised and sorted than her own. It was strange how these differences emerged in life. She wanted to say what she really thought: that the woman played terribly, and would never play well, because she was only trying to impress other people. You felt music in your bones, or you didn't, it was that simple.

'I've really enjoyed our lessons, thank you,' the woman added, pouring her tea down the sink without drinking it, and giving Rae an icy smile that looked like it had been practiced in a mirror. Her mobile pinged again. Rae thought it was best to leave quickly.

Instead of going home, she drove to Heron Court, her father's care home. She didn't want to see him while she was so angry, but knew she was impatient for answers. However, after signing in and walking to the end of the residential wing, she discovered his room was empty. The bed was made with the sheets turned over but there was no sign of him. She stood, poised, wondering whether it would feel like this, on the day that would inevitably arrive, when she would come to clear away his possessions. To stand here and be faced with his absence. The room was already full of what it would deliver, in the future. Emptiness. Not even the smell of him remaining, because old age had already taken that away. Yet his absence was powerful and strange, she gravitated towards the few photos that her father had reluctantly allowed to be displayed in his room. Specifically, a photo of her as a young girl, on holiday with both parents. A stony beach somewhere in the West Country, with her mother crouching down to put an arm around her waist, her father standing a little to one side. Rae's mother had died five years ago and, here, she searched in her mother's expression, now reading in it a great deal of silence; a hidden pain that had never been revealed. And then Rae looked at the little gap that was hardly noticeable in the photo, making her father stand apart from the rest of them. It was a gap small enough for a child, similar in size as herself, to fit in.

She found her father in the conservatory extension to the day room, his wheelchair had been angled to face the garden. His preferred option. Seeing him like this, isolated, prone – with the brakes clamped shut against the wheels just in case he rolled somewhere – made her soften towards him. There wasn't much left of her anger, and she was glad about that. She rested her hand delicately on his shoulder in case he was asleep. He looked up at her, grey-eyed, a little vague. This time in the afternoon, just before their evening meal, was often the time when he was most gentle. In the mornings he was angry, then grew frustrated during the day, but by late afternoon the fight was largely out of him.

Rae sat on a broad window shelf by his side, after making space for herself, while a caterer wheeled a noisy trolley through the room. There was a photo of a sunset next to her on the window, with 'peaceful days' written across it. She shoved it away, hoping the gesture might also get a bit of approval from him. He raised his eyebrows and a flicker of a smile played across his lips, before he started to chew on something.

'Are you eating?' she asked.

He opened his mouth and she saw the glossy red lozenge of a boiled sweet on his tongue. 'They don't allow it,' he said, with satisfaction. Rae smiled with the sense that her father had his ways of getting round the systems. Contraband boiled sweets, from some unknown source. His life was now peppered with these minor victories. For a moment she was intensely relieved, that her father's rebellious spirit had never quite faded. She was where she belonged, sharing a moment with the last remaining part of her family. But the feeling didn't last. The rollercoaster of her thoughts over the last twenty-four hours demanded attention – their conversation yesterday felt like a residual charge between them, now.

'I've been thinking about it, of course,' she said. Her father faced her, not quite looking in her eyes. He clearly knew she'd be coming back with questions.

'I got upset yesterday. I'm sorry,' she said.

'It's understandable.'

Rae took a breath, not quite knowing how to coax an openness in him. She decided to be direct. It's what her mother used to do, and it often worked. 'But I need to know more, Dad. I need to know what happened.'

'It's a long time ago, Rae.'

'I realise that. And I don't want to upset you. Of course I don't. But you're the only one that can tell me.'

He acquiesced, tight lipped. She could tell he was weighing it up, and suspected this might be her only chance to hear the truth. It might never be mentioned again. 'You need to tell me, Dad.'

He looked affronted. 'I don't need to do anything.'

'OK. But you *ought* to tell me. I think I deserve it.'

He pointed to some of his stuff on a nearby side table. 'My glasses.'

She opened his glasses case and slid them carefully onto the bridge of his nose.

'Better,' he said, looking at her with a concentrated expression that reminded her of how he used to be, always. 'You sure you need the details?'

She nodded, not wanting to interrupt him in any way, now.

'It was difficult to understand, at the time. I still don't quite understand it.' He stopped, and she heard him rolling the sweet around against the back of his teeth. She wondered whether he was going to say anything more, and was about to try and encourage him, when he suddenly continued: 'But it wasn't quite as simple as your twin not making it. Medicine wasn't what it is, today, and now, if it happened, I think it would be a very different outcome. But back then, there was an element of choice, as far as I can understand it.'

'A choice?'

'I believe so.'

'Between the two of us?

He gave half a nod, non-committal.

'But why was I never told all this? Why didn't mum tell me?'

Her father faced her with steely resolve. 'We thought it best, Rae.'

'Why?'

He cleared his throat, which used to be his precursor for telling her off. 'Because you were a difficult child, with problems. You're still difficult.'

For the second day in a row she wondered whether she'd be leaving her father, choked with emotion, to go and stand in one of Heron Court's non-spaces, stranded with panic and hurt. But this time she held her nerve, reaching forward to put her hand on her father's wrist.

'I'll come and see you soon,' she managed. He nodded, almost apologetic, but then slowly turned to gaze out of the window once more.

It was only in the car park, welling up with tears, that she allowed herself to dwell on the ramifications of what he'd said. An element of choice. How had her mother lived with that all those years, and then decided and stuck to the decision never to speak about it. Was there some degree of shame there? Or was it something else. Had her mother been worried about her daughter's fragility? The daughter who wandered around speaking out to imaginary friends? As she reversed her car out of the parking space she was suddenly aware of the awful volume of spare seats and emptiness around her. Was the presence somewhere with her, now, in the car? At any moment able to make itself be known, or just to wait, near her, ready for a sign of weakness. For the first time Rae felt a sense of dread, that the presence she'd always known was actually not comforting at all, and was perhaps something more malevolent. All those failed relationships, each one driven away by some aspect of her personality that they latched onto. Each, in their own way, instinctively aware that being close to her was to step into a space that was troubling and unsettling. Like a vibration that surrounded her, that made them itch. All these years walking in step with this thing. It amounted to a haunting. She was a haunted person.

Back at her flat, wary of being alone, Rae played loud music on the stereo. She stood, swaying to the beat, her eyes half-closed, but knew the evening would be difficult to navigate. Why had the lawyer's wife ended their lessons? There didn't seem enough reason. Had she, also, detected an unwanted aura surrounding Rae? Trying to console herself she deliberately remembered the night before, Tom eager to be with her, leading her towards the bedroom with an easy self-confidence. She decided Tom was worth trying for, so she took out her mobile and began to compose a text. Play it light. Be breezy. She thought about it, then typed: *Plenty more takeaways 2 try. Let me know when you're hungry*. She wondered whether she should put *hungry for more*, or did that seem too flirty, and desperate? She replaced *2* with *to*. She didn't want to text like a kid or – worse – pretend to text like a kid. She typed several versions of the message, playing with the wording, then deleted the whole thing. She put the mobile on the table, quickly picked it up again and ordered takeaway sushi. Quarter of an hour later, knowing her mood was beginning to fall, she decided to go out. On Wednesday evening a local café had live jazz. It was a good place to sit at one of the wooden tables, order a glass of red, and pretend to listen to the music. No one would care if she was alone. When she got there she chose a table near the band, where it was loud enough that no one would come to talk to her. She felt positive, in charge of things. She took out her mobile and sent the jokey text to Tom, because that's what any single woman would do in her situation. She sipped her wine. She listened to the set. She checked her mobile every ten minutes or so. At the end of the evening, saddened by the wine, her ears ringing, she walked back to her flat, wishing she'd left the lights on so she wouldn't have to walk into the darkness. As she opened the door to the entrance lobby, she stepped over the takeaway sushi she'd ordered.

In the morning, she chose the outfit that tended to make her upbeat. Tight jeans. A slight lift to her heels. A top that had bright abstract colours. The mirrors were still covered in the flat, but she knew what she looked like. A music teacher, but not a tragic one. It was the day of the school concert and she was glad at the thought of being rushed off her feet all day. She helped get the hall ready, putting out all the music stands and pushing the piano into place, hoping she'd be able to face all the parents and convince them the money spent on the lessons was worth it. Still no reply from Tom. She tried not to think about it. But what a dumb message it had been – why had she sent that? It did sound desperate, now. He'd be licking his wounds like any immature man liked to do, and always did, despite claiming he wouldn't.

Before the concert started, one of the teachers asked her if she would mind coming to the school office. Rae said of course, then asked what it was about. In hushed, serious tones the teacher whispered: 'It's Joel and Jed. They've had a big fight.'

'Oh – I'm sorry to hear that,' she replied.

'It happens with those two. But they say they're not going to play in the concert.'

'What happened?'

'Jed hit Joel with a brick.' The teacher frowned with the gravity of it. 'Well, half a brick. From what I can gather.'

'So what can I do?'

The teacher shrugged. 'Talk to them? You seem to have a rapport.'

When Rae entered the school office Joel was sitting, red faced, his wrist bandaged in a bright white Tubigrip, while Jed sat next to him, slumped forward, looking at his shoes.

'Oh, boys, what's gone on?' she said, sympathetically.

Jed lifted his head reluctantly, but didn't speak. Rae was unsure what to say. The boys looked at her, calm and unafraid. She had the beginnings of a headache. A sudden, insistent pain.

'Are you going to tell me what caused this fight?' she asked.

Joel stared back at her, implacable. She held his look for a few seconds, then turned to Jed. His clear blue eyes and total calm was exactly the same as his brother. They faced her like a wall.

After the concert, Rae helped stack the chairs away, then took her chance to escape the school as soon as she could, not wanting to see any of the parents. She wasn't in the mood for that, there was an air of scrutiny nowadays that might seek her out. Instead, she drove straight to the school where Tom worked, parking her car under the row of trees, opposite the school fence. She slid low in her seat, watching Tom as he walked across the playground, chatting with a group of year sixes as they headed back to the classroom. His easy, comfortable walk, rolling on his heels, wearing soft trainers. A man who could run fast, choosing to walk slow. After the kids had gone into the building he sauntered back across the play area, bending down to collect the brightly lit cones where they had done their football drills. The marks on his face were becoming faint, already much less of an issue. He put the cones in a net bag slung over his shoulder, then began to wheel the goalposts back towards an outside store. She waited until both goals were neatly stowed, and he'd fixed the padlock, before she called him on his mobile. From the car she saw him reach into his tracksuit pocket, as it vibrated. Watched him take the mobile out to see the caller ID. He lent casually against a low brick wall, crossing his ankles, and she wondered what to say when he answered. Then, abruptly, she heard the dialling tone stop, as Tom slipped the phone back in his pocket, pushing himself away from the wall to head back to the store.

That evening she dragged the furniture in her flat to the centre of each room, and then began to push it all back in an entirely different order. The sofa was left at a diagonal across the living room, and her armchair was pushed away from the reading light and left abandoned near the entrance to the bathroom. She rolled the rug and swapped it with the one in the bedroom, then took down the pictures and lent them against the wall. The activity made her feel galvanised, less of a victim to her mood swings, but as soon as she'd run out of things to reposition, she began to worry that it had all been a big mistake. The flat now seemed alien, transformed to a space that had little connection to her. All her possessions, haphazard and making no sense, as if it had been ransacked. Now, the rooms had new empty spaces that felt unknown and strange. Oh no, she thought, perching on the end of the oddly placed sofa, lacking the energy to put it all back again. She thought of the last couple of days and the feeling that she'd only just been keeping above water. Tom, crossing his ankles, looking at the mobile, then slipping it back in his pocket. Her father turning back to the window, preferring a view of the care home's accessible garden rather than deal with the free-fall of emotion that his daughter always displayed. Even Joel and Jed; mysterious and explosive hatred between them, but a powerfully united front against her, and during the concert they'd sat at the side of the school hall, sniggering at a private joke between them. Both, arms crossed, as if trying to make themselves even more identical than they already were.

Resigned, Rae went to the dining table, in its new place by the wall. She poured herself a glass of water then, on impulse, poured a second glass and placed it opposite her. Nervously, she looked at the two drinks, daring the presence to make itself known. She took a sip of water, then resumed her gaze at both glasses. The room was dense and oppressive. Another mistake, she thought. This was unnerving. Her heart was beating fast, and as she rested her hands on the table, either side of her glass, she saw her fingers trembling. In her glass, a quiver of movement flickered across the surface of the water. She tried to calm herself, lifting her hands free of the table and noticing how the surface of her drink gradually stopped moving. She held her breath. Then she checked the other glass. Continuing to hold her breath, being as still as possible, she saw the surface of the water begin to shiver with life.

In her dream that night, she returned to the mixed emotion of comfort and indistinct threat that had woken her before. But this time it felt less temporary, with a sense that it might be held onto when she woke up. In her dream, there was a coalescing presence in her bed, just beyond reach. If she moved, the presence moved too, mimicking her, maintaining a distance, but watchful and curious. If she tried to reach towards it the presence became elusive and fragmentary, but then gathered itself, collecting, pouring over her like a suffocating shadow.

She woke in pain, stumbling from the bed and rushing to one of the covered mirrors in the hallway. She tore the fabric off it and stared at the scratches across her face. Livid lines, deep and vengeful, aimed at her eyes. She thought she was going to faint, to fall backwards with fear and dread. Her heart was racing and there were multiple pains and aches all across her body, deep and troubling and with no reason to be there. She forced herself to push away the panic, steadying herself, and began to gaze at her reflection, wondering what she should even think about when she saw herself. Slowly, she began to lean closer to the mirror, bringing her face towards the glass, then closer still. Her face filled her view, shadowed and uncomfortably near, only her eyes shining with the remnants of the fear she'd had. She held the stare, familiar with the reflection but at odds with the strange intensity of it, too, and then, deep within her eyes, she recognised something else. Someone she had never met before.

Scapegoat

The caravan was propped on bricks at the end of the garden with a hawthorn overhanging the roof and dark green mould rising up the sides. It must be twenty or thirty years old, Laura thought, but it looked much older.

'When are you going to get rid of it?' she asked.

Carly seemed distracted. She shrugged. 'Let it rot.'

'Is that all you've got to say?'

'Pretty much.'

Laura stared at her sister, trying to guess her mood. She thought about asking one of the many questions she had about who the old man had been and what happened at the end, but knew she'd get nothing but evasion. She'd wait for a better time to have that particular conversation.

'I'll – take my bag upstairs, then?' she said. Carly looked back at her blankly.

As soon as she stepped into the house it felt strange. It was so quiet, as if the air hadn't properly stirred for weeks. She paused in her bedroom doorway, reluctant to go in. Such a long journey to get here, she thought. Never get used to it. Always those last few miles growing impatient to be there, but not wanting to arrive, also. And now the house to deal with. The house, a rotten caravan, and a sister who seemed secretive and distant, more tricky than ever.

On the landing, Laura crept towards her parents' former bedroom. She touched the door handle with a finger. The slippery glaze of the porcelain reminded her of going in there as a child, unable to sleep, tiptoeing across the carpet to stroke her mother's hair in the dark. She braced herself, gently swinging the door open, only to discover the room had been completely emptied. Bare floorboards, curtains removed, and all the furniture gone. Only the old, patterned wallpaper remained, but now with dark smudges where the pictures had hung.

She went to the window, still trying to walk quietly after all these years, and saw the slumped shape of the old caravan. It spoiled the view. Carly was still outside, half-heartedly chipping mud off a brick path with the toe of her boot. She looked tired. Tired and faded like the jeans and sweatshirt she always wore. She'd sent emails and left voice messages about the old man, his illness and his decline. But now he'd died, she was hardly mentioning his name.

Laura dumped her bag and went back outside. The garden was badly overgrown, and the paths were covered with rotting leaves and brambles. She found herself drawn to the caravan again. The door was open. She was sure it had been shut before. As she walked towards it, she heard movement coming from inside.

'Carly?' she called. There was no reply. She stepped closer, slowly. Bright green moss had grown along the windowsills and the glass was clouded with grime and cobwebs. It stank of a sour, marshy odour.

Laura cupped her hands against the glass. It was dingy inside, piled high with newspapers and books and on top of them she saw old mugs and glasses, plates, and a kettle. Clothes lay in a rough heap and one or two of the cupboard doors had sprung open.

Right under the window was a bed covered in yellow material. Gradually, she realised the fabric was beginning to alter as something lying across it shifted position. In the shadow she saw the matted grey hair of an old man start to turn towards her and as she recoiled in shock he was suddenly there at the window. Only it wasn't the eyes of an old man. It was a goat, pale and ragged, glaring at her.

Laura found her sister slumped on an old sofa in the hallway.

'Could've mentioned the goat,' she said.

'Oh yeah – he's a bastard.'

Laura perched awkwardly on the edge of the sofa, as her sister didn't make any room for her. Carly sipped a mug of tea and seemed to be listening to the air shifting in the chimney. Eventually she spoke:

'I wish you'd come sooner.'

'Me too. Just couldn't, you know how… You look knackered, Carly.'

Carly exhaled slowly. 'I eat bad food.'

'Want to talk?'

'Nope.'

Laura sighed. She'd forgotten how maddening her sister could be. Eventually, impatience got the better of her: 'Well – this is pretty typical of you – to roll out the red carpet like this. Cheers.'

'You didn't exactly drop everything to come, did you? I called a month ago.'

They stared implacably at each other, waiting to see who'd back down. Laura shook her head with frustration. 'Well. I'm here now. So why don't we talk.'

Carly gave a shrug.

'So,' Laura began, 'you open the curtains one day and this tramp's down there, in the garden?'

'Yep.'

'That's it?'

'Wouldn't call him a tramp but, yeah, sitting on dad's old bench.'

'OK, and?'

'He said he knew dad, way back, but I reckon that's a lie. He dug a few weeds then before I know it he's got that thing towed up.'

'The caravan?'

'Yep.'

'You always were a sucker.'

Carly held her mug of tea, shaking her head. 'He was sweet. You shouldn't just – you've got this habit of thinking out loud. Victor didn't fit in – that's all. Nothing wrong with that.'

'Yeah right – until you find out the man's a nutter.'

'Well how would *I* spot that?'

'OK – I'm sorry, if…'

'Yeah. You should be.'

Laura sat on her bed, searching through her suitcase. She found her mobile and checked for messages. None. For a while she studied the ornaments and photos in her room – the room she'd had as a child. Pictures and sketches on the walls, some of her with Carly when they were young. In particular, one of them as teenagers, pissing themselves with laughter. Several rosettes from horse riding competitions. Curios on the shelves – bits of pottery, glass ink bottles, a ram's horn.

She put her mobile on the windowsill and noticed the goat had wandered out of the caravan. The daylight was beginning to fade but she could still make out its grey back moving across the lawn. It reached the compost heap and climbed unsteadily, cautiously placing each foot. She picked up her phone, put on her coat and went outside. Immediately, the goat stopped chewing. It was old and skeletal-thin, with straight sides, a high anvil-shaped rump, and a long wiry coat, mottled down the spine. It stood rigid, refusing to look at her. Then it suddenly turned to face her, and for a moment she was afraid. It had pale eyes with thin black pupils. The hair on its head was long and wild, with tobacco-stained whiskers around the mouth and large horns lying swept back across the skull. She stepped away, and after a while the goat lowered its head to resume foraging. She saw a dull leather collar round its neck connected to a coarse-linked chain. Its breath came and went with a damp, rattling sound.

'Hurry up and die,' she muttered.

The goat was standing on potato peelings, and although the light was almost gone it seemed the compost pile was subtly moving, as skins slipped over themselves. Some of the skins were greyer, darker than the others, and she realised a small army of snails were working the pile, lifting up the peel. The goat grabbed indiscriminate mouthfuls, crushing the shells with a sickening crunch.

Laura dialled a number on her mobile, and took a deep breath. He answered almost immediately:

'Nick – where are you? OK… look I've packed all my stuff in boxes, right, so you won't have to feel guilty about anything… no – not now – I'm at my sister's…yeah. I said it's all in boxes… I mean how else can we do this? I am *not* starting.'

Laura listened while she watched the goat, trying hard to calm down.

'She's alright – don't know, giving me the usual runaround… Don't know. Tomorrow?' She hung up and with a wave of anger hurled the phone onto the lawn. Distantly, she saw Carly walking up the drive, bringing fish and chips in a plastic bag. Laura found her mobile, wiped it clean and headed for the house.

While they ate, Laura asked whether the old man had any other friends round here.

'Nope,' Carly replied. 'Said he grew up locally but no one really knew. I mean even I didn't know.'

'And no family?'

'I suppose – I was his family. I fed and washed him till the end. Wasn't anyone else going to do that.'

'Well, he might have been…'

'…You're going to say *looked after*, aren't you? In a pissy care home. With a social worker asking nosey questions. I don't really see it happening.'

'What questions?'

'Eat your chips, Laura.'

Laura suspected the old man's death had caused more of a toll that she'd expected. 'We'll clear it out tomorrow?'

'Whatever.' Carly screwed up her chip-paper and stared at the tabletop. 'You're judgmental, that's what you are.'

'Oh come on!'

'A man like him – he doesn't have to live like you and me – he doesn't have to live his life any way other than his own.'

'Yeah – I wasn't saying…'

'…Probably been misunderstood all his life. You think about that. All his life.'

'Carly – what's got into you?'

Her sister glared back, then let out a brittle laugh. She pointed at the window.

'Look,' she said, 'at what's out there. I mean it – go and look out the window.'

Laura went to the window and gazed across the soft featureless bushes. Against the dark, she saw the pale side of the caravan.

'I don't know what I'm meant to see,' she said.

'Interesting.' Carly sounded bitter. 'Do you *feel* anything?'

Laura wondered whether her sister had had a breakdown. Those emails had described a weird friendship with the old man. It couldn't have been healthy.

'You don't get it do you?' Carly added. 'You've forgotten what this arse end of nowhere is like.'

Laura went to put an arm round her sister, but stopped short. 'I can't cope with this flashpoint – every time we meet. I don't need all this right now.'

'Has your boyfriend called?'

Laura shook her head, tight-lipped. 'Weren't you worried, Carly, ever?'

'Not really.'

'Even at night? Didn't you think he might be – I don't know – you locked the doors, right?'

Carly went to get a bottle of cider off the pantry shelf, and came back with a photo. It was of the old man: long-haired and blurred – moving fast when the shutter went.

'It's the only one I've got,' she said.

'That is one scary bloke.'

'Yeah well no one gave him a chance round here either. There's this woman in the estate, she says her kids had dreams about him. That he'd been in their room at night.'

'Shit.'

'Bollocks isn't it? Anyway, so Victor heard the rumours and he had this great idea – we made this pact – him and me, that I'd feed him, do his stuff. And the rest of the time, you know, I'd chain him up.'

'Chain him?'

Carly pointed to her ankle. 'Wasn't necessary, mind. He was really losing it by then. Could hardly move.'

'You actually locked the man up?'

'His idea. Like I said.'

'How often?'

'Every night. You say his name round here they go nuts. Done this and done that, you know, they say he was bad, you know, a *bad man*. That's why they brought me the goat. A couple of days after he died they brought it up the track and tethered it there.'

'Why?'

'Local crap – they think the goat will soak up the bad stuff. Like a scapegoat.'

Laura lay in bed, sleepless, thinking about the long drive to get home. She thought about the flat she'd left behind in total disarray, and the boxes of Nick's stuff that she'd piled in the hall. The boxes had looked final and irreconcilable and she knew that would annoy him. She listened to her sister snoring through the wall and wondered whether she'd confront her in the morning, to suggest she sees someone. A grief counsellor. But it would be difficult to broach that with Carly, who prided herself on doing things her own way.

Laura picked up her mobile and played one of Carly's voice messages:

> *'Victor said he's had times when he's been off the rails, you know, so this illness wasn't clear till recently. But he's acting strange, now. Sometimes he sits in the field or even sleeps out there, in the mud. Then he goes off for days and I don't hear anything till someone brings him back in a car. And now this old cow in the estate's getting shirty. Says don't I know about him and am I protecting* him. *What's she on about? They're saying he follows people. This last week he's not been out in the day, but at night – there's always noise in there, always a light on, or I'll see the end of his cigarette glowing out there in the garden…'*

Laura thought of the garden, at night. The bushes and tress, a veg patch in moonlight. The dull gleam of the caravan with a light on inside, smoke rising from a cigarette through the windows, a glimpse of old grey hair, shaking rapidly.

When she switched off the lamp she listened to how silent the country was. A silence she'd grown unfamiliar with and something which now made her uneasy. Fields and trees made their own kind of noise. Even an empty field of ploughed soil seemed to add a dull thickly distant sound. What had Carly meant, when she said: 'do you *feel* anything?'

It was very dark and in the silence she listened to the goat's chain dragging through the garden, pulling over the caravan's doorstep, catching on the clutter inside as it rummaged through the old man's stuff. And when Laura woke it was still dark and she could still here the chain moving, and gradually she realised it wasn't the chain but the sound of the goat's hooves on the stairs inside the house, climbing, slipping on the bare wood.

When it reached her bedroom door she heard the stab of horns catching the handle and after several attempts she watched the door beginning to swing open in the half-light. The goat came in, treading on the floorboards like it was standing on stilts, his brittle hooves slipping as he approached the bed.

Laura kept perfectly still, trying to hold her breath and the terror she felt.

The goat stopped, staring directly at her. The gleam of its pale eyes shone like flint. It made no sound, as it seemed to be listening. Then suddenly it leapt onto the bed. She heard the panic in the tight yell she let out and then it all went quiet, the goat there, standing above her, its head still and its legs trembling against the give of the mattress.

Round its neck she saw the rough leather collar and the sharp edges of metal where the chain had snapped. Its beard was wet and matted. She smelt its damp unwashed odour of animal sweat and rotten food. An earwig uncurled itself from the hair of its chin and dropped next to her onto the pillow, and with the sound of the insect falling the goat seemed newly interested in what lay below him, turning and dropping his head so he could look down. It was like a hideous puppet, examining, angling his head to one side. Looking directly at her now, moving his head closer, beginning to curl his upper lip into a cruel snarl to reveal a dull, chalky row of tiny teeth, livid gums and, behind them, a black tongue.

First thing in the morning, Laura was out in the garden, hauling papers and old clothes from the caravan, then dumping them on a fire she'd built. She wore a new pair of marigold gloves because she couldn't bear the thought of touching the old man's stuff. The goat was nowhere to be seen, but the chain stretched out from the doorway into a patch of bushes, occasionally going taut as it dragged over the threshold.

Carrying yet another filthy bundle from the caravan, she saw her sister had come to stand by the fire.

'Don't start,' Laura said.

Carly looked affronted. 'I'm not.'

'I'm sorting you out.'

'Right.'

'OK?'

Carly shrugged with indifference.

'Tell me everything about him,' Laura said, trying to control her anger. 'The truth.'

'Whoa there.'

'Now.'

'Why?'

'Because – because you need to tell someone. This disease. What was it?'

Carly seemed secretly amused.

Laura continued: 'So why send all the emails?'

'Cause you live a dull life with Nick. I don't know!'

Carly pushed the fire with her boot, then bent down to pick up a snail from the grass.

'Hello little fella,' she said.

Laura looked daggers at her, fed up with the games.

'Victor took pride in living off the land,' Carly said, 'you know – berries and that. Sloe gin, and this pumpkin rum which – bloody hell. Then mushrooms from the woods, but – it was the snails that did it. He picked them after it rained and boiled them up, only the old fool didn't do it right. See, you have to starve them first – the snails. That's what the French do. Well Victor didn't know about that. And he got ill, in the head.'

'From eating snails?'

'Little bug in their stomach. Funny the things that get us. Mind you – not a nice end. He went crazy.'

Laura lowered her voice, bothered by how close they were to the caravan. 'What if they were right, you know, what if he did…'

'I don't know,' Carly said, 'I think he probably *did* follow people. Why are you whispering?'

'You're lying. *Why* are you lying to me?'

Carly seemed to weigh up how to respond. 'There was this night I had to find him – like, his chain must've broken or something. I saw him climbing through a window on the estate. I waited till he was in there, then I – sort of tapped on the glass. He had these pale eyes. He was really crazy.'

Laura stared at her sister, thinking she could see the tiniest of smiles at the corner of Carly's mouth.

'Shit Carly – stop messing with me!'

Laura marched into the caravan, fed up. She sat on one of the bench seats, defeated by the amount of mess around her. It was incredible to believe a man had lived in here. Black mould had spread across the wallpaper and damp had buckled the veneer from the cupboards. There was paper everywhere. Loose and in piles, or trodden into the muddy carpet or shoved into drawers. A heap of clothes had stuck together with grey fungus and when Laura tried to lift a jumper from it there was a noise like a sticking plaster being ripped from skin.

'This is unbelievable,' she said, as Carly came in.

'There it is,' Carly replied, pushing away a plate to reveal a large ring bolt fixed to the floor. 'That's where I chained him.'

'We've got to burn all this.'

Suddenly the goat's chain dragged heavily through the caravan. The metal links sprang taut and Laura realised that it, too, was fixed to the same bolt in the floor. A second later the goat appeared in the doorway. It glowered at them, then forced its way through the mess to sit on its bench.

Carly smiled at it with an affection that unnerved Laura. The goat grabbed a pile of paper and tugged away a mouthful, beginning to chew a child's sketch of a house and garden. Laura saw it too late, and suddenly tried to wrestle it from the goat's mouth.

'That was – that was mine!'

Slowly, the goat stopped chewing. It straightened its neck, inhaled, then let out a phlegmy cough. Laura could clearly see the collar. Could clearly see the chain was secure and had never broken.

'What's going on here?' Laura said, 'What the hell's going on?'

By nightfall they'd managed to burn all of Victor's stuff from the caravan. Carly dragged up their father's old bench so they could sit by the embers, drinking a couple of cans of lager.

'It was shocking, the night he died,' Carly said. 'I think he'd gone berserk in there. It's just so sad, how anyone can end up like that.' She looked up at the smoke rising into the sky. 'You know, with all his stuff gone – it's going to be like he never existed.'

Laura spoke quietly: 'Remember how dad made that scarecrow out of mum's old clothes, after she left him? Maybe you were too young.'

'Nah – I remember that. And I remember he was a lazy bugger.'

'Right.'

'At least he got to die in a hospital.'

Laura was affected by her sister's honesty. She was struck by just how much Carly had faced, alone. Briefly, she thought she should put her arm round her, but then stopped short, afraid she'd be pushed away.

'Here,' Laura said, offering Carly another can of beer.

Against the garden's growing darkness she saw a glint from the goat's eyes, shining back at her.

That night she was afraid to sleep. Again she heard the chain dragging through the garden. She was determined to stay awake. In the morning she'd leave. She'd think carefully about what Carly needed now. But despite her efforts to try and stay awake she knew sleep was coming, and at first she thought she might take just a minute or two to take the edge off her tiredness. Leave the light on. But her head felt warm and drowsy and sleep seemed so easy, so natural. She could hear the chain moving but it didn't bother her.

When she woke she was standing by the caravan. It was pitch black and she was in her nightclothes. Her mouth was dry with fear but she took some breaths and began to take control. I'm dreaming, she thought. I fell asleep and now I'm dreaming. She placed her hand on her other arm and pinched it hard. *Wake up*, she said out loud. *Wake up in your bed.* But nothing happened. She was cold and there was a fine drizzle falling. It was all too real. Too certain. The door of the caravan was open and, inside, a dull greasy light was shining. She thought there was movement in there. *Back you go now*, she whispered, but took a step forward, touching the damp doorframe before going inside.

The goat lay on the couch facing away from her. Its breathing was difficult and noisy.

She stood looking at the animal, quietly wishing she could turn away and walk out of there. Wishing she might wake up.

She watched the goat gradually tense its spine and drag its hooves across the fabric. She held her breath.

Suddenly the goat was awake and staring at her. She could see the dark, tight rim of lips through its hair and the small row of teeth. The goat lifted its jaw in a tight snarl and, half chewing, half twitching with effort, spat out the words: '*Leave – us –*'

She reeled towards the door but fell instead against the pile of clothes. Beneath the clothes she glimpsed several photos of her and Carly, as children. A close up of Laura, aged thirteen, holding out an equestrian rosette. The goat was standing in front of her. Silently watching her, waiting for her to move.

Slowly it began to snarl again, making a deep growling like a dog, and once more she heard the voice, forming the words: 'Leave – us.' It was the sound of the goat, but unmistakably the voice of an old man, a sick old man speaking through it.

She stumbled from the caravan and ran down the brick path. Locking the front door she went straight to her room. Her bed was still warm, the light she'd left on was still there, in the corner. *I'm dreaming. I'm dreaming*, she said, panicked. *I will lie here till I wake up and then I'll know. I'll stay here, in the quiet, and sooner or later I'll wake up. I'll get dressed. I'll leave.*

But she waited for a long time, and gradually it began to lighten outside. *You can't wake up*, she said, *you can't wake up because you've not been asleep.*

It was before dawn when she burst into Carly's room.

'Carly! Get up Carly! I'm going. Right this minute.'

Her sister woke and looked back at her, confused. 'Calm down.'

'*Calm down?* You've done nothing but freak me out, Carly. You and that shitty goat of yours. And you know what – you're not the only one with stuff going on – I'm, I've got to – I've got to get back to the flat. I mean why the hell did I ever come back here? This isn't my home – it's *never* been my home. You understand?'

Laura went back to her room and sat on the edge of the bed, confused and upset. She felt irrational and overtired. Her bag lay on the floor, but she left it and slumped back against the wall, drawing her legs up and holding her head. She picked up her mobile and read the text message: I'VE DROPPED MY KEYS THROUGH THE LETTER BOX. ENJOY. N.

Downstairs she could hear Carly making coffee. She took a deep breath, picked up her bag and went to the kitchen, defeated. Carly was pouring coffee into a thermos. A radio was playing quietly.

'Alright?' Carly asked, gently.

Laura sat down, exhausted. 'Not really.' She looked at her sister. 'You've always done that.'

'Done what?'

'Lean against the sink. It's one of your things. It's how I imagine you.'

Carly smiled thinly. 'I think of you in an office, in nice shoes.'

Laura waited, listening to the birds outside. 'I wish you'd called me, before you chucked out dad's stuff.'

Carly didn't answer.

'Where did it go?'

'Car boot, mostly.'

'You didn't even call me.'

'That's right.'

'I could've, you know, had something to remember dad with.'

'How about his ashtray – that's what killed him.' It was said in a matter-of-fact way, without bitterness.

Laura accepted it, quietly. 'Ever see mum?'

'What's the point. You?'

'No.'

Laura looked sadly at her sister. 'Carly – you should talk to someone, you're in a bad place…'

‘…Thought that might be coming.’

‘There are people that can listen to these things. They can help.’

‘I’ll manage.’

‘You don’t have to manage. You can get help. Help to move on.’

‘Maybe I don’t *want* to move on.’

Laura stood. She looked at the photo of the old man, still on the table.

‘I’m going to go now,’ she said.

Her sister nodded her head, refusing to look her in the eye: ‘You always do.’

First light was spreading across the sky, but the garden looked like it was made of ashes. Laura climbed into her car and locked both doors. Her headlights blazed across the garden and out into the blankness of the open field beyond. She took a moment to look at the brightly illuminated dashboard. Listened to the calm sound of the heater. She started to turn the car around, watching as the headlights swept across the side of the caravan. It had slumped onto one side like a wreck, sinking. And for a moment she stared through the smeared glass of the end window, thinking she saw the silhouette of horns and the glare of eyes reflecting the light.

The Marl Pit

Liam knelt down in his big Parka and blew gently into the fur. The hare's body lay across two of the field's furrows. With its head turned into the soil he could see the throat had been cut, or possibly bitten. A faint trickle of blood had seeped into the earth below its neck, leaving a damp oily stain. The hare was straw coloured, coarse and gleaming, and as his breath parted the fur he saw a soft downy undercoat.

It was a large animal and must have been running fast across the field before the attack, because several ridges of the furrows had been scuffed as it fell. He wanted to touch it. Lightly, he put his finger onto its flank, and as he did this one of the hind legs thumped with a muscle spasm. Once. He recoiled, shocked, then rested his hand on its body. It was still warm.

He stood. The field was one of the largest in the area. All the original hedgerows had been torn up and, rising as it did into a shallow crest, it seemed to stretch forever. Like a desert, it had its own horizon, and you couldn't see beyond. It was a harsh winter morning. There was no one around.

In front of him was the marl pit. He wasn't really sure what marl was, but he knew it had been dug here for centuries, and after the pit had been abandoned it had never been filled in. It was a deep hole, about forty feet to the bottom, filled with young trees packed round steep sides. He'd never tried to get down there, but had seen through the trees the bottom of the pit was filled with dark greasy water. The pit spoiled the perfect symmetry of the field, and that was partly why he kept returning here, through all the seasons. He set his camera on the tripod and checked to see what the sun was doing. The early morning light was already changing, the furrows were losing their slippery, dewy sharpness. It had been ploughed over the weekend. He looked through the viewfinder and framed the marl pit, as he always did, but instead of taking the picture he looked at the hare once more. What could have killed it?

He blew on his hands, took the photo and was immediately dissatisfied – as usual. He'd taken pictures of the marl pit all year long, and not been pleased by any of them. There, in the field, the sense of the marl pit's isolation, of it sinking deeply through the impeccably neat plough-lines, of it like an inverted island, all this was tremendous, but none of the photos had conveyed it. Oddly, the photos themselves were nearly always marred by something he hadn't seen at the time. Either misty or unfocused, the marl pit was often obscured – and he wasn't sure why.

Back at the cottage he went straight to the darkroom and ran the film through the developer. As soon as the strip came out from the wash, he held the negatives to the light. The lines of the field looked good and crisp, but the marl pit was again blemished. To the left of the trees it was hazy and indistinct. He blamed himself for being too hasty with the thought of losing the early sun, but wondered also whether light was somehow getting in the back of the camera. A few shots earlier he saw the hare's eerie outline – still in a position of flight – as it stretched across the snow-like grid of furrows. He remembered the way the leg had twitched and – in the moment after – wondering whether he was being watched. And yet the field had been totally empty. He thought harder. Open spaces – they make you vulnerable. But this didn't seem enough of an explanation. He'd sensed an unknown cruelty, vaguely formed but intensely focused, approaching.

The darkroom encouraged this kind of paranoid thinking. It was converted from the attic above his bedroom and it could be claustrophobic at times, actually quite gloomy, not because of its cramped size, but because it meant long hours hidden away from the rest of the world. He slid open the hatch to let some air in and looked down the rungs of the stepladder into his bedroom. He noticed the things that had eaten away at him for months: gaps where rugs had gone from the floor, nails left in the wall where pictures had once hung.

She'd left in the middle of the night a year-and-a-half ago. Returned in a hire van a week later. On a brilliant spring morning. She'd taken her stuff, driven away, and life had continued in that vein for her: sunlit, filled with movement and direction.

The mist returned a few days later. He woke suddenly knowing it was outside, and though it was still before dawn there was a difference to the light already. He looked through the curtains into the indistinct shadows of the garden, battling a rising anxiety, not because of what he saw, but because some deep-rooted problem – shapeless and unrevealed – had surfaced as he came out of sleep. And he'd felt scared.

Not for the first time he knew all this was a waste of his time, as he set off through the village. His boots seemed to make too much noise on the tarmac and his tripod seemed as cumbersome and as foolish as if he was carrying a set of golf clubs. He went the long route so he could pass Meg's house at the end of the estate. He saw her light on in one of the downstairs windows. It made him smile. He picked up a piece of gravel and chucked it at the glass, but the stone fell short, and he decided he wouldn't try again. Instead, he took a piece of chalk from his pocket and wrote DOUGHNUT on the pavement. Nearby, were the smudged messages he'd written before, over the last few weeks. He winked at her window and quickly moved on, heading to the field. What exactly would he say if someone asked what he was up to? What he'd really been doing all these months. Taking photos of a field. Nothing else. It wouldn't make sense and – having to say it out loud – probably wouldn't make sense to himself, either. There were plenty of people who'd spent their lives painting or photographing one particular view. Like Cézanne and his mountain. But the opinions about them tended to reach the same conclusion: they'd become obsessed. Even driven crazy by it. It's as if the view wouldn't let them lie. He instinctively knew obsession unchecked led to other things – paranoia, phobia. He didn't know these things but was afraid of them nonetheless. Fear is arriving all the time, wanting to get in.

He reached the field. Not that he could see much of it. The furrows of soil stretched away from the road and seemed to tip off into the mist. The thin glare of the sun pierced through the mist like it was coming through cathedral windows. It was an inspiring sight. He entered the field and followed his own footprints of three days before – his quickest way of finding the marl pit. At one point he stopped and listened to the silence. It was immense. Even the birds weren't singing. He looked at the footprints ahead of him, and those behind. Both sets disappearing after fifty feet or so into the mist. He saw the field for what it was, a patch of dark, featureless soil fading into damp cloud. His footprints looked pathetic in their determined, pointless line. Where had he gone wrong, he wondered? But to turn back now would raise questions he knew he couldn't answer, so he pressed on, till he saw the trees of the marl pit loom from the mist like the broken masts of a ship. In the soil below him were the marks of his tripod from the other day.

The hare had gone. He took a photo and hastily bagged the camera without waiting for the light to change or the mist to lift. He just wanted to leave. Maybe the obsession with this view was breaking after all – or perhaps it was defeating him. He didn't want to think about it. But then there was that other possibility – that he was beginning to get deeply unnerved by the marl pit. Perhaps it was the vastness of the field that made him believe he was being watched. But maybe it was something more than that.

There wasn't much on the negative, so he threaded it through the enlarger and framed it on the mat below. In the precise square of lamp light he saw the field slipping into the mist, and the trees, once more like the wreck of a ship. The sunlight fell strangely through the mist. He exposed a print, counting to fifteen under his breath, then slid the paper into the developing tank. Slowly the image emerged. First the trees lifting gradually from the fog, next those shafts of light, and then something utterly confusing – a tall dark shape to the left of the trees, standing in the field. Yet again, a blemish on the negative, but as the image grew he knew it was something much more alarming. A man, standing by the marl pit, trying to hide his face from the camera. He rushed the print into the stop-bath, and after a few seconds rinsing he put it in the fixer. Then he snapped on the main light. The photograph was grey in the tank, and what had seemed like a man in the red glow of the safety light now seemed much less conclusive. A haphazard alignment of the furrows perhaps, or a tarpaulin the farmer might have left out in the field. But there was something very formed about it – and it was easy to reconstruct the shape of a man – a rough coat, long hair, a sleeve in front of his face.

At noon he was standing in the alleyway behind the bakery, leaning against one of the refrigerator units. Meg had come out to see him, wearing her front-of-shop apron, hair net and Doc Martens. She was leaning against the bright blue fly-screen, smiling at him.

'You crack me up,' she said.

'I was there half an hour, and there's no way I missed him. No way.' He held her gaze. 'You tell me if I'm crazy.'

'Want to know what I reckon? There's too much of that –' Meg tapped the side of her head, playfully, '– and not enough of the other.' She dropped her eyes to his crotch.

He laughed. 'Been said before.'

She took a drag on her ciggie, and tried to blow a smoke ring. 'Impressive, huh?'

'Gets me every time,' he replied.

She stubbed the fag out, and looked back into the shop. 'Well – I got cakes to shift.'

'Heh – sorry,' Liam said, trying to keep her from leaving. 'Look, I don't wanna sound like a nut, but' – he reached into his photo-satchel – 'take a look, will you?' He brought out a selection of prints, then decided he couldn't just hand them to her. 'Wait a sec,' he added, parting the beaded fly screen and going into the back room of the bakery.

'You can't come in here,' she said, but he was already laying out the pictures on the zinc counter. The photos of the marl pit were always taken from the same angle, throughout the year: the stark skeletal trees in winter, the young wheat breaking the soil, the stout full heads of the harvest crop, the evening after the combine had been, with the dust still hanging in the air.

'Look,' he pointed. 'And here. And in this one.'

Usually in the trees – just the merest hint of an odd shadow, or leaves overlapping enough to suggest the rough outline of a man, or a blur by the edge of the marl pit as if something had rushed in when the shutter went.

A couple of the shop girls were looking at them, trying to wind Meg up. She tried to ignore them, but he saw a flush of embarrassment rising on her cheek. It was clear some sort of running joke was going on. And they were getting to her.

'Let's do this tonight,' she said, hurriedly.

'Yeah. OK – sorry. I'm going mad. I didn't mean to get heavy.'

'Chill out, Liam. You still want that doughnut?'

He nodded, why not. He was grateful she was still interested in him. 'Sure.'

She shook her head, pretending to admonish herself, then got him a doughnut from the shelf.

'Meg,' he said, beginning to leave, 'there wasn't anyone there.'

That evening, on the way to the pub, he passed by the field. He stopped at the gate and raised his middle finger at the marl pit, then breathed into his palm to smell his breath. He imagined Meg checking herself in the mirror, putting on that Goth makeup that made her look a bit too old. The smoky ring above and below the eyes. Lips the colour of an old bruise. The makeup set she'd shown him, laid out in a small plastic coffin that opened on a hinge. She was a great girl, he thought.

The Green Man wasn't a quaint pub with beams. It was functional and cheap and more than a little bit naff. It had a patterned carpet that could start to swirl if you looked long enough at it, and a fruit machine that woke itself up every five minutes or so with a flutter of noise and flashing lights. He was sitting at a small round table near the window, looking at the several empties in front of him. He felt bulky, perched on the low stool, and thought it was a mistake to have left his coat on all night. The door to the toilets opened and Meg started to walk back towards him, arms flat to her sides, looking in that instant a bit self-conscious of her weight.

'Thought you weren't never coming back,' he said, trying to joke, but realising it was probably not something he should voice. You give these things airtime, and they begin to stick. She took a quick drink from her glass, even though it was already empty.

'Liam – you gotta move on, you know that, right?' Being in the Ladies must have given her a fresh perspective. She looked at him like a nurse would, sympathetic but also in charge.

'I reckon this is the first time all year you've not been sat by yourself at the end of the bar.'

'You calling me a lost cause?'

'Not yet.'

He played with one of the beer mats, peeling a layer of card off it, unsure how to react.

'You're unusual, Meg.'

She gave him a sarcastic smile. 'Great.'

'In the best way. I meant you're special. You care.'

'Keep going.'

'Ahh – I'll make a twat of myself.'

She smiled, but it faded quickly, and he saw a troubled expression flash across her face. She took a deep breath.

'Actually – I'm the one making a twat of myself, aren't I?'

'Don't –'

'– I mean, what's going on here? You gotta admit it's a bit weird, Liam. You're – I don't want you thinking I can't handle anything, but – you're like my dad's age.'

Liam bowed his head, nodding, aware that a couple in the front room of the pub had noticed her raising her voice, and were looking his way. Probably keeping a check on him.

'Shit,' Meg said, making the effort to backtrack. 'I always – you know.'

'You're all right.'

'Thanks.'

He watched her, quietly, making sure she wasn't getting more upset. Her face was pale and powdery with makeup. He felt a lot of kindness towards her.

'I'm not expecting anything,' he said.

'Same.'

He gave her an encouraging smile, then leant forward, conspiratorial: 'You know what? Let's get really pissed and go out there.' He pointed at the window.

'Where?'

'Marl pit.'

'Yeah. Right,' she said, loading as much irony into it as she could.

'I'm serious.'

She leant back, weighing it up. Weighing him up, too. Under all that vulnerability and insecurity, she was a calm person, and she didn't rush her decisions. So her sudden smile was unexpected:

'Thought you'd never ask,' she said.

He bought a couple of bottles of wine as takeouts, and they'd already drunk the first one by the time they reached the field. He used his thumb to push the cork into the second one, because he didn't have his penknife with him. When he took a swig he felt fine drizzle on his face, as soft as steam. His skin was hot and numb, as if none of this was really happening. Not the field, not the dark, not the marl pit itself, ahead of them. The pit was darker than the night, without form, without shape, as dense as oil.

'You sure about this?' he asked, hearing an unpleasant slur in his words.

She shrugged, cold and silent. She hadn't said much since they left the pub.

'Are you pissed?' he asked.

'Any cows in here?'

'It's a crop field.'

He pushed the gate open and started to walk over the soil, feeling a strange sense of inevitability. Why was he bringing her here? Obsession is solitary. You share it and then you'll lose it. He had a nagging suspicion that things would change for him, after this. He could hear her stumbling across the furrows, behind him.

'This is going to fuck my shoes up,' she said.

'Nearly there.'

He led them towards the marl pit until its dark absence seemed to spread and wrap itself round them. He stopped.

'There,' he said, whispering.

She caught up, reaching to hold onto the sleeve of his coat, unsteady.

'What do you reckon?' he asked.

'Well – it stinks.'

Meg leant against him, then turned her face up towards him. He glanced at her and saw that she looked girlish and expectant.

'Is this where you take all the girls?' she asked, putting on a flirty voice.

'Nah –' he began, then felt her finger touching his lip to stop him speaking. She moved a little closer to him, and he smelt wine and crisps on her breath.

'I'm – I'm not ready,' he said, confused. He immediately noticed a stiffness in her, backing away from him. Something like humiliation and shame, and he thought about the girls in the bakery and how they were taking the piss out of her. A nineteen year old, hanging out with the oddball.

'I'm gonna go in there,' he said, trying to resist the magnetic pull of the marl pit.

'And leave me here?' she replied, suddenly brittle. 'Don't think so.'

He'd been there to protect her, at least that's what he thought, from the crush of problems she faced. But he knew, right then, that he'd become just another one of her problems, too. 'Go home, Meg. You shouldn't be out here.'

She stared at him, dark-eyed, upset. 'Don't come to the bakery anymore,' she said. 'It's too weird.'

'OK.'

'In fact –' she stopped. She hugged herself, against the cold, then turned and began to walk off.

He watched her leave, sadly, then walked forward and soon heard the thin branches of the trees brushing against his coat. A mossy softness, underfoot. Soon the earth sloped down and he slid a little, grasping for branches that were sometimes there, sometimes missing. The ground fell away and he slipped badly down the pit, sensing what he thought must be tree trunks nearby. He landed in mud, thick with water. There was a strong unpleasant odour. Decayed and pungent. And when he regained his balance he noticed a silence that was thick and absolute. He tried to keep still, fearing the water somewhere in front of him.

Whatever it was, this marl pit seemed to have its own microclimate, like a true island, inverted, forgotten and raw in the centre of the field. A rotten place. For the first time he realised it had never been the image of the trees he'd wanted to capture; it was the marl pit itself. What it meant to him. A pit. A hole into a darker, more menacing underneath. Dug out, abandoned and never re-filled, it attracted lost causes. He thought about his life with all its negative spaces which couldn't be filled and at the pit and what it had done to him, over the months, forming the mania which had become an obsession. He hurled the wine bottle in front of him, expecting it to splash in mud or water or smash against a tree. But the bottle made no sound at all. It was as if the marl pit had wrapped it in a soundless void, making it vanish. Either that, or the bottle had been caught mid-air.

In the middle of the night, Liam walked back along the road into the village. He stopped beneath the glow of two orange streetlights, taking in how the lane came out of the darkness and then sank back into it. He stared a little too long at what might be out there. He felt muddy and calm.

At the estate, he walked up the paving slabs and sat down beneath Meg's window, leaning his back against the bricks. In front of him, the garden was full of rose beds, pruned hard for winter.

He spoke quietly, not wanting to wake her. 'I had a really great time with you tonight,' he started. 'But you're right, Meg, that place is just messed up. You're right.' He wanted to tell her about what had happened before he started taking the photos. How she'd left him in the middle of the night. Then come back a week later in a hire van. Taking her stuff and leaving him broken.

'Are you at the shop tomorrow?' he asked, almost too quiet to be heard. 'I won't come in. I'll call you. Alright?'

The fog returned the next morning. He'd been awake most of the night seeing it grow steadier and thicker, thinking about the pit's foul water, how it marked the level of a dark watercourse which must flow under the whole county. A massive cistern of darkness and decay under all things.

When he set off for the marl pit he nearly forgot to take his camera. His mouth was dry. He marched into the field, completely surrounded by whiteness, and he knew he never wanted to set foot in there again. When he reached the marl pit he could only just make out the trees in front of him. He hated them. Hated the pit and all the time he'd been there over the year. Hated himself for ever believing he was doing anything worthwhile. And he was deeply scared. He raised the camera and stared through the viewfinder and began to take photographs, first of the pit's murky outline, and then increasingly of the fog surrounding him. Picture after picture, pointing blindly in all directions, winding on rapidly, afraid to lower the camera, not wanting to look at the marl pit but afraid to turn his back on it. And a growing sense – a terrible growing sense of approaching danger – of something getting closer, almost touching him. He stumbled back and tried to catch his breath, knocking back the fear, trying to be rational. Calmly, he stared into the total whiteness of the fog, raised his camera and pulled the focus as close as it would go. He took the picture and ran.

Back in the cottage he shut the front door, kicked his boots off, then returned to the door and slid the bolt across. He set the camera down and put the kettle on, then went to the kitchen window and stared into the garden. The fog was even thicker. What on earth had happened in the field? He looked at the camera again – at the gaffer tape he'd put on the back to stop light getting in. There was one picture left on the film. He took it of the fog through the kitchen window.

Developing the film settled his mind, and by the time he pulled out the wet strip of negatives he was annoyed with himself for getting in such a state. The film was blank. A total waste of time and effort, with only the faintest shape of the marl pit on one or two pictures. He dried the film and ran it through the enlarger, deciding he'd print the last photo he took in the field because it was of nothing at all and would sum up exactly what he thought of the marl pit after all these months.

On the measuring board there was no image at all, but as soon as he put the paper into the developing tray a darkness spread across its centre and in quick succession the features of a man's face began to form. A face one or two feet away, filled with rage, teeth barred as if he was going to bite.

Liam screamed and in panic switched the main light on and in an instant the paper flooded with dark streaks and the face of the man disappeared. He stared at the blank paper for a long time, till he slowly regained control. Then he quickly looked at the last negative on the roll. The one he'd taken of the fog through the kitchen window. He switched on the safe light again and framed it in the enlarger, focusing it on the mat below. It was of nothing but the window, with the sink, washing up bottle and a couple of mugs on the sill in front of it, all in sharp focus. But when he slid the paper into the tray the same wave of panic gripped him once more because there was the man again, with dead rabbits and hares strung on wires round his neck, climbing through the open window.

He scrambled for the darkroom hatch and threw it open and immediately couldn't make sense of what he saw because the whole house was filled with the same, dense fog. The bedroom below was just a series of indistinct shadows. The rungs of the stepladder sank into it, and as he slowly climbed down he felt the wood was dripping with dampness. He crept through his room with his heart pounding in his ears, past the formless, sinister shapes of his bed and desk. Onto the landing, where he saw a couple of chairs looming through the mist. He turned onto the staircase. Each step plunged further into the thick shadows of the fog. There was an earthy smell in the house. A smell of soil. Compelled forward, he went down the stairs, noticing the dampness on his face and smelling the stench of the marl pit all round him till he reached the kitchen window. It was locked shut. And suddenly there was a juddering as the air began to reverberate with sound and the utensils and crockery on the work-surfaces started to vibrate and then the air compressed near him and he held his ears and stared through the obscuring layers of mist and he saw the glint of a long carving knife, trembling with crazed energy on the work surface, trying to lift, trying to spring towards him.

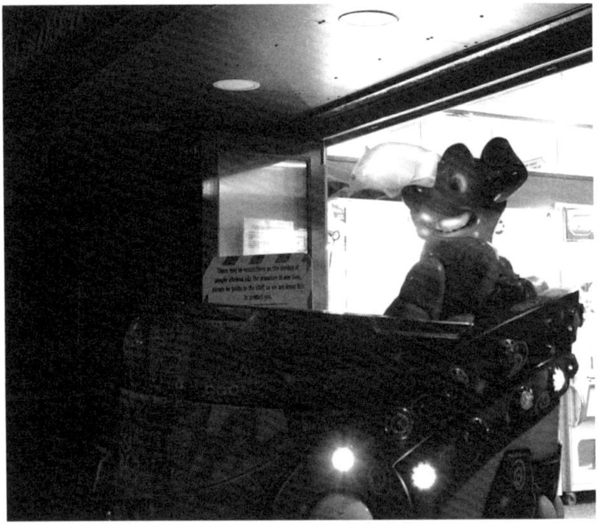

Hen

There were eight of them in the back room at Pirandello's, around a table littered with glasses, wine bottles and party popper streamers. Mandy sat at the head, still wearing her HEN PARTAAAYYY! sash, although it was ripped and hanging off her shoulder. She was flanked by her two oldest friends from school, Donna, shrill and unmarried and proudly outspoken, especially on a night like this, and Merc, large and bossy and high-spirited, but kinder natured. Further round the table was Chica, a small Portuguese girl Mandy had met on holiday in Wales, three women from Bramwells estate agents – Sharon, Angela and Mo – and at the end of the table, slightly under sufferance, Greg's younger sister, Charlotte. Being the sister of the fiancé marked her out, but she took it gracefully, and the others had made an extra effort to make her welcome.

Pirandello's was the third stop of the night. They'd already ticked off *Butler in the Buff Afternoon Tease*, and the nail parlour where a couple of them had paid extra for facials. Now they were loading up on carbs ahead of the dancing. Throughout the meal there'd been regular visits to the loos to sort outfits and reapply makeup, and Pirandello's waiters had picked up on this new vibe, swarming round the table, plying them with drinks. It had become loud and crude and the waiters, outnumbered, loved it, pushing the boundaries with suggestive comments, then making big shows of innocence when the women called them out. One of the waiters claimed to be the owner's son, and it gave him extra licence to make smutty remarks, probing for reactions around the table he could build on. Only Chica squared up to him, pointing out some sort of Latin familiarity that put him ill at ease, although it was widely suspected Chica wasn't that interested in men, anyway.

Mandy's glass had been refilled from both sides, she sat increasingly red-faced and unfocused while trying to keep up with several conversations at once. Her tiramisu was half off the plate, and she began to eat it from the tablecloth with a finger as her old school friends, Donna and Merc, led the Mr and Mrs honesty game. She rattled out the answers. Favourite holiday: Florida. Favourite meal: this one. Then, inevitably, what were Mandy's favourite sex positions? A big raucous cheer went up. Apparently, Greg had put his answer as reverse cowgirl but Mandy said no, that's crap, it's her on top, every time. Donna banged the table demanding the details and it soon became a list of Mandy having to rate all her previous sexual partners. Who was 'had all the gear, but no idea?' That would be Mitchell. Correct. And who 'always farted when he came?' Tom. No. Simon Boswell. Simon did that, too. There was a lot of shouting and wolf-whistles, stoked up by the school friends reliving their school days, enjoying making Greg's sister cringe and knowing it was all going to be dead embarrassing for Mandy when she was back at Bramwells on Monday, organising the spreadsheets. With a new round of drinks ordered, Mandy was given mystery presents. She quickly guessed that Merc had bought her the vodka in a water bottle, because that's what they'd done on their girls' holiday to

Alcúdia after sixth form, and Donn's present was – obviously – the glow in the dark condoms. Chica had given the bottle of port and box of natas, Sharon, the Sticky Rib pot noodle – because that was Mandy's go-to lunch at the office, the chocolate body paint had come from Mo, Angela had given the hand cream, and the small pot of expensive moisturiser had come from Greg's sister, Charlotte.

With the bill paid, and the waiters lined-up in an impromptu guard of honour to let the hens out of the door, the party spilled out onto the seafront. It was a bitter November night and Yarmouth was half-deserted. A sharp wind tore along the road, coming from the sea, picking up the grit of sand from the beach. A couple of Styrofoam chip cartons blew along the pavement, sticking then lifting off the damp slabs, and an empty lager can rolled madly across the street, accelerating, then bucking loudly when it hit the gutter. The women hardly noticed as they laughed, staggering on heels, divided into a couple of groups as they headed towards Stardust, the biggest of the nightclubs. It had rained heavily while they were in Pirandello's, and the multicoloured lights from the arcades and overheard awnings along Marine Parade shone off the wet pavement and trembled in the puddles.

Instead of going straight to Stardust, part of the leading group peeled off onto a side street, and when the others caught up they discovered they'd been led to some sort of clairvoyant's hut, built in a former shop. It wasn't part of the schedule, but Merc explained they had time and, besides, we can all find out a bit more about Mands, can't we? No one objected. The group consensus was easy to manage, and it was a good place to keep out of the wind.

Inside, the women filed boisterously through an ornate archway into a small room. It was gaudy and overfilled with tasselled curtains and fairy lights, a bit like a Gypsy caravan, a bit like Santa's grotto. The party crammed themselves in, bunching up around a table set in the centre. Glad to be out of the wind, but now giggling, trying to be quiet, this was clearly something no one needed to take seriously. Mandy sat slumped, pissed, saying she didn't think she wanted to have a fortune read. On the table was a menu of services: Angel, Oracle and Tarot decks. Palmistry. Psychic readings. Clairvoyancy. Soul connection. Fortune telling. Astrology. Crystal ball. Animal connection. Mandy tried to focus on the list before shoving it away, then rallied herself with: 'Right then ladies, bring it on.'

A soundtrack – new age and mystical – began to play on concealed speakers and, as a curtain pulled back to reveal a hidden entrance, a man stepped forward into the room. A couple of the women burst into giggles. The man was slight, androgynous, with black eyeliner and slicked-back hair in a ponytail. He wore a cheap purplish suit and some sort of small cape that looked as though it came from a party store. 'Jesus Christ,' Mandy muttered, trying to avoid eye contact.

'Wow, there's a lot of you,' the clairvoyant said, in a reedy voice that sounded like it had never quite broken.

'Shit,' Mandy said, stifling a laugh.

'Just her,' one of the school friends said, taking charge. The clairvoyant cleared his throat and gazed calmly at Mandy, as if gearing up for his act with a theatrical stare. Then he flipped out the cape, flamboyantly, and sat at the table, creating a space among them. He angled his knees to the side, in a feminine way.

'And what reading would you like?' he asked.

Mandy jabbed a finger onto the table: 'The one that says this time round I'm not making a big mistake!'

'You're the one getting married?'

'Oh, you're good – just how did you know that!' she answered, sarcastic.

'Congratulations.' He looked around the group, gauging the mood and taking his time. Again he cleared his throat before announcing: 'Well, good evening to you all. My name is Lorenzo and I shall be your guide between the two sides of life, what we have here in the room, and also from the spirit side. I would appreciate your patience and silence, as the spirits may present themselves with a degree of fragility. You may hear things that you are unaccustomed to, but I assure you it is all quite normal. If there is anyone who is uncomfortable at any time then they are welcome to leave. There is a small seated area you may have noticed on your way in.' He paused, rearranging the cape on his shoulders.

'Is Lorenzo your real name?' Sharon asked.

'It is.' He smiled, then raised his hand to pre-empt any more questions. He addressed the hen: 'So. Let us start. Please, may I have your name?'

'Mandy.'

'Hello, Mandy. Would it be possible for you to hand me something? Something that belongs to you. A personal item?'

'Phone?'

'Maybe.'

Mandy opened her bag, rummaged about in it, before deciding on a lipstick tube, which she put on the table.

'Perfect,' Lorenzo said. He rested a slender finger on top of the tube, and studied Mandy closely. He shut his eyes several times and made a few swallowing sounds. One of the women held in a burp, but he ignored it.

'I see suitcases around you,' he said. 'Nice luggage, and you're excited. You like to travel, and you have high hopes for this trip.' He continued to gaze at Mandy, making sure he had her full attention. 'And I'm aware of an elderly gentleman coming forward, from the spirit side. He would like your attention, because things were not settled when he passed. Does that make sense to you?'

'Not really.'

'And I'm aware of your lower back and I wonder if you have a weakness there?' Mandy gave a non-committal shrug. 'And tell me, do you have some kind of aching in your knee, your right knee?

'No.'

'But someone you know has problems with their knee?'

'Yeah. My dad.'

'His right knee?

'I think so.'

One of the school friends interrupted. 'Yeah, my dad, too. And everyone's dad.'

'Please,' Lorenzo frowned. 'A little silence.'

'Go on,' Mandy said.

'Do you have a scar, a tattoo or some kind of mark?' She nodded. 'I thought so. Now, in a few weeks, I'm seeing changes and opportunities. And Mandy, you will need to grab this new venture with both hands.'

Donna leant forward with a dismissive sneer: 'Amazing. She *is* getting married.'

Lorenzo didn't flinch. 'Again, congratulations.' He smiled,

then closed his eyes again. 'I feel like you want to settle down. Does that make sense to you? This may sound strange but I have the sense of an accident? I'm also aware of a lady who passed very suddenly. I am hearing singing, perhaps she was a singer, or played music? Also, do you have problems with your right foot?'

'This is bullshit,' Donna whispered.

Lorenzo raised his hand again, until the room was quiet. 'No problems with your right foot? Then I think it's a sign, that you are about to step forward, to something exciting.'

'What about the love life?' Merc asked.

Taking his time, Lorenzo smiled and nodding to himself, as if he was listening to something no one else could hear. 'Well I know that you have been fussy with your choices. You get annoyed by people's habits…'

'Yeah I am fussy,' Mandy said.

'But you are making the right choice, now. You will be happy Mandy – and if –' Lorenzo jolted, and his eyes sprang open. 'Whoa,' he said, breathlessly. 'Shit.'

Mandy looked back, anxiously.

'What's going on?' she asked.

Lorenzo lent back from the table, drawing his arms tight across his chest. He looked nervous. 'I'm afraid we have to stop.'

Donna, already fed up, leant aggressively towards him: 'What the actual –'

He cut her dead. 'I'm sorry. We have to stop.'

She glowered meanly at him: 'Well, this has been a total waste of time. We're not paying.'

'I understand.'

'Yeah? Come on Mands, this is a shitshow.' She urged the women to get up. 'You're full of bullshit, man. What a waster.'

Mandy started shaking her head: 'No – Donna – wait a sec. If he's seen something...'

'He's seen nothing. Look at his shitty little outfit here.'

But Mandy was sitting still, spooked. 'What is it?' she asked.

Lorenzo stood, wavering slightly, looking uncertain. He seemed genuinely upset. Slowly, he pointed to one of the women from the office, Angela, sitting at the side of the table. 'It's her,' he said, quietly. 'She's in trouble.'

Briefly, the room fell silent. Angela stared back, afraid to move. The atmosphere felt thick and expectant. But singling her out was a big mistake, because outrage quickly spread through the group. The women started to get up, huddling around Angela in a protective circle, and a couple of them shoved Lorenzo away towards the edge of the room. He reacted badly, squealing in a high-pitched voice, and holding his hands close to his face as if he was about to be slapped. Someone knocked the table over in the rush to get out and Lorenzo – taking an opportunity – scuttled off behind his curtain as they hurled insults at him.

Out on the pavement, the sense of indignation and anger pulled the group together, surrounding Angela to make sure she was alright, and saying what a creep Lorenzo was, pulling a stunt like that. Angela stood among them, stunned with embarrassment, as they made her promise to forget it. It meant nothing, absolutely nothing, and it wasn't going to spoil anyone's night. Angela nodded obediently, accepting the goodwill with a brave smile, trying her best to shrug it off.

'It's probably some part of his weird act,' she said, breezily.

'Seriously, hon,' one of the school friends said, slurring her words. 'I'm making a complaint about him, first thing Monday.'

'Yeah,' Angela replied.

'You work in Hel's office, at Bramwells?'

'Different department, but yeah.'

'Nice to meet you.'

The others stood around, blood up with undirected outrage, ready to lay into the clairvoyant if he dared to come out of the shop. Angela tried to laugh it off, uncomfortable with being the centre of attention. She was just about to speak when she noticed the group already starting to walk off towards the nightclub.

Angela let them move away, her heart still racing, before deciding to follow. So far, the hen night had been nothing but torment for her. She'd hated the nail parlour – the chemicals had given her a headache, and *Butler in the Buff Afternoon Tease* had made her anxious, especially when he'd gyrated in front of her chair. At the restaurant she'd found herself sitting too close to the rowdy school friend, Donna, and been intimidated as a result. She couldn't compete in the same oxygen, couldn't be smutty when the others had expected it, and had ordered a dish that ended up covered in shaved truffles, which she hated the taste of. When she spoke it had seemed slightly out of sync, missing tempo with the rest of the group, and she thought it was only a matter of time before they'd notice it. Even laughing along to their jokes, their dirty outrageousness, she hadn't been convincing. Her suspicion was that she'd been invited on the hen night to make up the numbers, and because she worked at the same island of desks where Mandy's better-known colleagues, Sharon and Mo, sat. And now that moment in the clairvoyant's crappy back room, when he'd cruelly singled her out and, briefly, made her the absolute centre of attention. It was horrible. She just wanted to shrink.

Catching up with the others she felt drunk and emotional and unable, now, to retreat to that place of awkward anonymity which, at least, had been safer. She kept noticing little acts of sympathy, such as one of the women putting an arm round her, or a voice in her ear saying 'just forget it, hon,' even though that's exactly what she'd promised them she was going to do.

Luckily, they soon reached Stardust and, after stepping into the huge carpeted foyer, queuing up by a roped-off VIP entrance, then facing a row of amused, implacable bouncers, she knew the group had quickly begun to forget her. From the top of a steel and mirror staircase a powerful regular beat thumped down towards them.

'You alright, darling?' Mo asked, her closest colleague from the office.

'Yeah – it was weird, but – I mean, what a creep.'

'Hundred per cent, babe.'

Angela hoped that would be that last of it. They filed in through the cordoned-off area, past the bouncers who adjusted their ties like they were at a wedding, and were met by a scantily clad girl on roller skates who handed them a tray of shots. The hen party congregated round it, dutifully downing the drinks and slamming the glasses back on the tray, making the girl slightly lose her footing. Then they climbed the staircase into the nightclub. Stardust had the cavernous quality of an airport lounge, darkly lit, with wheels of lights spinning above a huge dance floor, and Angela watched the others beginning to jig with the beat as they walked towards it, pushing their way into a busy crowd. On the other side of the dance floor she spotted at least two other hen parties.

Led towards a private booth, Angela saw the rest of the party were already downing more shots. She felt drunk and not quite able to take in her surroundings. But opting out would make her stick out so she downed the colourless, fiery liquid, and quickly accepted another one straight away. Dizzy, disorientated, she followed the others back to the dance floor. The lights flashed and spun aggressively above her, and blasts of dry ice swept up from vents at ankle level. It was too loud to talk, or to explain that she didn't really want to dance. Among the crowd she saw Mandy stumble to one side before laughing it off, still flanked by her school friends, and the small Portuguese girl, Chica, bopping around like crazy, shaking her hair and punching fists in all directions. A pocket of bewildered space developed around Chica, which only encouraged her more. Staggering, trying to move to the beat, Angela worked her way to the edge of the crowd. She lost her balance where the floor met the carpet, and fell against one of the upholstered booth seats. She stood up again and walked off, embarrassed, heading for the toilets. There, she locked herself in a cubicle, sat on the toilet seat bracing her head on her hands, wanting to stop her vision from spinning. Nauseous and distracted, she tried to focus on a problem that she couldn't quite formulate. Why had the clairvoyant singled her out like that? Was it just some cheap way of saying he didn't want their business? But why her – it could have been done a hundred different ways without being so personal. Perhaps the clairvoyant had picked up on her being slightly separate from the others, and targeted her as a result? Hen nights were a particular wound for her. She'd had one herself, three years ago, but no wedding to follow it. The onset of Craig's illness and his sudden death had been so shocking that, even now, she was afraid to think about it. Luckily, the others didn't know this about her. That particular part of her history belonged to another workplace and another set of friends, most of whom she'd moved on from because just to stay in touch with them reminded her of that acutely painful time.

From the other side of the cubicle door she heard some of the women from the hen party, chatting at the mirrors, and she waited with dread for them to mention her name. But they were laughing about something else, or weren't even from her party at all, and after a few minutes they left. Angela flushed the toilet, walked briskly past the row of mirrors and returned to the vast, thumping darkness of the club. Pushing her way through the crowd she headed for the stairs, held out her wrist to get an ink stamp from one of the bouncers, and within a few seconds she was out on the pavement, walking fast in the cold wind.

When she reached the clairvoyant's kiosk she saw with dismay that it was already closed, with a security shutter pulled down across the window. She rattled the door until she saw movement inside. A light turned on and she heard the lock turning, then the door opened a fraction, held on a security chain. Without his eyeliner, and now wearing some sort of Adidas sports jacket, she didn't immediately recognise the man as Lorenzo.

'What do you want?' he asked, matter of fact.

'I'm Angela. I'm the woman you pointed out.'

'And the shop is shut, now.'

She didn't know what to say, and hoped her breath wasn't too alcoholic. She put a hand on the door jamb, trying to steady herself.

'I think you owe me an explanation,' she said.

He frowned, disagreeing, but made no attempt to close the door.

'I've come back – I've left the others, just to come here.'

'So what do you want?'

'I told you.'

He sighed. 'You're drunk. Do you want me to make you a coffee?'

She nodded. He unlatched the door and let her in, then led her through the clairvoyant's room to a small kitchenette. It had a kettle, a microwave and a few theatrical props in open cardboard boxes. He popped the kettle on, then shifted to the back of the room, leaning against the counter top with his arms crossed.

She held the door frame, not quite wanting to go into the kitchenette, fighting the drunkenness that was making the surfaces spin.

'I wanna know what it's all about,' she said, impatiently.

He looked at the floor, shrugging: 'The way of the spirits is a mystery –'

'I don't want the act. I don't want that, OK?'

He nodded quietly, and she realised he was almost pressing himself against the end wall, as far away from her as possible.

'Are you a fraud?' she asked.

He cocked his head to one side, considering the question. 'Am I a fraud?'

'Yeah.'

'It's difficult to answer.'

'Lorenzo –'

'My name's Dave.'

She hesitated. In his tracksuit trousers and sports jacket, without the eyeliner, he didn't look much like a clairvoyant at all. He looked like any one of the sketchy misplaced men that wandered around the town. Someone you'd walk past. Someone you'd ignore.

'I'm not going to have a go at you, Dave,' she said. 'I just –'

'When you're this close to death,' he said, suddenly, 'there's a new energy.' Raising a hand, he demonstrated a kind of trembling motion in the air. Then he looked at her, seriously. 'You have it.'

'What do you mean?'

He maintained his stare, looking at her warily. 'It might not make much sense to you,' he continued, 'but just before death, or when death is really near, the body begins to alter. Like it's building up a charge. It's like a shimmering.'

She stared back, deeply unsettled by his sudden seriousness.

'It's in the room now,' he added.

She took a deep breath. 'You're crazy,' she replied, anger rising. 'You've got no right saying this kind of stuff.'

'I'm sorry.'

'You bloody should be.'

The kettle came to the boil and switched off with a loud clunk. He made no attempt to go towards it. 'So that's your explanation,' he said. 'I need you to go now.'

'Why?'

'Just go. I don't like the feel of this. I'm worried.'

'*You're* worried?'

He shook his head, not wanting to say anything more. He looked awkward and uncomfortable, trying not to look at her. But she stood in the doorway, blocking his exit, not going anywhere.

'When you're like this,' he said, choosing his words carefully, 'it's… risky. To be this close to you.'

He backed off even further, until he was leaning into the corner. Angela was stunned, and suddenly without fight. He was treating her as if she was radioactive.

'I'm going to die?' she said, incredulously. 'You mean – tonight?'

'All I said, is death – it's near you.'

'Will it go?' she asked.

He looked back at her, kindly, but not masking his concern. 'It might.'

'How will I tell?'

He shook his head and said nothing.

Five minutes later she was back at the nightclub, showing the entrance stamp on her wrist and trying to wipe a couple of tears off her face with her sleeve. She knew her makeup was a mess, but the brisk run along the seafront had at least helped to sober her up. She went straight to the toilets, forced herself to be sick in one of the cubicles, then ordered a coke from the bar and headed towards the cordoned-off booth to join the others. She sat with them, avoiding eye contact, hoping no one had noticed her absence, and when someone slid her a shot of vodka she politely refused.

'Go on, doll, only live once,' a woman said.

Angela looked up and realised she didn't recognise any of the women sitting in the booth. It was a hen party, but not her one.

'Oh, sorry,' she said, getting up to leave.

'No worries,' the woman replied, while the rest of the party looked at her sympathetically. 'Have one on us.'

Angela shook her head, excusing herself, clambering out of the booth as quick as she could. The music thundered around her, and among the dry ice and swirl of lights, she couldn't find her group anywhere. She looked for the baby pink of Mandy's HEN PARTAAAYYY! sash among the crowd, catching the light, but the crowd was packed and confusing. Everyone looked like someone she half-recognised, yet clearly didn't, and everyone was shrieking or dancing in groups or mouthing along to words with hands in the air. She kept moving, clutching her coke, knowing she only had a limited time before someone noticed she was all by herself. There were men hanging around on the periphery of the dance floor, in tight polo shirts and skinny jeans, nodding to the beat and scanning the crowd. It was obvious and predatory, and it made her keep her eyes low as she kept moving, pretending she knew where she was going. She tried to hide, briefly leaning against a pillar, looking for anyone from her party, and when a spotlight flashed across the top of the crowd it momentarily caught on bright red hair, she thought she saw Merc, the tall school friend, aggressively snogging a man. Angela stepped out from her hiding place just as the couple broke for air, and she realised it wasn't Merc at all, but a much older woman, whose face looked desperate and skull-like. Angela turned, her foot got caught on something, and when she glanced down she thought she saw the baby pink ribbon of Mandy's sash, discarded and trampled upon, among the debris on the floor. She stumbled forwards and – trying to look where she was going – looked straight into the face of one of the men that was watching the crowd. He studied her, direct and shameless, with wolfish interest. Turning away quickly, she threaded her way across the dance floor, but knew he'd latched on to her vulnerability. She went straight to the toilets, locking herself in a cubicle and putting a foot up against the hard surface of the door. This was relentless, she thought, a night that was slipping out of control. Threats emerging. Entrapment. And where were the others? If she found them, then more of the same: being on the edge of the group, or suddenly at its centre. Both options were excruciating. She stared at the graffiti on the back of the door and tried not to dwell on that man's expression – the man from the dance floor – judging her attractiveness, her potential, his chances – all in a micro-second. It made her sick. Him, and all the others like him, on the hunt. She felt renewed alarm about what the clairvoyant had told her. The danger she might be in. The man by the dance floor had looked at her with a sneering half-smile, only barely concealing an underlying shadow of something far more ugly and death-like. Abstractly, Angela nodded to herself, thinking of her fiancé, Craig, three years ago, who'd developed a terminal illness soon after they'd become engaged. He'd told her, as she'd nursed him in those last few weeks of his life, that he was seeing similar shadows of illness in other people. He'd never noticed it before, but among a crowd, he could now see people who were near death themselves. Similar illnesses, rising like a shadow through the flesh, declaring themselves. And sometimes one of these people would look towards him and he would simply panic and try to escape, because he knew that eventually, in one of those faces, he would encounter something mysterious and frightening: death itself, stalking him.

Angela burst into tears with the hotness of the memory. Those final weeks. She left the toilet and ran from the nightclub, not stopping until she was several minutes away along the near empty seafront. She paused in a small pedestrian area, taking deep breaths of the cold night air, near a closed-up café kiosk and a line of empty benches. The café had a large fiberglass model of a cone of chips stuck to the roof, with arms sticking out from the sides, and a cheeky, winking face poking out of the top. It looked surreal and eerie in the dark. Next to it a plastic model of a half-eaten doughnut stood on cartoon legs, running, headless. Angela calmed herself, regulating her breathing, and considered sitting on one of the benches. During the day she'd seen skateboarders here, doing stunts on the sloping terraces and paved areas while, on the other side of a low fence, she'd seen old people sitting on a similar row of benches, eating sandwiches within an ornamental flower garden.

She wasn't entirely sure where her B&B was. She remembered it was off the seafront, among an indistinct row of other guesthouses, but the seafront was long and repeated its mix of chip and burger stalls at regular intervals, so she might have easily overshot her particular street. And although she'd been to this pedestrian area earlier in the day, she couldn't quite remember what route she'd taken before, or after. Around her, the adverts for trips, souvenirs, food and toys were gaudy and overwhelming, absurd without anyone to read them. They seemed, to Angela, to be like a memory of a vanished life, which she was somehow led back to view one last time, as if the world had ended and she was looking for clues as to what it had all been about. Fun and holidays, but joy that never truly lasted, because it never does. She walked away, partly to escape from the sense of unease, but also drawn to an empty boardwalk that led towards the beach. Stepping onto the boards the sea air stiffened around her, blowing from behind the storm shelters, and the sound it made became empty and strange and difficult to determine. The beach lay in front of her, vast and deep. The spill of Yarmouth's streetlights faded in a long blurry line along the stretches of sand. Beyond that was a thick impenetrable darkness. She heard the sea, somewhere in front of her, waves surging against the shore. She clutched her arms to her chest, against the cold, and concentrated on the point where the lights from Yarmouth faded into featureless dark. A girdle of shadow, miles long, surrounding the town. Like a frontier between life and death.

All the streets looked the same. The same mix of railings, guesthouses, VACANCIES and NO VACANCIES signs hung in the windows, the same assortment of names and front doors. She retraced her route several times, looking down the streets leading off the seafront, looking for signs of familiarity, and was hugely relieved when she finally saw the hanging baskets of plastic flowers either side of the Glendale's front door. Freezing cold, worn out, she let herself in. The guesthouse was quiet and still. Only a couple of sidelights had been left on, and the foyer led off into a back area that was shadowy and unpleasant to look at. Angela took her shoes off and quietly started climbing the stairs, aware of the middle of the night quality of a building that seemed to be deserted. There were many half-landings and dead-end corridors. Her room was on the top floor, one of two off a tiny attic landing, and when she rounded the last flight of stairs – she halted with shock. Her door was wide open. Alert with anxiety, she crept towards it. Inside the room, someone else's luggage had been chucked on the bed. A half open suitcase, with women's clothes and a makeup bag spilling out. There were several bottles of spirits, half drunk, on a desk.

Angela quietly returned downstairs until she reached the ground floor. Not knowing what to do, she explored the darkly lit back area of the building, and found a door marked MANAGER. It was locked, no one was in, but on a nearby table she saw an envelope with her name written on it. Opening it, she found a key, and a note explaining there'd been a mix up with the booking, that her original room, a double, had in fact been booked for weeks. Would she mind moving to the single room next door? It was very apologetic. Having no choice, and exhausted from the day, she went back upstairs and let herself into the second bedroom off the attic landing, where she found her luggage and a small box of chocolates with a second note expressing an apology.

Soon after getting into bed, she heard noises coming through the wall from the room next door. Some sort of argument, restrained but vicious, followed by a series of mysterious knocks and thuds. A woman laughed, brittle and cruel, then stopped laughing. Angela thought she heard crying. Once, almost a scratching noise, like long uncut nails dragging along the wallpaper in the other room. She lay on her bed, startled and afraid, knowing she should try to find out what was happening next door, but was too scared to move because of what the clairvoyant had said. Threat seemed close. Very close. She held her hands against her ears until she fell asleep, but was awoken by a persistent knocking on her door. A grey light, pre-dawn, was coming through the gaps above the curtain.

'Who is it?' she called out.

The knocking continued – insistent.

'I'm sleeping!' she said.

A man's hushed voice answered, speaking close to the other side of the door.

'I'm very sorry. But you will have to leave.'

Angela struggled to wake up, trying to make sense of it. She tried to focus but her head felt heavy and numb.

'It's so early.'

'I'm sorry. But you will have to do this. Please get dressed. I will explain.'

'Are you the owner?'

'Yes. I left you the note, for when you came in.'

She heard a strange beeping noise and sounds of other people moving on the stairs.

'What's going on?' she demanded. He didn't answer. Hurriedly, she got out of bed and pulled on a pair of jeans. She put her jacket on and zipped it up tight. He knocked again.

'OK. One second.' She slipped her shoes on and went to the door. Again, she heard sounds of other people out there, speaking in low voices.

'Who's out there?' she said, close to the door.

'Are you dressed?' the owner asked.

'Yes.'

Immediately a key started turning in the lock, and the door opened. She tried to push it shut, but the man put a foot in the crack and held it. The owner's face appeared, pale and apologetic.

'Please, this way,' he said, kindly. 'The police are here.'

She stepped, obediently, onto the half-landing. Immediately, she saw the body of a woman, fallen on the stairs. A jacket had been placed over her face and head, but her body was in an unnaturally twisted shape where her neck had made contact with the wall. Angela could see the woman was young, half-dressed in nightclothes. Several policemen were standing near her, talking to a paramedic in low voices. She realised the beeping she'd heard was the sound of their radios.

'What happened?' Angela whispered, to the owner.

'We don't know, I'm afraid. You can wait in my office.'

A policewoman came up the stairs, passing the woman on the floor, offering to help guide Angela down.

'This way, Madam,' she said. 'Keep going. Don't look.'

Angela did as she was told, stepping carefully past the hand of the fallen woman. At the turn of the stairs, she gazed up at the bedrooms, both with their doors open.

'That was my room,' Angela said.

The policewoman stopped, interested: 'Your room? Do you know her?'

Angela shook her head. 'I mean – it was meant to be my room, but we had to swap. I was put next door.'

'OK. We'll probably need you to make a statement.'

'Was she attacked?'

'Let's just get you down, first.'

But Angela was reluctant to move. The nearness of the dead woman, lying on the stairs, compelled her to stay. There was a connection between them that she didn't fully understand, demanding her attention. 'What if I hadn't swapped?' she said, then was ashamed for voicing it. She looked up the stairs at the open bedroom door, confused, emotional, remembering fragments of what she'd heard during the night. Violence erupting, uncapped and fierce, a few inches away from where she was lying on the bed. It had been the proximity of death, approaching, occurring like a pulse of energy that sparked, mysterious and unannounced. With a tremor of fear she glanced towards the woman once more. A jacket had been placed over the woman's head, but it had been done in a hurry, and it left several gaps. Beneath the material Angela saw a shadowy glimpse of the woman's frozen stare, appallingly focused, aimed directly at her. Blue, lifeless eyes. Violence, now passed, like a shimmer where life releases its hold. And what it had left behind was this: a clear-eyed accusation from the dead.

The Murder of Crows

The bird had been scratching for hours and Sal could do nothing about it, other than sit in bed with the duvet wrapped tight, watching Mitch's back in the dark as he pressed his ear to the wall. The cottage was built right in the middle of the oak wood and it had a bricked up fireplace. 'Can't do nothing,' he said, every so often, sighing with sympathy, 'it must have falled down the chimney. I ent smashing a hole with a crowbar cause that's gonna kill it anyway.'

He always called the shots. There was an air vent on the chimney breast, and he was trying to peer through it to see the bird. He shone a pocket torch, angling it between the slats of the vent, just to show her he was trying to do something. Soon as he stops trying, soon as he gets back in bed, that bird is as good as dead, she thought. That's the way it is. Mitch is going to solve it, or no one will. Any minute he might give up, saying it's gonna die and it's gonna die soon.

But the bird very clearly *wasn't* dying. It was deep behind the plaster in some damp throat of soot, flapping against the bricks, falling over, stumbling in the dark. Occasionally, a chirp of panic. This might go on for days, she thought, a slow death of thirst or exhaustion or battering itself against the bricks. How could she bear that? And after it died it would be in there forever, filling first with maggots and then rotting and then there'd be a skeleton, always, in the wall.

'I think that's it,' he said. It was a stock phrase of his – the kind of thing he said if the car broke down; the kind of thing he'd also say if he then managed to fix it. He stretched his arms and stepped calmly to the window. He was a large man, happy to walk around in boxers even though it was cold, always looking through the window as if answers – true answers – only lay outside. He stood there, one hand on the back of his neck, the other tucked down the front of his waistband, his usual stance, and said:

'Don't you get in a state about this, yeah?' He sounded defeated. He sounded like they'd already been arguing about it. 'I don't wanna scene.'

'Sorry,' she replied.

He got back in bed and scratched his stubble. Immediately, the bird started moving in the wall. A fluttering, restless noise, then the sound of a beak tapping the bricks. She pictured its eye tilting up towards the chimneypot, and the sight of the sky, no bigger than a coin. Sal listened, as the sounds of Mitch's breathing grew heavier, and she wondered – she wondered whether the dark mist would come today, rising from the stain on the carpet.

When she woke in the morning, she realised Mitch must've carried his clothes out and changed in the living room, then taken the handbrake off to let the car roll down the slope before he started the engine – so as not to disturb her. He was considerate that way, yet selfish in almost every other way. People thought he was a free spirit – that he couldn't be tied down. Driving off, he'd be glad to get away from her. He'd be travelling all day selling lawn seed and he'd enjoy every second of freedom he had, stopping for a fag and a fried breakfast in one of his usual places. He claimed it was tough sitting behind the wheel all day and tougher still to face a salesman's bed at the end of it. But she imagined his long back stretched out on a soft mattress in a Travelodge, and it seemed to her in that instant that his life was just a long string of treats.

She made a mug of tea, crossed yesterday off on the calendar and looked up the section in her book which was titled 'Week 32':

> By now your child will have usually turned into an upside-down position (Cephalic). This may not change until birth. He or she will have well-developed eyes and hearing. Sometimes the child may suck its thumb or scratch its own body.

She dialled Hannah's number.

'Hi Hannah,' she said, quickly, 'I was just looking up in the book – it says at this stage the child can have dreams at night. Isn't that weird?'

'Is it?'

'Well – what's it got to dream about? I mean, there's been no experiences and all that.'

'Suppose so.' Hannah seemed cheery, but often got distracted within seconds. 'We still meeting up today?'

'Let me just check,' Sal paused, trying to make a joke. 'Yep. Nothing else planned.' She tried to sound casual as she looked through the kitchen window at the trees. Crows were in the high branches and she could see them crashing about like devils up there. 'I'll see you later,' she said, and hung up.

She arranged five acorns into a row on the table, then twisted the cap off one and sniffed the green smell of the tree. She made another call – this time to the mail order company. The computerised message made her wait, but even this was all right, she thought, as she thumbed through the range of cots in the catalogue. I'm important, she reminded herself, tapping an image of a brightly lit cot with a finger. Eventually someone answered and Sal started asking questions about sizes and mattresses and drop-down sides. It made her happy to talk about the details. She felt good, to be listened to like that. She sought her reflection in the chrome-sided toaster, wondering if she looked like a mother yet.

After placing the order for the cot she picked up her mug of tea and stepped outside. The stink of the wood was overwhelming: an autumn dampness full of fallen leaves and wet earth. The crows were screaming at something, crawling like rats from branch to branch, wings thrashing out like axe heads when they lost balance. She looked back at the cottage, imagining it was the first time she was seeing it. Such a quirky little place. Knapped flint walls and odd pointy-shaped windows. A woodsman's cottage, a couple of hundred years old but, really, who'd ever want to spend their life surrounded by all these dark trees?

With a trowel she scratched around in the mud till she found an earthworm, then rolled it onto the blade with a twig, not wanting to touch it. She was being extra careful with hygiene now. She carried the worm inside, went to the chimney breast in the bedroom, and eased it through the vent. It fell without sound. The bird, also, was silent. She sat there for a while and thought about the early morning, how she'd gone to sleep thinking about the bird dying inside the wall. Then she looked at the patch of carpet where the dark mist always rose from, and was amazed that it looked so plain and unremarkable. Just a stain on the carpet, like a can of oil had once stood there. She'd tried scrubbing it using a variety of methods, but it always came back.

As Sal walked into the café at the farm shop, Hannah pointed guiltily to the remains of a fruit scone on a plate in front of her: 'Just couldn't stop myself,' she said. 'Oh –' she added, looking surprised: 'You look tired, love – is it the baby?'

Sal smiled and read the menu. She sensed the scrutiny of Hannah's gaze and tried not to think how lovely Hannah's skin was. Five months pregnant and her skin was glowing like honey.

'I've gone right off coffee,' Sal said, happily. They'd met every Monday, since that day in the factory car park when Hannah had rushed out to give her a leaving card and slip her a tenner. 'You'll need it,' she'd whispered, showing kindness where no one else had. And then both of them pregnant within weeks of each other.

But five months later Sal knew her friend was beginning to find their Monday morning coffee a bit of a chore. They'd counted up the weeks together, but now Hannah was beginning to count down and make her individual plans, any Monday seemed like it might be their last. Apart from their pregnancies they didn't have much in common. 'We'll bring the kids here,' Hannah had once said, but Sal knew that would never happen.

'How's the cottage?' Hannah asked.

'Don't know – I mean, fine, but it's really quiet at night. Really dark and I don't like the woods. Guess I'm still getting used to it.' She always did that, gave too full an answer to a question which wasn't really being asked. She tried to be brighter: 'Anyway, it's cheap for the next few months, and we've got to pull the belt in. Rowells gave me five hundred redundancy, but that's not gonna last.'

She knew Hannah from the canning factory. Hannah worked labels while Sal pushed the frankfurters into the beans – which was easily the best job on the line. All the women loved that job – it was suggestively rude to push the sausage into the beans, and the factory was a rude place – but for Sal it seemed she wasn't even up to that. She wasn't up to being the centre of attention like Hannah was. If Hannah had pushed the frankfurters into those beans, it would have been a right laugh, every day. But Sal did it quietly, almost shamefully, and the girls on the line said things like *is that sausage not doing it for you, babes?* Sal knew they were mocking her. Mocking her for not making rude jokes when she'd been given such a golden opportunity. Why hadn't she been allowed to do the labels – the kind of job no one noticed? Then she might have stayed at Rowells instead of becoming what it had said on her redundancy letter: 'Difficult'.

'How's the factory?' Sal asked.

'Same old. Twelve weeks left then I'm out of there, for good.'

Hannah's fella was a builder called Jason Jones and he'd once carried an injured deer back to the village when he'd been out jogging. Slung it over his shoulder, apparently. All the girls at the factory had heard that one.

'Sal, when do I get to meet him?' Hannah asked, with half a wink.

'Who?'

'Your man!' she said, and there was a touch of impatience in her voice that Sal didn't like. 'Can't keep him *all* to yourself.'

On the walk back the handles of the plastic bags cut into her fingers with the weight of the shopping. Had it sounded suspicious when she'd replied that Mitch would probably be away for weeks? 'Everyone's after lawn seed,' she'd said. That was a dumb thing to say. But there again, Hannah wasn't the sharpest tool in the shed. She probably didn't pick up on anything. Pregnancy re-wires the brain, she thought. Hannah was soggy with it. She swapped the bags from hand to hand and looked at the oak wood across the pasture. Trees mostly leafless, the wood rose across its own hill like unkempt hair on an old head. The trees are too close to the house, she thought. They press round it with their dark shadows and foul breath.

No need to scare yourself, she thought. But those crows, if only they'd fly somewhere else. A parliament of rooks, and a murder of crows, that's what they call them. What did they do all day, apart from scream at each other and thrash about? Gathering there, guardians of all things barren and all things poisoned.

In the cottage she listened to the radio, grew restless, made too much tea, read a magazine she'd already read, decided that was pointless, closed the curtains before it was dark and eventually spent the evening sitting on the floor in front of the chimney breast, trying to hear the bird. She wondered about Mitch, remembering how they'd first met, when he'd walked her back to her rented flat near Rowells and kissed her in the pub forecourt. How they'd banged teeth because he was drunk and how his leather jacket had hung off his shoulder nearly dragging on the cement. She'd told him his jacket would get ruined and he replied that he didn't care, he never felt the cold, and he thought his jacket looked cool like that, full of attitude. But to her it just looked like he was drunk. He'd put his hand up her skirt and unbalanced himself, dragging her into the empty street, both of them stumbling off the curb. And she remembered seeing the pub sign wet with the drizzle above her. The Green Man. The sign had an impish face painted on it with leaves sprouting from its cheeks and eyebrows. And now, as she remembered that pub car park, she imagined the dark mist lifting from the shadows like a pile of old leaves swirling up in a gust.

It's coming, she thought, the menace that started at some unnoticed point in the day, some comment or sight or half-remembered thought which caused it; a menace that spread like a stain, discolouring everything, and there was nothing you could do to drive it away. It would come tonight. It was unavoidable.

In the middle of the night Sal realised she was awake, staring intently at a shadow rising from the carpet. The shadow became rich and malleable, as if fungal spores were drifting, gathering into a dense rich vapour. The mist darkened, bruise black, elongating into a twisted, hunched shape. Sal drew her legs up in fear as the mist thickened, straightening then bending towards her across the bed. An odour emerged: a musty unwashed smell of old clothing, of damp woodland, of roots and leaf mould. Among the mist she saw a thickened cord of darkness, like a wooden staff, with an outline of knuckles curled across the top, contracting in tension.

Sal let out a despairing cry as her wrist was gripped by a strong force. She tried to shake it off, but the grip was too strong and she was pulled swiftly from the bed. She twisted and fell against the chimney and heard a cough from the bird trapped inside. The dark mist stood in the half-light, creased like bark. Then Sal was being dragged into the corridor, out through the front door, into the oak wood. She heard herself moaning with fear as she was pulled through the bracken. The air was dense with the smell of acorns, leaves, bark and soil, and as the boughs hung above her she realised she was being pulled towards the silhouette of a tree she'd never seen before.

The pressure on her wrist relaxed as they reached the tree, but then Sal felt the rough bark against her face as she was pressed against it. The old oak was like stone and then with a sudden release it yielded, Sal was being pushed into the tree, the bark softening like folds of dough, a living texture that was strange and suffocating. Around her the darkness of the wood was being replaced by a greater, closer darkness as the tree swallowed her.

Sal stood in the middle of the oak. Above her the tree vanished into a complicated darkness. It was peaceful and silent. The tree surrounded her with an enormous pressure, making her ears hum and pushing at her like it was a giant living throat.

She woke on the floor, her duvet wrapped round her tight as a tourniquet. She was damp with sweat. She breathed deeply, trying to calm herself. Everything was going OK before the pregnancy. Putting a little by each month, that evening-course she took last year, those thoughts of getting a qualification in home design. She was good at that, everyone always said she was good at that. A nest builder. And now the child inside her was filling her head with fear and doubts. *They don't dream*, she said out loud, *they just fill your head with fear. They're inside and they're stuck and they think there's no way out*, and she realised the very thought of what she was saying was making her cry. Why wouldn't he just call – why couldn't he just go to a phone box or use his mobile or ask someone if he could borrow – I mean it doesn't matter – as long as he calls and just – just is there, on the other end, that's all I need…

She went to the kitchen and started to flick through the pages of a glossy magazine about interior design ideas, fast and angrily so the paper was almost ripping. She stopped to gaze at a photo of a beautiful room. A penthouse apartment floating above a city. There was an espresso cup on a table, and she noticed on that table there was another glossy magazine just like the one she was looking at. The magazine had been casually left open as if the owner of the flat had gone to pick up a phone that had been ringing. A call from a boyfriend: *Dinner at where? No – really? You're spoiling me. Then I'll wear my you're-in-danger dress…* Sal pictured herself sitting in that apartment, listening to the girl on the phone. A sweet breeze coming from the window through a drape of muslin. Sal imagined a smell of coffee and a hint of perfume. Something expensive. A soft, clean warmth to the light she's never seen in any house she's ever been in. This must be in London, in an exclusive development, in a riverside apartment. From somewhere beyond an open bookshelf the girl giggles on the phone and Sal sees a glimpse of an exquisite summer dress and some long blond hair hanging as the girl cups the phone under her chin. *I think I know what you like*, the girl says suggestively and there's the merest flash of a private smile, through the veil of her hair, then Sal gets distracted by what's on the shelves: a camera, some woven baskets, car keys in a tasteful pot, some dried seed pods a little like the thistles that grow along the path. And suddenly the fantasy collapsed and Sal was back in her cottage thinking about the thistles, looking at the kitchen table she'd found in a skip. She saw a bill from the rental agency, a universal credit claim form, the pregnancy book opened on its spine from yesterday.

She went to the kitchen drawer, brought out his pair of motorcycle gloves, and put them on the table to die.

Later on, she decided to venture out into the wood. Taking the initiative. She set off to find the tree, the huge oak from the night before, but she kept going in circles through the bracken without coming across it. Her morale began to slip. *Careful* she said, out loud, knowing she was becoming scared again, *let's go in now*, but as she turned back she saw a glimpse of her cottage through the trees and for the first time she felt spooked by it. Those pointy windows and the moss-covered roof. She couldn't believe she'd ever decided to rent it. Why had it been vacant for years? No one knew its history or who'd lived there, or if they did, no one told her. That smarmy bloke from the rental agency had said it'd been on the books a long time, it was cheap because it clearly wasn't everyone's cup of tea – that alone should have rung an alarm bell. She decided to call him tomorrow and put him on the spot. She could be good on the phone. Be direct and ask him, and if he's hiding something, then… suddenly she stopped dead in her tracks. Someone was staring back at her from a few feet away. The recognition was awful. It was herself, her own wooden face mapped out and mirrored in the bark of a tree. Her instinct was to reach out, but as she stepped forward the alignment of the bark shifted and the recognition vanished.

The dark mist was waiting for her in the bedroom, poised for her to fall asleep, souring the air with cruelty. Sal climbed quietly under her duvet while it gathered over the carpet, deepening and amassing until it hung over the bed.

Several times as Sal started to doze off she startled herself awake to see it peering down at her. *Its eyes, as black as a crow's wing, a crow's wing, as black as its eyes…* Sal felt a stab on her face as if she was being prodded with a stick. There was a foul energy in the room as the dark mist twitched above her, unstable and overbearing. Again, there was an awful unwashed smell. Suddenly, the mist lurched to one side, twisting into a point to strike the chimney breast. Chips of plaster and brick dust spat across the room. Sal cried out for it to stop – shouted out that she didn't want it there, didn't want to see what was in the wall, but the attack continued with manic effort, till a dark crack appeared and Sal smelt the enclosed stench of the chimney as the bricks were pulled loose and a hole grew, piece by piece, and Sal yelled again because there, through the rough broken shape of the hole she could see the slumped skeleton of a woman, collapsed upon itself with age, her skull caught between her own ribcage, legs folded unnaturally, and across the pelvis of the skeleton, the lifeless figure of the dead crow.

*

Sunlight was streaming through the curtains as Sal woke to hear a car bumping its way across the meadow. Crows stirred in the trees outside, cawing as first one door then a second slammed. Sal got up from where she'd slept on the floor and looked anxiously through the window. Parked outside, she saw a builder's van, bright red, with the name Jason Jones printed on the side, and BUILDING YOUR DREAMS written beneath it. Everything to be proud of. Jason was there, leaning against the van door in a fleece and faded jeans, lighting a cigarette and staring across the meadow.

Hannah rang the bell and immediately followed it by banging on the door. Sal heard her name being called. She let the curtain fall back into place and saw how bloodied her knuckles were. On the floor by the chimney was the crowbar she must've used to pull the bricks out. The doorbell rang again and she thought about hiding and knew she couldn't and knew it was only a matter of time before one of them came to peer through the bedroom window.

When she opened the front door, Hannah had a finger raised to press the bell again. Her face was set as the thin-lipped, disapproving woman she would one day become. Yet, suddenly faced with Sal, she was clearly struggling to understand something.

'What the hell's happened?' Hannah asked.

Sal looked down at her bruised hands, wondering if it was possible to break knuckles, and she realised her hair must be wild and matted with plaster dust.

'A bad night,' she replied.

Hannah glanced at her husband, seeking support, and he

gave her the tiniest of nods before she pushed past Sal into the house.

'So,' Hannah said, 'we received a cot today.' Her voice was tight with anger, and Sal knew that the man outside had probably already had an earful on the way over. 'What are you playing at?'

'It's a gift.'

'Right.' Hannah walked to the kitchen table and picked up the mail-order catalogue, like it was evidence. 'Thing is, when's it going to stop, Sal? The stroller, car seat, the changing table – it's been going on months and you clearly can't afford it and anyway even if you could we don't want it, we don't want any of it.'

Sal was still holding the front door. 'Is that your husband?' she asked.

Hannah ignored her. 'I'm taking this,' she said, stuffing the catalogue into a pocket of her coat. Through the window Sal could see the builder calmly blowing smoke into the air – enjoying what a man does best, being one step back from the action, but being ready in his fleece and jeans in case he's needed. Totally in control. Sal tried to imagine him carrying that injured deer over his shoulder – carrying it miles back across fields to the village, knowing it would be the making of his reputation. Something he could live off for years.

'I'm sorry,' Sal said. 'I thought you'd like the cot.'

'We've *already* got one,' Hannah said, wearily.

'It was my boyfriend's idea – see, Mitch, he's making good commission with the lawn seed and he knows what good friends you and me are.'

Hannah was shaking her head. 'So where is he?' she asked.

'Who?'

'Your so-called *boyfriend.*'

'Why are you so angry?' Sal asked, but it wasn't heard.

'Sal,' Hannah was saying, 'you've got to accept it, there's no boyfriend. There's no bloke selling lawn seed, is there? The guy was a loser – just some greasy biker.'

With sudden clarity Sal remembered how she'd woken that morning in her old flat near Rowells because Mitch was revving the throttle of his motorbike in the yard below, and before she could get to the window he'd ridden off, gunning it down the street and she'd seen the bike lurch as he changed gear and there was a flash of the morning sun off its chrome mudguard and a moment later he was gone, turning the corner and out of her life.

'Oh, *no...*' Hannah said, lifting Sal's special T-shirt off the back of the chair as if it was a dead animal. And as she began to pull out the padding that had been carefully stitched inside it she didn't have the strength to hide her disgust any longer.

'Is this – is this revolting thing what you use to pretend you're pregnant?' she said, letting it fall onto the tiles. Hannah began to cry, holding her hand over her mouth, and Sal heard her say something like *you sicken me*, but all Sal could really think about was that morning when Mitch had ridden off on his Honda. In his haste Mitch had left his motorcycle gloves behind, left them on the kitchen table, and she'd looked at them all that morning, afraid to touch them, looking at how the old leather had formed its own dark cast round the shape of his hands, the fingers of the gloves slightly curled as if they were still gripping the handlebars.

After the bright red builder's van had driven away, Sal sat on the tiles and pushed the padding back into the hand-sewn pocket of the T-shirt, before pulling it over her head. She tried stroking the belly. A small but pleasing shape. And as she closed her eyes, imagining a baby's unborn dream, she smelt the musty woodland odour of the dark mist as it came into the room behind her.

Ice

Gradually at first, ice crystals began to rise in the water, glinting like fish scales. The water became greasy and thick, and when the breeze stirred across the lake its surface seemed dull and unpolished. All year round the lake had a rich vegetative colour but, now, like a great eye going blind, it became cloudy. The ice formed into granules, hardened, then large flat plates started to grow into each other, before the lake froze into one continuous sheet, as tight as metal.

The last night in November. Sam had watched the lake freeze many times, and it always filled him with wonder. Wonder and fear. But this was the date when it had happened. If it was going to come again it would be tonight.

He began to hear the ice attaching itself along the side of his boat. Fingers of it, feeling their way along the steel hull of the barge, as if it knew he was in there, listening. Soon the ice would connect him to the bank and the boat would stop floating. It would be set in stone, sharp and clear, and Sam would be fixed to the land he'd left behind. He'd have to face what he'd never come to terms with after all these years.

He shovelled more coal into the stove and took a swig from a hip-flask. No good. Rough brandy. The stove was smoking and the air in the cabin was thick and stale with it. His eyes were smarting and he was cold to the core. People said he had a troubled face: old before his time. They kept their distance, and it suited him. But his solitary way of life had made him a reluctant talker; a man who stared too much and said too little. He made others uneasy. Some people called him slow-witted, but it wasn't that at all. He just didn't know how to be with people.

He sat on the edge of his bunk rubbing the back of his neck with his hand. His hair was long and straggly and he tried twisting it round a finger, trying to calm himself. He'd grown a beard, too. He never left the lake. There was no fight in him to leave. Grown sluggish like the water, he thought. Move from the table to the bunk, to the wheelhouse, it's all the same. He could watch a floating leaf for hours or stare at a heron standing motionless on the bank until the light faded. The only thing which disturbed him was this ice, and nothing would stop it now. *Sam*, he thought, *you got to be ready for her this time.*

At midnight he lifted the hatch and stepped out on deck. A full moon was up above the trees. It shone with a piercing winter clarity across the perfect white disk of the lake. Along the riverbank the grass was leathery with frost. He climbed onto the jetty and stood quietly on the old boards. It was the only jetty for the lake, and as he looked down at the wood he was overtaken by a warm memory of children running barefoot along its planks in the hot summer months, jumping and yelling and tumbling off the end. How they seemed to hang in the air, suspended, for that fraction of a second before they hit the water, enough time for him to see the flies hovering a few inches above the lake's surface, the seeds and pollen floating like dust, and then the children, crashing into the water and shouting and laughing and their hair would be stuck flat across their foreheads. Hair as slick as an otter's, all of them. He remembered the smell of the wet planks drying in the sun – and wished he could still see their footprints.

He pulled his coat tight and sat at the end of the jetty. The last two boards were worn smooth by the hours he'd spent sitting there. He rolled a cigarette and looked over the lake. Not much more than a cricket pitch in size, and about as round, fringed by thick woodland going right to the water's edge. Ash, lime, willow and alder, all standing in thick mud so that the water could only be reached at a couple of places. The river passed somewhere beyond the trees. Boats passed too, but you never saw them. It was a forgotten place.

Mist was emerging from the trees. *Here it comes,* he thought, as he watched it rising and collecting on the far side. He watched the vapours anxiously, waiting for it to happen, and gradually he noticed strands curling in on themselves below a small clump of willows. The mist coiled into a pillar and then began to unravel. A small figure, light and delicate, formed, vanished, then pulled through the mist, rushing beneath the trees at great speed.

The man stared, clenched with fear. Though he'd waited for it he couldn't believe it was happening again. After all this time.

What he saw was a young girl, around twelve years old, gliding from shadow to shadow. An apparition which flashed briefly into the moonlight then suddenly came to a halt beneath the trees. For a moment it seemed like she'd vanished into a pool of oil. But then the girl came forward, this time venturing into the lake, until she was far from the trees in the full blaze of the moon. A small girl, so thin and pale she was almost translucent, moving cautiously across the ice, testing its thickness. Gradually she became more confident, lifting each of her skates in turn and sliding her legs forward, shifting her weight from side to side. She wobbled off balance, an arm waving out like a puppet, then at one point she tipped forward at the waist, and the man prepared himself to react, anticipating her fall. But she regained her balance and came onward, closer now to the jetty, perhaps heading for it and the man didn't know whether she had seen him or not and he didn't know whether to stand up or wave or call out.

About thirty feet away she stopped to examine her skates. A lace was dragging. The man saw the lace and the tiny crumbs of ice cut up by each blade, and the soft cloud of her breath as she tried to reach down. Her cheeks were flushed with a mixture of cold and heat, and suddenly she was standing upright again and sliding over towards him with her arms raised out ready to grab the jetty and he moved and stretched out his hand to try and stop her coming any closer. His throat tightened with fear. She noticed him then, right at the last minute, her eyes widening with fright as she tried to stop, nearly tripping over as she ground her toe into the ice.

'Stop!' he called.

The girl stared back at him wildly. He saw the narrowness of her mouth and the look of panic in her eyes. They stayed like that for a long moment, him gripping the edges of the planks and her a few steps away. The air seemed frozen between them. Slowly her expression began to change, began to be replaced by something more fleeting, a shy smile perhaps, but she was against the moonlight and he couldn't be sure. Then suddenly she turned and skated in a straight line across the deepest part of the lake, once more disappearing into the mist.

It had happened again. The girl on the ice, just as he'd expected. The lake fell silent. It was too shadowy against the dark trunks to see whether she was still there or not. Trails of vapour wound themselves loose from the body of the mist, but not enough to reveal the apparition or prove it had gone. He imagined he saw the glint of her skates, but it could be many things and he didn't trust his eyes. But his assumption was that she was there, on the ice beneath the willows, watching him.

There was a path that side of the lake. A cinder path which led from the water's edge, through the wood, then eventually out into the pasture in front of the hall. Earlier that day the man had picked his way along the banks to reach it. In the thin sunlight the ice had glowed between the tree trunks. It seemed a miracle how such tea-brown water made such pure white ice. Coots had been venturing onto the frozen lake. Confused by it. The twigged joints of their legs and blue webbed feet had looked disproportionate and strange.

It had been difficult to reach the path. The mud had a brittle crust but it was black and greasy underneath and the tree roots were as slippery as glass. Snow had blown into the ruts and some of it had fixed as ice. In the trees and in the air was the sharp dry smell of more snow arriving. The woods had been incredibly still, but occasionally he'd heard a stirring, followed by the sound of ice tinkling in the branches.

The trunks had been dark and wet and as hard as stone. Ash green lichen had been the only colour, it clung to the bark like it was in agony. This was where the frogs mated in the spring, turning each marsh and rut into a sliding, boiling movement of legs and backs. The tadpoles that came filled every damp footprint, making the ground wriggle with an oily sheen. All that activity. The snakes that arrived, a few weeks later, hunting with ease, filling their bellies, and then slipping into the water to swim across the lake. Pike hunted in the pools beneath the hanging branches, barely moving as they waited for the perch to come to them. Winter had taken all that away. He was the only one, now, the only witness to it all.

Eventually he'd emerged onto the cinder path, but instead of going direct to the water's edge he'd crossed over into the trees to see the site of the old ice works. A large pulley and block was still there, lying against the one oak which had been chosen to anchor the gear. The anchoring chain was now deeply embedded in the trunk. A trestle and preparation table had long gone, but the two iron rails were still lying flat across the ground from the tree to the bank. Roots had lifted the rails in places, but they were still intact and resting on the sleepers. For three or four weeks each winter, one man had worked the ice, edging his way across the lake on planks which spread his weight, breaking the ice with a lump hammer, attaching grappling irons to each piece and winching them back to the bank. On the table the ice was sawn, cleaned and wrapped in straw and canvas before it was strapped to a horse and the load led up the cinder path to an ice house – little more than a brick cellar built deep in the wood beyond the flood line. The ice would last for six months if it was stacked well, and the hall never ran out. They had ice in their drinks right up to August. The worker lived on a boat at the lake all year, and when he wasn't cutting ice he'd be tending the reed beds, coppicing the hazel, managing the fish stock and in summer he hunted teal and duck for the hall's larder.

A good system. Until that one tragic November night, when thick ice had covered the water. Immediately afterwards, the hall had been closed up, sold, the thought of continuing to live there had been intolerable. The heart had been lost from the place. Now, ninety years later, the hall was a series of privately owned flats and holiday lets. No one remained to tell the history of the lake, yet somehow – clearly – an air of tragedy had never quite left the place. No one ventured there. It was a bad place. They didn't have to be told.

The man continued to stare at the other bank and before he saw the girl he heard her skates moving in the dark. She emerged from where she'd been hiding under the willows and came boldly towards him, swinging her arms from side to side as she pushed each skate forward. Her hair was shining in the moonlight but her face was obscured by its shadow. She picked up speed and aimed directly at him, her eyes dark and unknowing, staring at him, lifting her arms out to grab him.

'What do you want!' he shouted.

The girl ground her toe into the ice, forcing her to stop.

'Who are you?' she asked.

The man was startled to hear her speak. It wasn't right, he was unable to grasp the implications. Things like this brought about a thickness of mind in him, tongue-tied, unable to act, unable to think.

'Just keep away,' he replied.

'Why?'

She was oblivious to the sound of ice beginning to stretch below her. 'Who *are* you?'

'I live in the boat,' he answered, pointing to the black shape of his barge under the row of willows. 'Get off the ice,' he said. 'It's young ice, it ent good.'

'Come on.'

'What?'

'On the ice.'

He stared at her in fear, shaking his head. She hesitated, then whispered: '*It's alright.*'

He looked down at the poles of the staithe going through the ice. A small ring of black water remained round each post. Until the staithe supports were entirely set he knew the ice wouldn't be thick enough.

'What do you want?' he repeated.

The girl frowned back and but chose not to say anything.

'I know about ice,' he said. 'It's good and strong here, but there's these currents even in a lake this size – the flow make it weak – see, the ice gets these cracks in it and it can sheer up like ploughshares and slide you in.'

'You'll tell my daddy, won't you. I'm not meant to be out.'

He looked back at her, confused.

'I'm eleven. Daddy says I tell stories.' She smiled at him, but seemed sad. 'Because I'm an only child.'

'I *know* who you are,' he said.

Again the girl frowned. She glanced questioningly at the man and he looked down at his coat and boots. She was dressed entirely in white. Soft and delicate and as clean as a burial shroud.

The girl took a step back and raised her arms to beckon him. She gave a half smile. An invitation that seemed to lift him, the weight going from his shoulders, urging him, and before he could stop himself he was slipping off the jetty onto the ice below. There was an unpleasant squeak and he grabbed the wood as he saw the ice sink against the posts. Water as dark as blood welled onto the ice and collected round his boots.

The girl skated away from him in a wide circle, excited, then slowly she returned and – a little way off – signalled for him to come forward. He let go of the jetty and stepped cautiously after her, aware of the ice bending under his weight and thinking how like a skin it was. A living, breathing skin across the lake. As brittle as glass but not like glass at all.

He walked slowly after the girl, aware of how heavy he was in comparison – her, tiny and light in front of him on the fine ridges of her skates, him, in his coat and thick leather boots. His boots – iron capped and hobnailed – the weight of his boots alone would break the ice on some parts of the lake.

Always, she kept slightly beyond reach. And he began to imagine he was in the middle of a great glowing light, coming up through the ice, as he followed someone or something he couldn't understand. Below him, air bubbles scurried away from his weight. Cracks spread like filigree under each step. When he looked up, the girl had stopped a few feet away. They were in the middle of the lake.

'You're the girl ent you?' he said. 'The one who drowned.'

The girl gazed back, silent, her face hollowed by shadow.

'Agnes, weren't it?' he continued, 'from the big house.'

The girl shifted her weight uneasily. She glanced at the trees far away from her, then back at the man.

'Don't play games – I seen you many times out here over the years. I ent afraid of you no more.'

'What girl?' she asked, quietly.

'His daughter. Only one. Come down one night with them skates on. No one down here but this old boy who's cutting the ice and he's blind drunk anyhows. She goes on the ice and he sees her out there in the moonlight and that's it – it crack and she go right under…'

'… stop it – shut up,' the girl said, suddenly.

'… and he tries to save her – but he don't crawl out on the boards like he learnt to do – he just goes runnin' cause he's so scared and that's something he shunt have done cause he goes in an all. You hear? He gets her but it's too late. He fall in the lake and he's got her – arm round her waist, and he's thinking he's saved her – but there ent nothing to do. Ent no way out. He just hold her and they fight the ice for some time and then they just look at each other and slip down through the water.'

The girl glowered back at him, cheeks flushed with anger. Their bodies had been found in the reeds a day later and they'd been buried at the church near the hall. Her, in the family vault, him, under a simple wooden cross in the corner of the graveyard.

The man looked at the fringe of dark trees along the banks. Then above them, at the cold burning light of the moon that seemed to pour down at him from a hole in the sky. For a moment he was weightless, as if the moon was the lake itself, shining far below him in a dark unlit county. The lake as it was, eighty years ago, as it retreated back from him through time and space.

Suddenly the ice was splitting beneath his feet.

'I told you to get off the ice!' he yelled. *'Why won't you listen!'*

The ice rose in cruel edges around him, then shattered, the echo of his cry vanished in circles like ripples from a stone. As he plunged into the water he saw the lifeless figure of Agnes below him – turning in the darkness amid the cloud of her hair – her face as white as marble. The delicate tinge of life still in her cheeks. Turning towards him she opened her eyes. He saw her blue lips spreading into a smile. Her mouth, already full of water. And he felt her sudden grip as she pulled him down.

The girl screams as the ice sheers away from her and one foot plunges into cold water and she's falling and scrabbling and suddenly she's racing across the lake for the trees. She rips her boots off and runs in her socks up the path – looking back only once at the man still flailing about in the ice and water. His arms rise desperately among the shattered edges of ice and the steam of the lake. She runs up the path – the sharp cinders stinging her feet and twigs whipping her legs until she's in the open pasture and running as fast as she can for the house. She can hear the sound of music coming from inside. Some of the flats still have lights on, but the one where her parents are staying is dark. She lifts the sash of the window and shouts for them, crying for them, and she sees her father stumbling out of the bedroom, hardly awake, he tells her to calm down. The light goes on and her mother's suddenly there, too, telling her father not to shout. She blurts out what happened and though it makes no sense yet they know they have to act – it takes them a couple of minutes to be dressed and then the three of them are running across the field. She leads them along the path between the trees to where it heads down to the lake and when they get there both her father and mother shine torches across the ice. The beams are strong and straight and full of the deep eddies of a mist they can't otherwise see. Her father stands silently, grimly determined to see what's out there. As the torches sweep back and forth the eyes of birds shine brilliantly like an eerie constellation where they huddle on the ice or roost in the trees. But there's no sound.

Her father bends down to her and asks where the man is. Where did he fall in? He wants to know, exactly. Afraid of his tone, she points to the centre of the lake and the torches shine together, overlapping in a blaze of white mist and ice. The girl steps forward because it doesn't make sense and her mother holds her back from going onto the ice.

'Are you sure?' her mother asks, softly. The girl points to the exact spot and yet they can all see that the ice is solid and smooth and there are no cracks. The torchlight drifts from side to side, and returns to the spot, but there are no signs at all.

'Now listen to me,' her father is saying as he squats in front of her. 'No one's out there.' He breathes heavily as the tiredness catches up with him. 'Will you tell me who the hell this man was – I mean, do you know where he comes from?'

The girl looks down at the ground – waiting to be told off, wondering what they want her to say.

'The boat', she whispers. 'He said he lives on the boat by the jetty.' And the torches shine over to the jetty and along the bank where they light up the willows. But there's no boat there.

The girl cries for an hour back at the hall until she's so exhausted she falls asleep. Her father's anger is now spent, and he's dealing with some of the other flat owners who heard the commotion. He's explained her knack for making up stories. After their concern has embarrassed him, it's beginning to annoy him. His wife senses him about to snap and whispers that they should carry their daughter to bed. They're in a communal part of the old hall and the father gathers his sleeping child up and carries her into their flat. There are old photos on the wall here, and as his wife goes ahead – turning the lights out so as not to wake their daughter – they fail to notice the picture of the lake. Summer, 1935, it reads. A group of children are jumping off the end of the jetty. In the background is the lake-man's barge. A heavily built man sits on deck. Smoke rising from his stove smudges across the photo's background as if it's erasing itself from view.

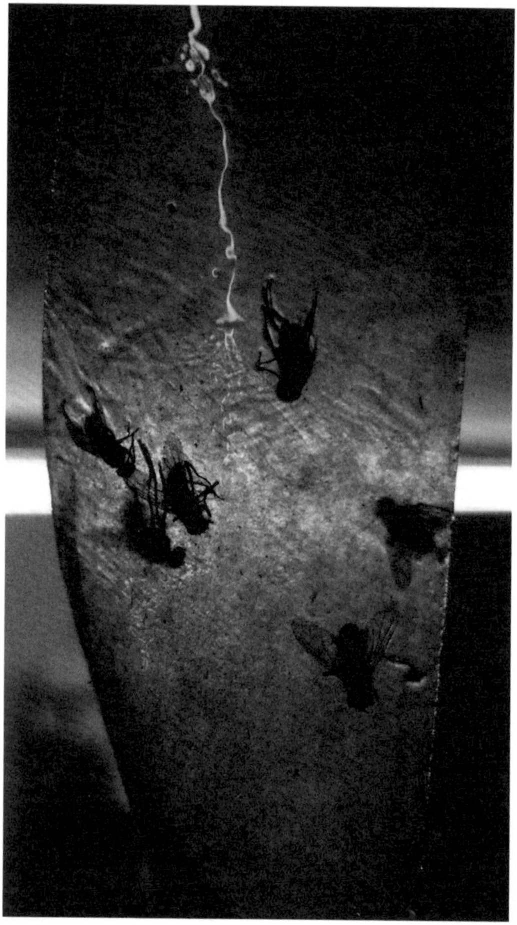

For Dr McBride

11th November

So I'm starting this journal at 3am and I'm in the kitchen coz right now there's no way I wanna to be in my room. It's gonna pass – I get it – but I've just had this nightmare and I'm not happy about the thought of getting back in bed. Being in here's better coz the stove's on and the kitchen feels normal. And I've got this crappy exercise book with me because you told me to write these things down. Write them down, you said, and then we'll take a look and see if we can make any sense of it all. I mean – that sounded so patronising and I really wasn't going to bother with it. But – well – maybe the dream's made me think.

I'll describe it: I was standing in a wood, and in front of me was this deep hole, with fresh cut sides like someone's dug it out. I was looking into it. Then suddenly I was in there, lying at the bottom. And there's this rough chicken wire that's been dumped on top of me. I mean, you're saying all this is in my head, right, but I knew just how cold that wire was, and the way it was almost cutting into my face, and the rotten smell of the soil. It was so *vivid*. I was lying there being totally still, and there was no noise at all, apart from the crows up in the trees and some distant twigs breaking in the wood. Then suddenly there's this loud noise nearby and something falls on me. I don't know what it is then more stuff falls down and I realise it's soil being shovelled in. Soil and twigs and bits of bracken, and it starts piling up on the wire and it's all getting heavier and it begins to press down on me. And I'm like – trying to scream out – but I can't. There's just nothing coming out of my mouth. I'm in this hole and then it starts to go dark and I try and push the soil away and I can't because it's so heavy and then… then it's the sound that really scares me – the sound starts to get all muffled and distant like I'm sinking deeper and deeper and, yeah –

Like I said, I don't really wanna go back to bed at the moment.

Thing is, I know the dream's because of Mr Greaves, and everything I was telling you about. But it still scared me. When I woke up I was sweating, and then I got really cold. So I'll just sit here and look at the things in the kitchen. I'll warm my hands up. There's a nice hum coming from the fridge.

I've sat here for about ten minutes. I think I'll go back to my room now.

12th November

Course, didn't get a lie in. Mum woke me up banging on my door – *just* to tell me she was going out, which is something I don't get, ever. Can she not Let Me Sleep! Anyway, I got my own breakfast and left all my stuff in the sink for her to deal with. She says some results came back from the hospital but I had a look at them and I can't work out what they're saying. I think they wanna do more tests. The best thing to do is keep on with the journal and jot down when it happens Rachel, that's what mum told me, as she was walking out to the car. I mean – like it's all that easy. When it happens. It's not like she's got any answers. You *are* jotting things down aren't you? she says. Yes Mum. It's just *so* annoying.

Anyway – she says I know how to wind her up, so she drove off in a bit of a huff and – I don't know – I couldn't wait for her to get out of the house but the minute she's gone I didn't feel that good. This house doesn't sound right when it's empty. You start listening for things and it's so quiet that it just makes it worse.

First thing I decide to do is get out and take my bike up the lane towards the wood. When I'm nearly there, I push it in the hedge and walk the last bit, climbing over the gate and walking over the horse field.

Now, just standing in that place brings it all right back, because the wood looks just like it did in that nightmare I had. Dark black trees and thick shadows.

I could hear Mr Greaves hitting something with a hammer. The thing about farmers is they're always doing something. Every time I see Mr Greaves he's doing some job with screws or he's bending wire or he's fixing some knackered old tools. I mean, I've never seen him move fast but he never – you know – stands still, either. Never in a hurry. So I hear this banging and I immediately get a sharp pain in my head, so I stop and lean against a tree until it goes. There you are, Dr McBride. That was about 10:30am and I had a pain in the left hand side of my skull. You said about that scale from one to ten, and I'd put it down as a seven or eight. Not that bad, not like that one I told you about a few weeks ago, but it was still nasty. And it was only a stabbing pain, right, I didn't *see* anything. Not then.

Anyway, the sound of the hammer stops and the next thing I see is Mr Greaves limping down the path and I see him stop there, in the shadows under the trees, and he just waits for a while, standing there with his eyes shut. He's such a tall man and that faded jacket he wears hangs off him like a disgusting sack – either he's had it for years and years or he doesn't feed himself. So he's just there with his eyes shut and his head angled up towards the branches, and I'm there leaning against the tree, and I don't want to move in case it gives him a shock. Then, he does this strange thing coz after a while he just turns to me and says *season's changing Rachel.* Just like that, like he's known I was there all along, and he's looking right at me with those pale eyes of his that have got milky grey rings round the iris like there's some kind of fog growing inside him.

'Come and have a look at what I've found,' he says.

Mr Greaves is always like that. Says these dramatic things. I think it's because he's basically lonely. Then he gives me this creepy smile and says: 'Were you alright there, by the tree?' I noticed his eyelid was twitching.

'Just a headache,' I tell him.

Anyway, he says it'll only take a minute, so I walk along the path with him. I think he owns the wood. There are signs saying PRIVATE nailed to the trees and there aren't any other huts. Just his. It's right in the middle, in its own clearing. I mean it's not a big hut at all – more like the kind of place you'd build if you were going mad, to shelter in, before you realised you couldn't stand spending any time in it.

When we get there, Mr Greaves takes his boots off in the porch. 'It's inside,' he says. 'That alright with you?'

I give him a shrug like I don't care. Actually, I've never been inside, and I know it's risky doing stuff like this, but he's pretty old and fragile, especially with that limp of his – I mean I could push him over if he tried anything – or just run off. I'm way faster than him. The man can't run at all. Plus – well – I really wanted to see what it was like in there.

So we went in. The first thing I notice is how dark and quiet it is. There was this old clock on the wall, ticking heavily like it was about to break, and the air was like it hadn't changed for years. It smelt of carpets and old wood and I think he must smoke a pipe when he's there by himself. There was this long gold strip of flypaper hanging from the roof, looking like a dry old bit of bark, and when I get closer I can see it's covered in dozens of gross dead flies.

Mr Greaves drags this box across the floor, making a big deal about how heavy it is. It's like some sort of chest. 'Here,' he says, pulling up one side of its lid. I can see a large bird wedged up in the corner at the bottom of the box. 'It's a jay,' he says. 'Found it in the wood.'

The bird's panting and has jabbed its beak into the side of the chest. Mr Greaves had put a saucer of water in there and some worms, but the jay hasn't touched them. It's knocked over the water and the worms are all curled dry and muddy in the other corner.

'What are you going to do with it?' I ask.

'You best get back,' Mr Greaves replies, pressing the lid back down and going off to another part of the hut as if I'm not there. I don't know what I'm supposed to do. I can see him through this old doorway, sitting on an old sofa, looking at his hands resting on his knees, like they're too heavy to lift.

After a while I decide to go over and check if he's OK. Like – ask if I could get him anything? His eyelid was still twitching. Then for some reason I start telling him about the other night – you know – waking up and going to sit by the stove and how in the dream I'd smelt the earth and the cold chicken wire. Mr Greaves didn't seem to be listening and I'm there beginning to wonder if he's, like, a bit senile? You know, forgetting I'm there? So I stop telling him about the dream and say: 'I don't know why I told you all that.'

It's so quiet and creepy in that shack and I thought someone was watching me, even though Mr Greaves is still looking down at his hands. I wished I'd never gone in there, but didn't see an easy way of walking out either.

Then Mr Greaves looks up at me and says: 'You're not the first one round here to have that dream.'

13th November

I've just come back from my appointment with you, Dr McBride, and I want to get a few things straight. First, I think my mum's got a thing for you, and that really pisses me off as well as it being disgusting, too. She puts her date-night perfume on when she goes to see you, and it's all a bit cheap and obvious. Next time I don't want her sitting in the room, especially if you're examining my head. Second, I think this is all a complete waste of time. I know you're a doctor, but I also think you're a bit of a shit doctor, with no clue about what's going on. You sat there reading my journal, but I'd didn't get the sense that you were having any ideas. So I reckon it proves you're just a small town GP and mum's doing this thing of thinking you're something special. Like today, when you asked me if there'd been any pain, and I said yeah – a bit yesterday. You asked where and I pointed to the left side of my head. Like – where it always is. And I watched you jot down a couple of lines on an index card that you put in a brown paper envelope. Is that's it, I thought, job done? 'Remember, Rachel,' you say, 'I want you to continue with the journal and I want you to write down anything that you think might be out of the ordinary. Anything you can't quite make sense of,' and I'm there thinking, yeah, the only thing I can't make sense of is why mum's gagging for you. It's pretty silent going back in the car, I tell you. Mum says her bit about everyone just wanting me to be well again and then she has this little cry near the roundabout and all the cars get pissed off trying to get past her.

As if that's going to make anything easier.

But I do want to tell you about what happened next. So on the way home we're coming down the river lane and through the hedge I can see Mr Greaves standing in the middle of the horse field like an old scarecrow. I'm watching him through the gaps in the hedge and he's turning to watch the car as it passes. It's like he was trying to catch my eye. So I get mum to pull over by saying I felt sick. She pulls over immediately coz one thing she hates is the thought of someone vomming in her car, so I get out, saying I'm gonna walk the last bit home, like I need the air. It always works. She drives off and I can see her looking at me in the rear view mirror with the kind of frown that's going to leave her with lines on her forehead if she's not careful.

Mr Greaves sees all that, then he comes over to me and asks where I've been.

'Doctors,' I say.

'You shouldn't bother listening to them. I can see in you you're all right and that's all there is to it. In fact, I was having a laugh about you just now.'

'Thanks a lot.'

'Just up there in the wood I was, laughing.'

'Well, I'm walking back now,' I tell him, a bit pissed off. I thought maybe he'd been drinking.

Then he rubs his chin and starts grinning at me. He seemed a bit younger – dressed up, like he'd had a shave.

'You're an odd one, aren't you,' he says.

'Whatever.'

I started to walk off but was really unsettled by him, so I asked: 'Why'd you have to say that?'

'Haven't got many friends, have you?'

'I don't suppose you do either, Mr Greaves.'

'I do alright,' he says. I'd turned my back on him by then but I can feel him smiling at me in this creepy way.

'Here lass – about that dream of yours. You should know something.'

I stopped.

'Come an' look over here.' I turn to see him walking towards an old sheet of corrugated metal on the ground. He shoves it to one side. Underneath there was a small round hole with a thin cage of wire at the bottom.

Now I'm really scared because it was just like in my dream. 'What's that?' I ask him.

'Bird grave. Bird graves all round here. Sometimes just one

bird buried at a time but more often half-a-dozen. Always the same – bird's caught, then pushed into a wire cage like this, then it go in a hole – maybe an old burrow or badger's set. They're in there flapping about crazy, then the hole's filled in.'

'In this hole?'

'That's right. Buried alive. Lots of other holes.'

'Why?'

'The old beliefs. Burying them like that is good for the earth. Keep everything else young.'

'That's disgusting.'

Mr Greaves just says nothing – like he's forgotten I'm there. He's looking past me and I can see – in the distance – mum's waiting by our front gate. From the way she's standing, with her tote bag over her shoulder, I can tell she's getting pissed.

'I gotta go,' I say.

I ran over the field and down the track to the garden where mum was still waiting. I can see she's been crying again, so I'm thinking that's another thing I'm gonna have to deal with.

'What were you doing, in that field?' she asks.

'Talking to Mr Greaves.'

Mum just looks at me in a very odd way and she says: 'No – no you weren't.'

I mean, crazy, right? 'Mr Greaves,' I say. 'He's just up there by the gate,' and mum's going: 'Hang on Rachel, are you having one of your things? One of your moments?' There's something really strange about mum sometimes, as if she doesn't even see the world that's around her.

'So, what was Mr Greaves saying?' she adds, making sure I've heard every word.

'This and that. Telling me about the area.'

'Dr McBride just said you mustn't over-stimulate yourself. You know it's not a good thing running about. You've got to take each day as it comes.'

14th November

I'm sorry I wrote those things about you yesterday, Dr McBride, because today I'm glad I've been keeping this journal. And right now I need it because what happened today makes no sense to me at all. Especially after yesterday and mum not seeing Mr Greaves in the field. I've read what I wrote about it and tried to see if I was missing something, but I'm totally confused.

This is what happened today: I went up to see Mr Greaves and there I was walking up the track to the horse field and the first thing I notice is the gate to the field swinging off its hinges. Someone's left it open, I thought, but when I tried closing it the top bar felt slimy with moss and rotten through and I just look at it and think: *someone's changed the gate.* I mean, that's all I could think. Someone's come in the night and replaced a good gate with an old rotten one. It didn't make sense. And then when I look out over the field I can see the grass is high and weedy and I can't even make out the track that leads to the wood – the one that I always use.

So I make my way through all this long grass and thistles till I reach the trees, but when I walk into the wood and find the clearing I get the shock of my life. Because the hut – Mr Greaves' hut – *wasn't there.* Well, it was sort of there but only as a complete ruin. Stumps of wood and old planks everywhere. There was ivy as thick as an arm twisting up the posts and growing all over the roof. Or what was left of the roof where it hadn't collapsed. The sides had fallen in and the windows were knocked out or smashed. It looked like there'd been a fire in one half of it. I mean – just writing this down feels so crazy to me.

Anyway, I decide to go up to the porch where Mr Greaves had taken his boots off just a couple of days ago. But now it was full of old junk and piles of leaves and the door was broken in half and covered in moss.

Inside, there were these bits of furniture all smashed up on the floor and the main room was full of leaves and bracken, and some of the floorboards were smashed through and I could see this really dark earth beneath. And that's what I want to tell you about, because under the floor I'm looking at all these old wire cages full of pale bare twigs and I suddenly realise it's not twigs at all. The cages are full of bird bones.

And that's when I ran.

15th November

I've just come off the phone to you, Dr McBride. Sorry I got upset, and I probably shouldn't have sworn at you, but when you said I should have more tests, I just lost it. Deep down, I know you're just trying to help me, but I also think you don't know what to do. I mean, mum was tearing her hair out trying to listen in to the call, so I showed her what I wrote yesterday in the journal and now she's gone straight to the phone and has called the surgery. She's pulled the phone lead into the other room and I can hear she's getting frustrated with you for not doing enough. But you know what – I'm over the moon about that. Looks like she's seen through your little act at last.

I didn't tell either of you about what happened this morning because you'll only think I'm losing it. But here goes. And I think this journal is now more for me than either of you. It was still dark when I woke up, and something was outside my window making a strange screaming noise. I mean, not a person screaming. Something else. And this screaming was sort of faint, but insistent, and it wouldn't stop, so I went to the window and there – stretched out over the lawn – was this high net. I mean – it's hard to describe, but it was like a badminton net. And in the middle of this net was a blackbird, all twisted up and making this screeching noise.

And while I'm there looking at it, Mr Greaves walks onto the lawn with this kind of mad focus in his eyes, and he starts to pull the bird out. He's rough and impatient with it and I think he even goes and breaks one of the wings pulling it out because the bird suddenly goes limp and then a second later starts screaming *like mad*. He stuffs it in his side pocket and I can see the bird's outline flapping about in his jacket while he does up a button on the flap. And then the blackbird stops moving, like it knows it's got no hope.

That's when I realise I'm crying, so I banged on the window – you know – really banging with both fists against the glass, but Mr Greaves *doesn't even look at me*. Instead, he starts walking off, so I run to the front door and go round the side of the house into the garden. He's gone. I can't find him anywhere. Then I go back to my bedroom window and… there's *nothing* there on the lawn, either – no sign of the bird or Greaves or even that huge net.

But then the strangest thing happened. When I start to walk across the lawn, just where the net had been, I get this real feeling of something hanging in the air – I mean, I put my hand out and can't touch anything, but it's like the air had a little *memory* of what had been there. Then I try and walk backwards and forwards, trying to notice it again, and it's gone. I mean, what's happening? What's going on with me?

16th November

I'm ill. I've had terrifying dreams all night and I haven't gone out today. I've stayed in my room all morning. Mum thinks I should be on medication. I can't talk to her about it.

It's late afternoon now. I'm so scared I can hardly write. About an hour ago I felt desperate so I snuck out the house and I really didn't want to go up there but I just start walking up to the horse field and then I'm standing in the middle of the field looking at the wood. It was dark between the trees and I had a really strong feeling there was someone in there, watching me. You know, just standing there under one of the trees, not moving. This sickening pull was reaching out towards me, like some kind of hand had grabbed me, dragging me forward towards those horrible trees, and that's when I started hearing the sounds. I knew it was Mr Greaves. And I really wanted to go back home or shout out for help but I just can't stop myself walking in there, into the wood. And then I see him, through the trees in a patch of old bracken and brambles, digging a hole in the earth.

I walk right up to him till I can smell the sweat on his arms and see how his old grey hair is sticking to his head. He kept on digging this deep trench. I stood next to his jacket which was hanging on a branch.

I said: 'You're not really here, are you?'

He didn't even stop for a second. He keeps thrusting that spade into the soil and chucking the earth onto a pile.

I touch his jacket where it's dangling from the branch. It's like a piece of old carpet. I could see the pocket where he'd put the blackbird. But the bird's not there anymore.

'Mr Greaves?' I say, and I can hear how afraid my voice is. I thought I was about to faint. It was getting dark. 'What's that hole for?'

He stops digging.

'It's for you,' he says.

17th November

It's the middle of the night. I'm in the kitchen again sitting by the stove because I can't sleep. All night I've been listening to the sound coming from the wood of him digging. It's not stopping. That scary sound of the spade cutting into the soil.

It's beginning to get light outside. I've been awake all night. I'm going to go up there. I'm going to walk into the wood and confront Mr Greaves. I'll tell him to fill in that hole he's been digging. I mean, what can he do – he's not even real – he's in my head. It's clear all I have to do is tell him to go away and maybe that will be it. That's how I'll get rid of him and how I'll start to get better.

Can't hear the birds this morning.

I'm fed up with writing. I'm going to go up there and find out what this is all about. I'm going now. I'll write more when I get back.

Floaters

Patrick leant forward into the apparatus, pressing his jaw onto the smooth metal chinrest. The room was dark and cooled and, as he pushed his forehead against the restraining support, he saw the twin lenses of the slit lamp gliding once more towards him. The beam of light shone strangely, not quite into his eyes, illuminating his vision with a bright spectral glow.

'Still see it? the ophthalmologist asked, in a quiet professional voice.

'I think so.'

'And the other one, in the lower part of your vision?'

'Not right this second. But I'm not sure.'

The lenses shifted and the beam adjusted, flooding his eye with white light as the ophthalmologist trimmed the controls. Patrick held his breath, not wanting to exhale straight into her face. He smelt peppermint, and remembered how the doctor had popped a lozenge into her mouth before the examination began. After a few more realignments, with the beam shining at him from differing angles, the apparatus slid away and Patrick was told to relax. He was then asked to sit at a second instrument, a fundus camera. She asked him to stare at a small winking light and warned him there would be a bright flash. She pressed a button and Patrick's eye filled with a dazzling blaze. An image of his retina sprang onto a screen at the side of the room.

The spotlights in the ceiling came on gradually as the ophthalmologist rolled her seat over to the computer screen:

'The anterior and posterior structures of your eyes are clear. There are no signs of lesions associated with retinal detachment. Which is good news because it's something we can rule out. And I've checked for other issues that may have caused this. I'm fairly confident that what you are experiencing is a persistent floater or floaters due to regular age-related degeneration of your vitreous humour.'

On the computer screen, Patrick's retina looked like the surface of a mysterious planet, burnished red and ancient.

'You might need to simplify that,' he replied.

'The jelly-like matter in the back of your eye is usually transparent. But as you age there are chances that liquefaction occurs, or damaged cells might accumulate. They can gather together, causing faint obstructions in your vision, or cast shadows onto your retina – it amounts to the same thing, and it's very common.'

'And these floaters – can anything be done?'

'In some extreme cases there are surgical procedures we could consider, or laser treatment, but that's certainly not the case with you, and it's nothing we generally advise.'

'So I just get on with it?'

'In a large majority they either dissipate or fade over time. Otherwise, yes, that's pretty much what you need to do. It really is nothing to worry about. I have some reading material you might take with you.'

Because of the eye drops used to dilate his pupils, Patrick was given a pair of oversized plastic sunglasses to walk back to work with. He was told not to drive, and to avoid bright light sources for the next two hours, but in the street he removed the glasses and looked up at the sky. It was a grey wintery morning and the sky was filled with a blanket of cloud. He saw the familiar shape of one of the floaters in his vision – a faint string resembling a sticky, translucent cobweb. When he tried to look at it, it sprang away from view. But it was the other shape – that had been in his eyesight for the past month – that had made him go to the eye clinic. Against the grey sky he studied it. A dark, oddly shaped smudge. It looked like the outline of a hunched figure.

Back at the office, he dropped the ridiculous plastic sunglasses into the wastebasket and, after checking in on emails, went back to the drawing board by the side of the desk. For some reason the client had insisted on hand-drawn architectural plans rather than the more standard issue computer aided designs. The scheme was lucrative, but challenging: the conversion and remodelling of a medieval watermill, and the extra cost of doing the drawings could easily be built into the fees. Patrick slid the scale rule across the drafting paper, rechecking the measurements. He unplugged the drawing light, peered closer at the plan, then angled the whole board towards the window, for the daylight. It was still no good. With the tip of a brand new eraser he stroked the paper carefully just below the roofline on the front elevation. He'd noticed the mark there, before. A smudge that never entirely went. He rubbed his eyes and tried again. It was no use. Just below the roof, near the upstairs window, a persistent shadow on the paper.

By late afternoon he was safe to drive, so he left the office early, announcing he'd be at a site visit the following morning. He drove home carefully, and when he parked the car outside the house he squinted once more at the sky. It was getting dark and there was only a slight hint of one of the floaters: a smoky blemish. When he went in, he opened a bottle of wine and sat at the kitchen table with his partner, Simon, and repeated what the ophthalmologist had said. Simon listened, kindly, but then looked as though he was trying his best not to smile.

'What is it?' Patrick asked.

Simon looked closely into his eyes, trying not to laugh. 'The whites of your eyes – they're kind of – fluorescent?'

'Yeah – yeah,' he said, relaxing. 'It's the eye drops.'

'Oh – right. And will they stop being green..?'

'No – it's permanent. I'm going to have glowing eyes from now on.'

Upstairs, he could hear an argument breaking out between the twins, Joel and Jed.

Simon put a consoling hand on his wrist, while they listened to the growing intensity of the row in the upstairs room. Jed's guitar banged loudly onto the floor.

'Shall I go?' Simon suggested, gesturing towards the stairs. 'Or should I send in their monster dad, with his luminous eyes?'

Early next morning Patrick drove out for the site visit. It was only one of many schemes he was working on, but the remodelling of Oxthorpe watermill was a complicated project and he'd already had to go there several times. He wasn't keen on the place. This part of the county was desolate, with large un-hedged fields that were bare and lifeless, ploughed into harsh geometric lines for winter. The trees looked skeletal against the sky, or were being slowly strangled by ivy. It was easy to have miserable thoughts round here, and to get lost too, as the roads were narrow and barely signposted.

He turned the Audi onto the muddy track that led to the mill, then drove slowly alongside the river. Several old willows lined the track, leaning over the sunroof with thin branches hanging down towards him. In one patch the river had flooded, so he steered carefully to avoid the verge. The river swelled into a wide stagnant pool, he parked the Audi next to it, in the long grass of the pasture. Oxthorpe watermill was a curious building, partly hidden among trees. Much of it was Victorian but an older section dated to the original medieval mill. The brickwork was stained with streaks of damp running vertically up the walls and, as he remembered, there wasn't a straight line in the whole structure. Built on the soft banks of the river, the doorframes, windows and beams had all warped over the years, and every one of the floors was uneven.

Just before he left the car he pulled the sun visor down to check his eyes in the vanity mirror. His pupils had returned to their proper size overnight, and the whites had lost the faintly green tinge from yesterday. He looked at a patch of grey sky, but couldn't make out any sign of the floaters.

As he walked towards the mill, a sense of unexpected unease grew in him, and he reminded himself that this happened every time. After each of his previous visits he'd come away with a sense that he'd failed to notice something of importance. He wondered what it was. Was it the mill itself that bothered him, with its complicated mixture of additions and alterations over the centuries – a professional puzzle to untangle? Or was it something less tangible? Was there an element of spiritual disquiet that flowed through this part of the county? He paused to look down into the river, hunting for what was elluding him, and thought the water was unnaturally dark and thick with shadow. Long tendrils of cabbage-coloured weed drifted in a current he couldn't detect. This part of the river felt forgotten and neglected, with a damp vegetative smell, almost fungal, as if the air never changed here.

As he reached the mill, Blyth came out to greet him by the side of the former wheelhouse. Patrick liked Blyth. He was a man in his late fifties, who'd earned too much money and didn't really know what to do with it, but was a grafter, nonetheless. Gangly, with pebble thick glasses, he was a kind of hopeless optimist, readily amused at his own repeated mistakes, and you couldn't help but like him. He always wore the same faded blue boiler suit. He shook Patrick's hand enthusiastically. Blyth looked grey with plaster dust, and his eyebrows had grown long and unkempt.

'Still wrestling with the kitchen?' Patrick asked.

'It's a bastard. Dislodge a tile and a roof beam starts shifting. I've had the whole ceiling propped on Acrows.'

Patrick grimaced in sympathy, and followed Blythe into the mill. The kitchen had been hollowed out, down to bare brick, with most of the floor tiles dug up and a thicket of steel Acrows holding up the old beams. There were power tools in the corners, along with a portable generator and several LED work lamps on tripods.

'This way,' Blyth said, expertly threading his way between the steel props. 'Mind the cables there.'

In the centre of the room was a table, wiped clean of dust, with a kettle, teapot, and several types of biscuit neatly laid out. Blyth always took time to look after the small things. It was the big things that tended to escape his attention.

Patrick smiled at the gleaming tray full of cups and saucers. 'This is the only building site I've ever been offered leaf tea.'

'You actually have a choice of two blends, if you want,' Blyth replied. 'I'm all about the standards.' He popped the kettle on. 'Brought the plans?'

'May I?' Patrick replied. He cleared a space on the table and rolled out the copy of the front elevation, putting a teacup and saucer on each corner. Blyth peered at the design for the proposed remodelling of the front elevation, pushing his thick glasses onto the bridge of his nose.

'You've actually done me a favour,' Patrick said, stepping away from the table and going towards the hearth where the builders had hacked off the plaster. 'There's a complicated intersection of walls here, some of them dating back to the original structure. It's difficult to work out what's been left and what should have been taken away.'

'Building regs surveyor said the same,' Blyth muttered, peering over the plans.

Patrick examined the chimney breast. All these walls would have to go if Blyth wanted to open up the ground floor, as planned. The old lime mortar was damp and the laying of the brickwork made no sense at all. Some of the bricks were laid vertically, or made a patchwork among one or two flints, and evidence of previous coursework shot through the structure in diagonal lines. There were two, maybe three extra layers of wall that didn't seem necessary.

'You can see more of it on the stairwell,' Blyth said, still studying the plans but pointing towards the panelled door at the end of the room.

Patrick stepped over the rubble and climbed up several steps of a dark, narrow staircase. The exposed brickwork of the chimney breast leant at a strange angle, then became incorporated into a wider flank of the original building. There was a bulge in the wall, as wide as himself, as if something was pushing it out from within.

'What did building regs say?' he called. Within a patch of lime mortar, between two bricks in front of him, he saw the edge of something metal.

'Oh, yada yada, the usual stuff,' Blyth answered. 'They're doing some head scratching.' Patrick pinched the end of the metal object, and began to wiggle it loose. The builders had already partially dislodged it when they'd hacked off the plaster. 'Probably their way of putting a few extra digits on the bottom line,' Blyth added.

'There's something here, in the mortar,' Patrick called.

Blyth came to the bottom of the stairs, and looked up, eagerly. His eyes were bright and magnified by his glasses. 'Yeah – we came across a lot of them stuck between the bricks.'

'What is it?'

'Beats me.'

Patrick picked up one of the masonry chisels that had been left on the stairs and worked it into the mortar, loosening the metal object. It came out relatively easily. He brushed his hands clean and returned to the kitchen, where he showed Blyth what he'd found. It was a piece of dark rusty metal, wide and flat as if it had once been part of a large hinge, with a curious zigzag shape at one end. The opposite end was encrusted with blackened mortar.

'Any idea what it is?' Blyth asked.

'And you say there are others?'

'All round the chimney breast. Hammered into the mortar.'

Patrick turned the metal object over in his hands. It was heavy, roughly made, but didn't seem to have any practical purpose. At that moment he heard someone's footsteps walking across the room above them, and a few seconds later Blyth's son came down the stairs. Nine years old, shockingly pale, Caleb came into the kitchen and stood still, dressed only in a pair of pyjamas.

'Dad, I'm hungry,' he said.

'Caleb, not in your bare feet, love,' Blyth replied.

Patrick saw Caleb glance towards him. Every time he saw this boy he was concerned. Caleb looked worryingly ill, with gaunt cheeks and shadows beneath his eyes. His skin was bluish white, and he had a tendency to stare at people.

'What can I eat?' Caleb said, impatiently.

'Have a couple of biscuits. I'll take you out for lunch.'

Caleb turned away from them and marched back upstairs.

'He hates this place,' Blyth whispered, quietly amused.

After a few more discussions about the proposed remodelling of the ground floor, they went outside to view the mill from a spot on the riverbank. Some of the roof tiles had been lifted, and a large tarp had been tied across the area. Two of the windows had been removed and were blocked with plywood. The area to the side of the mill was deeply rutted with greasy mud, where the builders parked their vans.

'When are they here next?' Patrick asked.

'Tomorrow, hopefully,' Blyth replied with a shrug. The watermill was a tricky project, it tended to uncover new problems each day. Blyth was resilient, but it was clearly taking its toll.

Just below the roof, Patrick noticed a shadow flick across one of the panes of glass. He studied the window, closely. It was the room where Caleb slept.

'Is Caleb alright?' he asked.

Blyth nodded to himself, and sighed. 'Well, I think so. He's possibly anaemic. I don't really know what to suggest. He had some sort of fit the other day – his eyes rolled back.'

'That's worrying.'

'It was over as quick as it started. Back in London he's full of life. Part of the football team.'

Patrick continued to study the upstairs window, realising it was directly above the area he'd been investigating, where the oddly shaped walls congregated around the hearth.

'Blyth – that thing I found in the mortar – it's old, isn't it. My partner has a friend who works for the museum service. An archaeologist. I could show it to her, if you'd like?'

'Oh – would you? I'm dead curious.'

'We'll probably find more when those walls go.'

Blyth put his hands in the pockets of his boiler suit. 'You think Caleb's looking worse?' he asked.

'Well – he was very pale, but perhaps he was cold?'

Blyth looked down at the wet grass, thinking. 'Right, well, I'll go and fetch that bit of metal.'

Blyth walked back to the mill, light on his feet, trying not to slip in the mud. Life must be odd here, Patrick thought, Blyth and his son camping out in the upstairs rooms while the builders dismantled the ground floor. It wasn't the way they should be going about it.

His attention was drawn again to the upstairs window and – this time – he noticed the glass had grown darker, as if a figure was hiding several feet back in the shadows of the room. He rubbed his eyes and looked again. Then he realised this part of the building – just below the roofline – was exactly the same area where the strange mark appeared on the architectural drawing.

Driving back to the office, Patrick wrestled with apprehension he couldn't quite place. The car felt lonely and inexplicably full of emptiness. Passing the bare fields and leafless trees, he thought the countryside seemed unnaturally silent and without life. It was a curious feeling, like something was keeping track of him. Either watching him, or getting closer. He angled the rear view mirror to check the backseats were empty, then chided himself for being so jittery. It's just a decrepit watermill by the side of a stagnant river, that's all. Yet the sense that there had been something gathering in the reflection of that upper window made his skin prick with heat.

At the office, he busied himself with routine tasks, trying to distract himself, but the weight of unresolved questions felt like a barrier he needed to break through, so he brought out the strange metal plate from his bag and took it to the office bathroom. There, with a plastic nailbrush, he scrubbed at the metal in a basin of hot soapy water, which quickly turned dirt brown with rust. He scrubbed hard, but it looked as though the mortar would have to be chipped off. Lifting to inspect it from the water, the curious zigzag was clearer – a simply cut piece of metal, still sharp at the edges, as though its shape had been cut with tin snips. He held it up to the light to examine it, then noticed the reflection in the mirror. It was a letter M.

He dried it with paper towels and took it back to his desk, placing it on the side. Now it was the tubes of plans sticking out of his shoulder bag that seemed overly demanding of his attention. It was senseless to ignore them. He dried his hands meticulously, then rolled out the architectural drawing of the mill's front elevation, and immediately felt hot with panic. At the upstairs window, just below the roofline, the darkly clouded outline had become more pronounced. He saw a hooded figure. A shadowed face angled towards him.

He picked up the eraser, then hesitated, trying to calm himself. Getting scared like this was absurd, when all he needed to be was rational. He called over one of his colleagues and asked her to take a look at the drawing. It was one of the junior architects, who'd only recently joined the practice.

'Aisha,' he asked. 'You see anything on this plan?'

She studied it closely, then took a step back, wondering whether she was being tested. 'What am I meant to be looking at?'

'This area, just below the roofline?'

She looked closely, then shook her head. 'Have you tried to rub something out, there?'

'Yesterday I did. You think there's a mark?'

She smiled at him, but he could tell she was confused. 'Maybe. I'm not sure.'

His mobile rang, It was Blyth. He let it go to voicemail.

'Thanks, Aisha. I've been having problems with my eyes.'

'Yeah – I saw the groovy shades. No problem.' He waited till Aisha had gone before he played Blyth's message. Apparently the builders had come and made a few investigatory holes into the brickwork near the chimney breast. He should come and take a look.

That evening he sat on the sofa with his laptop and searched for information about Oxthorpe watermill. He found some historic black and white photos, with boats tied up along the side of the millpond, men with rakes making stands of thatch, and a packhorse standing by a cart. The building looked fresher and full of activity. Instinctively he studied the upper window, enlarging it on the screen, but found nothing strange about it. With a further search he discovered there'd once been a village nearby, but it had become abandoned, and all that was left of it was a single tower of its church and the water mill. Oxthorpe had been emptied in the eighteenth century, as far as he could discover, and was one of the many vanished villages in that part of the county.

Jed sat next to him on the sofa, rapidly flicking a bright red controller while, on the TV screen, a video game took him through various halls and corridors of what seemed to be a stone fortress. The point of view span dizzily as he went between the viewing modes. Oversized assailants loomed into view, coming at him with various weapons, and he dispatched them with prolonged bursts that made the screen splatter with blood. Joel slyly watched his brother's progress, but showed no encouragement, probably waiting his turn, while Simon caught up on social media in the comfy armchair, occasionally scratching his beard with amusement. Typical family life,

Patrick thought, everyone totally absorbed in their own worlds, but totally baffled by what each other was doing. He looked at Joel, again. He seemed more withdrawn than usual. Perhaps something had happened at school.

'Joel? You OK?' he asked. He got an ambiguous shrug in response.

Patrick squinted, bothered by something. 'What's that on your cheek?'

Joel put a finger to his cheek, absentmindedly, then took it away. Patrick thought there was a discoloration of the skin, just below the eye. A darkened smudge.

'Maybe it's nothing,' he said.

Simon looked up, noticing Patrick's concern, then gave a *who knows* shrug. Patrick closed his laptop, reached into his work bag, and passed over the strange metal plate from the watermill.

'What do you think this is?' He asked. Simon examined it, turning it round in his hands.

'No idea. You going to give me a clue?'

'It's from the watermill scheme. I was wondering whether I could show it to Iris – see what she makes of it?'

'Yeah. You should.' He didn't sound particularly interested. Patrick often experienced moment like this, where he realised he was getting obsessed with something that others wouldn't bother with.

'It was stuck between the bricks,' he said. 'There were lots of them, apparently.'

After the kids went to bed, Patrick fetched the toolbox from under the stairs and began chipping the mortar off the metal plate with a blunt chisel. He quickly exposed more of the shape, revealing a second, then third letter. In rough outline he saw MA and the beginnings of an L or T. *Malt?* he considered, wondering whether it was something to do with the milling of grain. He tried to shift the mortar from the rest of the word, but had little luck where the rust had grown thickly into the lime. Relieved to give up, he went to bed, but in the moments before he fell asleep he thought about Oxthorpe watermill, right at that moment, how dismal and unpleasant it must be. A gloomy unlit building surrounded by dark trees. He didn't know how Blyth and his son could cope with it. It was enough to give anyone bad dreams.

Skipping breakfast, Patrick drove out to the mill to see what the builders had unearthed, because until the purpose of those walls was resolved he couldn't go ahead with the plans to remove them. Turning onto the muddy track he was relieved to see the bright red van of the builder, Jason Jones, parked by the side of the mill, with the curious slogan of BUILDING YOUR DREAMS written in script on the side of his transit. A team of men were already working, knocking a hole in the side of the building to form the entrance to the new extension. The mill was noisy with activity, and as Patrick approached he listened to the sound of a pneumatic hammer competing with loud music from a radio, and the men calling to each other when the slabs of brickwork fell. It contrasted with the almost unnatural quiet of his last visit, and Patrick was glad of the change. He noticed Caleb, sitting in the passenger seat of Blyth's Land Rover, bundled up in a thick coat.

Blyth came out of the mill, walking fast, in his familiar boiler suit.

'Morning Patrick,' they shook hands, but Blyth hardly stopped. 'Gotta dash, I'm afraid.' He walked quickly towards the Land Rover.

'You want me to wait?'

'No, no,' Blyth replied, not looking back. 'Off to get Caleb some medicine from the pharmacy. Do take a look at the holes they made.'

Blyth drove off with his son, and Patrick walked into the mill by himself. He went straight to the chimney breast, where several deep holes had been hacked into the brickwork. Shining the torch from his mobile into one of them he saw a narrowing crack running deeply into the wall, before it turned a corner that he couldn't see beyond. He measured the depth of the bricks as over seventy centimetres – much thicker than it needed to be. Other investigatory holes revealed similar dead ends, but when he crouched on the narrow staircase he saw a hole made there led into what appeared to be a void. He shone the torchlight and saw – deep within the wall – the bricks gave way to an opening. He carefully eased his hand in, rolling up his sleeve so his arm could reach further. With his fingertips he noticed the surface of the bricks became smooth and damp, like the calcified wall of a cave. His fingertips stretched into the void, and he suddenly had an overwhelming belief that he was doing something very wrong. He pulled his hand out, and noticed an odd odour, marshy and unpleasant.

The staircase was an oppressive space, but instead of returning to the kitchen Patrick decided to climb to the landing. There, he peered into Caleb's room. He saw a low single bed on bare floorboards, surrounded by the boy's clothes and trainers. Patrick looked at the window and saw nothing peculiar about it. But along one side of the room he noticed a thickened shelf, and realised the curious walls had been capped off at that point with heavy beams.

From the car he called Iris, who worked as an archaeologist and cultural archivist. He described the things they'd found at Oxthorpe watermill, and asked whether he could swing by to show her. They met at the museum café, and when he placed the metal plate on the table he explained how it had been found wedged between the bricks.

She picked it up, assessing its weight and looking at its construction. 'It's a series of letters, right?'

'I think so.'

She pointed out a thin line etched within the letter M. 'That looks medieval – a kind of simple decoration made by a burin.' She viewed the plate from several angles. 'MALE?' she wondered aloud. 'Or MALADY?'

'I tried chipping off the mortar last night.'

'We use acid. You can get it from a DIY shop.'

He wondered whether he was wasting Iris' time. It could be part of a hinge, after all, or something that was hammered in there and snapped off when the wall was made. It certainly didn't seem to have any particular value.

'That whole area feels weird to me,' he said, suddenly wanting to share the unease he always experienced when he visited the mill. 'I don't know what it is, but I know I don't like it.' He stopped short of telling her about the upstairs window of the mill, the shadow that had appeared like a partial figure lurking behind the glass, or the smudge mark on the architectural plans that only he seemed able to see. Any of these things would sound crazy in the comfortable surroundings of the museum café.

'You're probably just freaking out because of the history,' she said.

'What history?'

She angled her head to one side, giving him a questioning look. He felt under scrutiny, and wondered whether Iris and Simon had had a private chat about him. The stress of his job. His vision problems.

'What are you referring to?' he asked.

'OK' she replied, bringing out a folder of papers from her workbag. 'When you told me where it was I immediately thought of these.' She passed several sheets to him, and he saw photocopies of medieval documents, some of them faded and singed at the edges, or water damaged. 'Not just there but all along the river, that part of the county was a hotbed for witch trials. I printed these off from the National Archives.'

Patrick tried not to show his unease. Perhaps it was a mistake to have approached Iris – she probably had her own obsessions when it came to research, and was naturally jumping to conclusions.

'Have a look here,' she said, pointing out an underlined section of the transcript:

> Among others afflicted with hysteria she was in step with her dread familiar and was thence taken to the river where upon hearing charges she proceeded to damn the village for the children to die until it is vanished.

'Is that about Oxthorpe?' he asked.

'It's not clear. The accounts tend to be loose when it comes to specific locations.'

'But it could be?'

She nodded, but looked unconvinced.

'What's this about the children?' he asked.

Iris gave a shrug. 'No idea.'

'Oxthorpe – the village – it disappeared.'

'Lots of villages have gone round there,' she replied, beginning to sound more rational than he was.

'So why are you showing me this?'

She smiled, like she was about to lay a winning hand at cards. 'Look here, a mill is mentioned.' She pointed to another part of the transcript.

> Her vile protestations were ended in the river and she has gone to the mill and hence the miller will keep her close.

Unable to stop himself, he imagined a woman being dragged into Oxthorpe watermill, bound, gagged, dripping with river water. Drowned or nearly drowned. Being entrusted to the miller, to be kept there. He leant back from the table. 'Looks like I'm going to have bad dreams, Iris.'

She laughed. His mobile started ringing, and he saw it was from Simon.

'The truth is,' Iris said, 'there's a story under every stone in this county. I wouldn't lose any sleep over it.'

He answered the call. 'Did you get a text from the school?' Simon asked.

'No. Why?'

'Joel's been sent home. He fainted, like he was having some kind of fit.'

By the time Patrick arrived, Joel was already asleep in his bed. Simon had drawn up a chair next to him, and was patiently keeping watch. Joel was pale, his skin clammy.

'What happened?' Patrick whispered.

'He's got no recollection – but they told me he started shaking, uncontrollably, then fainted. His eyes rolled back, apparently. They asked me about epilepsy.'

'He's not epileptic.'

'Yes. I know. It was during art.'

Patrick stood, awkwardly. There was no space for him near the bed, and nothing more that could be done for the time being. Joel's school rucksack was on the floor, where it had been dropped. Patrick zipped it up and moved it to the desk. Then he opened it and pulled out Joel's art sketchbook. Turning to the most recent page he saw a drawing of a building, much like the ones that featured in the video games. Joel liked to draw buildings. Then Patrick noticed something odd about the drawing. He tried to conceal his shock. Just below the roofline, a familiar smudge mark.

Patrick pulled out the chemicals under the sink and found the sulphuric acid they sometimes used to unblock the U bend. He took it to the shed and poured it into a Tupperware tray, then dropped the metal plate into it. The lime mortar started fizzing immediately, releasing a dirty white cloud into the liquid. He waited for two agonising minutes. Picking it up with a pair of barbecue tongs, the metal was now clear and gleaming. MALEFICI, he read.

When he searched on Google, it turned out to be Latin.

Be cursed.

He drove to the mill in fading light, the glowering smudge of the hunched figure constantly in his view. It revealed itself against the pale light of the sky, or flickered like a dark wingless bird through the bare trees.

Turning onto the track for the mill, he switched off his headlights and drove as quietly as possible, before parking in the pasture. The mill faced him, black and oppressive against the trees. A couple of windows were dimly illuminated on the upper storey of the building, but the child's room was dark. Next to the car was the glassy water of the millpond, stinking of marsh plants and weed. It was an awful place. Was this the spot where they had once brought the woman to the river? Was it right here where she'd stood defiant on the bank, cursing the local children, inflicting illness on them, while her accusers passed sentence on her? He was sure now that there was malignancy here, trapped and somehow held at bay, and knew it had recently been disturbed. It should have been left alone.

He crept along the riverbank until he reached the mill, then quietly pulled the tarpaulin aside where the builders had made the breach in the wall. A stench of old water and damp brick rose around him as, in near total darkness, he slipped silently through the kitchen space, taking care not to dislodge any of the tools or tread on the rubble. The air was thick with malevolence, he imagined the scenes that might have happened in this room: a woman being dragged roughly across the floor, then held against the chimney breast while the miller decided how he was going to keep her here. Patrick felt feverish, while a sinister presence grew around him. He shut his eyes, because he knew that if he left them open he would see her body slumped against the end wall: her face in the candlelight, muddy from the river and scratched by the stalks of the reeds, eyes wide open and staring, a mouth full of water. He stumbled forward, keeping his eyes closed, knowing with absolute certainty there was something very near and watching his every move. Something unnatural, bringing him closer, like a bitter flame that he had to approach in order to extinguish it. Whatever the malignancy was, it had been dealt with, sealed up and capped off. Dormant for years, possibly centuries, but recently awoken by the building works, and it was becoming more powerful. It had appeared in his vision and then spread to his family, as a warning.

He approached the door to the stairwell and eased it open, then traced the rough wall with his fingers until he reached the hole in the brickwork. Trying not to breathe in the strange marshy odour, he brought out the metal plate and pushed it into the wall, nudging it into the cavity until it fell, soundlessly, into the void.

Joel rallied in the night. The following morning he sat eating his usual breakfast, while his twin brother Jed took the piss out of him, mercilessly. Patrick sat with them, listening to the chatter and casual cruelty of family life, making a point of them all eating together. He took them to school in the car, then sent an email to Blyth, letting him know that the plans would have to change. He was still willing do the remodelling, but those walls were to be left untouched. If Blyth wanted a different architect to come on to the scheme instead, then Patrick wouldn't object. Either way, those holes in the brickwork should be permanently sealed and the whole area re-rendered. He pressed send.

Three weeks later, he had the first of the scheduled follow up appointments with the ophthalmologist. As with last time, he noticed she slipped a mint lozenge into her mouth before the examination began. Again, the twin lenses of the slit lamp slid towards his face, held immobile against the restraining bars of the apparatus. The lights spilled into his eyes at strange angles, flooding his vision.

'And you've not seen them today, at all?' She asked, glad to be dealing with good news.

'Not for three weeks,' he replied. 'Nothing at all.'

Room 13

Chloe's lying on the bed, looking at the strange patterns on the ceiling. It's a large room in a faded Victorian hotel: the plaster's the colour of old teeth, a filigree of cracks across the surface, cobwebs in the corners. There are stains too, pale melanomas, spreading into each other. She sighs, turns to one side – a stab of pain shoots across her shoulders. It passes.

None of the curtains are drawn. The hotel floodlights shine up from the car park and the rain catches in the glare like sparks from a fire, slanting in rows. It's a stormy night, and she can hear the waves crashing onto the beach below.

He's been gone a long time. That fits, she thinks. Can't stand still is his problem. Actually, it's not really a problem, it's the thing she loves about him. How he'll buy a paper, sit down to read it, then put it aside to do something else. He does that kind of thing all day.

She studies the room. It must have been grand once. But now the carpet looks old, with a woven design of port-coloured fleur-de-lis tangled up in a beige grid plan. It's ugly. She thinks of all the guests over the years, too many people walking to and from the window to look out to sea, too many suitcases hauled around, opened up, drawers pulling in and out – staying in hotels is spending time with ghosts, inevitably; the rooms belong to no one. They'd stayed at this hotel once before, ten years ago. On that occasion they'd been renting a cottage a few miles away, but on a whim they'd come here and asked for the best room going, enjoying the sheer recklessness of spending unnecessary money.

In the bay widow there's an out-dated coffee table. It's a draughty place to sit. And there are too many chairs in the room, all of them different and none of them looking comfortable and most of them facing the bed, which is something she doesn't like at all. She should have turned them away before lying down. She'll ask Saul to do it when he returns.

Saul's standing halfway down the corridor, peering through a small window overlooking the street behind the hotel. No one's about. He watches the rain blowing in squalls across the puddles. A pub sign is swinging wildly in the wind, flashing a square of wet light at him so he can't, in fact, read the pub's name. Something like The Lobster and Eel or even The Lobster at Heel. There's an easy chair next to him, though no one could ever have sat in this place, and a small table with a few leaflets on it for local attractions, arranged in a neat circle. A butterfly centre, a water park, boat trips to watch the seals. They use photos taken on hot sunny days. For him, the appeal of these places is to come out of season. The cold blast of wild sea air. He'd rather see a plastic bag blowing down an empty street, the multicoloured strings of promenade lights swinging in a gale, or feel a latch inside an old pub door while the wind tried to tug it from his grasp.

Where are all the people, he thinks? He and Chloe had arrived late, but not too late; it doesn't explain why the hotel is empty. They'd come in from the storm and waited, windswept and disorientated, at the reception. It had been warm, with carriage lights on the walls giving off a soft glow. There'd been a faint smell of tea and butter and furniture polish, and something more nostalgic like pipe tobacco. They'd stood at the reception and waited, but the office was shut.

'What do we do?' Chloe had asked. She looked weary, her skin was dark under the eyes, and she'd wrapped her coat tight round her – tiredness always made her cold. She leant in a way which looked uncomfortable. Car journeys do that to you, he'd thought. They bend you, then they break you.

'Do we ring the bell?' he'd asked. Stating the obvious sometimes worked. But he'd been reluctant to ring it. Hotels in the middle of the night were odd places, and you had to fit in with them.

On impulse he'd climbed over the reception counter.

'Saul!' she'd said. 'Don't piss around.'

'Welcome,' he'd replied, brighter with the role-play. 'Pleasant journey, Madam?'

'Really boring company, but what can you do?'

'Well, a good night's sleep is what you need. What number was it?' Then, dropping out of character, he'd added: 'Actually, what number *was* it?'

'Room thirteen, Saul. I shouldn't have to tell you.'

'You'd think hotels wouldn't have a thirteenth room.'

Behind the reception counter it had been surprisingly messy. There was a half-drunk beer bottle hidden below the eye line of the guests, and an open bag of makeup. It didn't take long to find the key to thirteen. He lifted it up by its thick plastic tag and held it like a prize.

Then as he climbed back over the counter he'd felt a terrific pain – a kind of tearing spasm right across the top of his chest. Chloe reached for him instinctively, as if she was trying to catch him.

'It's ok, Chloe,' he'd said, but he knew it wasn't.

Saul walks to the end of the corridor and pauses at the top of the stairs. The hotel is silent, totally silent. He feels weak. There must be staff somewhere, he thinks, surfing the internet in a backroom, or watching TV. He goes downstairs to the reception and, this time, rings the bell. It makes a very loud brass ding, and almost straightaway he puts his finger on it to stop the noise. No one comes. He walks to the bar but finds it's locked, through the glass panels in the door he sees chairs tilted towards the tables and bar towels draped over the pumps. It's eerie, so he heads back to their room.

He hesitates outside the door to thirteen. The corridor spans the width of the hotel. It's poorly lit, beyond their bedroom door it fades into a dark and impenetrable shadow. There's a glimmer of something at the end, which might be a fire exit, or it might be the rim of something chrome, but whatever it is the corridor makes him uneasy. Too tired after the long journey, he thinks, he's letting himself get unnerved. He can't help wondering why he'd felt such a pain as he'd climbed over the reception counter. Make the weekend a success, he says to himself, it's our last chance. The thought of it, of Chloe and him being here ten years ago, so eager, so carefree; their youth is like an obstacle now. Something to compare themselves with. Maybe that's why everything is so odd. Unfamiliar places ambush your senses, especially if you've been there before, and especially when the last time you were there you were so much happier.

As he opens the door to their bedroom he smells something strange. It smells like petrol.

He sees Chloe on the bed. She's turned to face the window and her hips are raised in a strong high curve in the centre of the mattress. The rest of her seems deflated and flattened, and her coat is wrapped round her legs to keep her warm.

'You've been ages,' she says, softly, almost asleep.

'There's no one about. I looked everywhere.' His voice sounds thin, lost in the big room. 'It's just you and me.'

'That's odd.'

'Very.' She has the ability to fall asleep anywhere, mid-sentence even, as soon as she's lying down. He's always been amazed by it. Before he sleeps he almost has to exhaust himself with thoughts, and right now, there's so much to deal with, to remember. Surely she's been thinking along similar lines? But maybe not.

He walks past her to look through the window. The North Sea looks murky, stretching away like a void, no border between it and the oil dark sky. The sea frightens him on nights like this. He can't see the beach either. But between the sea and the beach there's a line of dimly illuminated waves, lit by the spill of lights from the prom, and this division between two elements of the night is like a rift to him. A rift between the land and sea which feels like it might spread.

For a second he imagines what he must look like from down there – standing stiffly by the window in his thick coat, the room lit behind him like an unreal stage-set high in the darkness.

'Shall I draw the curtains?' he asks.

'I like them open. But Saul, move the chairs, will you? They're facing the bed.' She's more awake than he thought. She has her eyes closed and her expression's slack with tiredness, a kind of stunned look that's made her mouth oddly shapeless. The shadow below her eyes has spread to her temples and across her forehead, where there's a tiny knot of worry between her brows.

The chairs are heavy, too big for the room and too many of them, as if the room's been used for some kind of meeting. A séance he thinks, but decides not to say this out loud. She's on the edge as it is. He's worried for her, for that crease in the forehead that so often means a migraine is coming.

He sits in the last chair and stares at Chloe. She still hasn't moved. Ten years ago they'd got pissed in this room. They'd jumped on the bed doing karate kicks and air guitar solos and then whacked each other with pillows – it was a mad night. He'd rugby-tackled her on the carpet and she'd banged her elbow hard, and when he tried to say sorry she swung a pillow at him unawares, and they'd started fighting again. Laughing. Spit on their faces. Her hair was longer then, Saul remembers. They'd sunk an entire bottle of Malibu, which Chloe had nicked from the bar before they'd gone to the room, and they'd played trashy pop songs on the stereo and turned it up full. Chloe had done this strange little dance in the corner near the door, like she was caught in some small daft whirlpool, hanging her head down in her drunkenness and running on the spot in rapid, childlike steps. Saul's thought about the sight of her doing that many times over the years – her, lost in the moment – it was one of his reasons to suggest they came back here for a kind of reunion. Rekindle the fire. It's turned out to be something of a last chance for them both.

'Are you coming to bed?' she says.

'I don't know.' He knows he wouldn't sleep. 'Are you hungry?'

She doesn't respond. He sits there listening to the wind lifting the edges of the tiles on the roof somewhere above them.

'I couldn't eat,' she murmurs.

Something else very strange happened here ten years ago, and that's the other reason Saul wanted to come back to this room. He's gone over the event many times and has never made sense of it. Ten years ago he'd been hanging up his jacket in the wardrobe and suddenly felt as though he was being watched. Chloe had been in the en suite, and when Saul turned round he'd seen – for the briefest of glimpses – a dark figure standing in the centre of the room. The figure was only partially there, smudged at the edges and full of shadow but it also seemed, in that instant, to be just as amazed to see Saul. The apparition had wavered, in a rippling haze of shadow, and Saul had had an enormous sense of recognition, of absolute familiarity with it. As he stepped towards it the figure had tensed, as if pulled together by a rope, and as it vanished Saul had had a brief and disturbing realisation that the figure was actually himself. Himself, but different, a mirrored version who knew more than Saul did about his own life.

Saul had made the decision never to mention what he'd seen.

Chloe has propped herself up on one elbow. 'What's the matter?' she asks.

Saul doesn't entirely know. It's the hotel, he thinks. It's this room. Thirteen. They should never have come back. It's a mistake to try and go back to a time when you were happy.

'I think we should leave,' he answers. 'I don't feel right here.'

'Let's go first thing.'

'I don't want to wait that long.'

'But there's nowhere else to go. It's too late.'

Saul knows she's right, but it doesn't help. 'I don't like the corridor out there. It's spooky.'

She smiles. It's a pattern of behaviour they have – he gets more paranoid and she gets calmer.

'Can you smell petrol?'

She shakes her head.

'Something happened on the journey up here. In the car.'

'What? What are you talking about?'

'We – we had a row, and something happened. I think we crashed.'

She looks at him, alarmed. Her eyes are dark and the shadows below them look like bruises. 'I don't remember,' she says.

'Did we veer off the dual carriageway? I think we crashed.'

'You're not making sense.'

'I'm scared, Chloe. I think something terrible happened.'

'No – don't say anything.'

He's welling up with tears. 'We have to leave.'

'Come here,' she says, shifting on the bed to make room.

He lies next to her on the bed, afraid. The cover is cold underneath him, almost damp. He looks up at the ceiling plaster and sees the water stains there.

The smell of Chloe's hair calms him.

'Do you remember that bottle of Malibu I nicked?' she whispers. 'I can't believe I did that. I was a wild thing.'

'You still are.'

'I'm not really, though, am I?'

He doesn't really want to take this further. There's been too much talk in the last few months about their relationship and what has happened to it.

'I remember that dance you did, over by the door,' he says.

'What dance?'

Outside the window a seagull glides close to them on an updraft, like some ghostly puppet caught in the floodlights. Its wings don't move as it rises then falls off to one side.

'I'm cold,' she says. 'Hold me.'

He thinks things will calm down now. He can put his arm round her waist and wait till she falls asleep. Falling in with the rhythm of her breathing will settle him. He'll sleep too. But as he reaches his arm across her – she vanishes. Just fades away, unstoppably. He panics and cries out as his arm strays into emptiness. For a moment he lies there, in total shock, before urgency sweeps around him and he jumps from the bed. He stands, afraid, his heart pumping in his chest and a sweat covering his skin.

He stares at the room, disorientated and scared. He takes a couple of steps towards the door. The carpet seems enormous – it seems to stretch forever around him. He sees darkness growing around the walls – the walls themselves becoming something other, the confines of the room not important enough anymore. There are glimpses of shadows there too, glimpses of places in the dark stretching out from this room in strange wide corridors, pulling away from him.

He's on the verge of a great understanding – that time and place don't need to be fixed, but are instead fluid and transparent, and that that is their true nature. This room and this moment – he floats free from it, disembodied, and immediately there comes a longing to make a final comprehension of what is happening. But there's an urgency, too, because he's fading, needing to leave this place for the strange world emanating away from it beyond the walls. It's a world he suddenly understands, that wants him to be part of it, and that's the moment when he sees himself – ten years younger, hanging up a jacket by the wardrobe, staring back at him with shock. Staring back with recognition.

Low Ebb Feathers

'Fish don't trust no one, right? They got you sussed. There ent nothing on your bait that get them excited. That dab – one example – that dab you got last week – that must have been hooked every week of its miserable life.' Billy chuckled to himself, lying back on the shingle, propping himself up on one elbow so he could drink his lager. It was his third can.

'Here he come – them fish are sayin' – trying it on with a half-drowned rag worm – I ent going *near* that when I got me a tasty peeler crab on that Billy's line.' Billy pointed a grubby finger at Owen, making sure he got the message: 'You got to lure them in my friend, there ent no other way.'

Owen carried on threading his hook onto the paternoster, smiling at the way Billy went on and on. It was Friday evening and this was the usual way it went each week. Him tending to his gear, while Billy lay down on the shingle, goading him. Further along the beach there were ten or twelve other fishermen already set up, most had their rods up on the tripods, a bag of stones hung off them to weigh down the rig. The regulars cast out as soon as they could, but others – the tourists, the faddists, the fiddlers, all with their brand new kit – some of them could spend an hour getting the tent up and organising the bait box before they even looked at the sea. In the height of summer there'd been upwards of thirty men on the beach, but tonight was different: it was sharp with an early winter chill, it was just for the die-hards. Three days of a northeast wind had brought the fish in closer, Owen could tell that by the amount of interest the men were giving the sea. They'd all been sniffing the weather – some of the boys came out two days ago, but the real fishermen had waited, because the big fish waited, too.

The beach slanted steeply into the water, the November tides had already given it a scoured, wintry look. The raw wind from the last few days had made the shingle greyer and more shiny than usual. The only colour came from the battery lamps glowing through the multicoloured backs of the tents, like a string of Chinese lanterns pegged out along the bleak curve of the shore. A nice sight, it looked like companionship of sorts, although there was also an unwritten rule that the men kept themselves to themselves. Some brought along radios but most preferred to listen to the sea, how it changed, how the receding tide would begin to subdue the waves, how the currents became thick and lifeless as the low ebb arrived. All these men were men without women, or had women who were no part of this, it amounted to the same, really. He'd never known a woman to fish here, not in ten years.

Owen zipped up his jacket tight round his neck. Putting on weight, he thought. He looked at the fishing conditions. There was a touch of surf, but nothing too distracting for the fish. They'd be in close and hungry tonight. If only there was a moon, then the hunter fish would come right up to the shore where the water was grey with moonlight. They'd be easy pickings.

He'd been one of the first to set up, and had quickly got his long cast out with a try of ragworm on a single-hooked impact weight, erected the bivvie against the breeze and scooped shingle round its base to cut out the draughts. He liked scooping the shingle, it gave him the sense that he was dug in for the night. And he liked the thought of his hook already out there, sitting on the seabed, while he made it ordered on shore. By the acid light of his storm lantern he'd put up his folding chair, assembled the second tripod, wrapped the bait, checked and changed the batteries in the LED light on the rod's tip, stood his thermos in the shingle, then set to work on rigging up the close rod. That's when Billy had ambled over. As always, Billy carried a single beach rod, plus the bait box strapped across his back. He didn't fish with anything else, and spent most of his time lying on the shingle watching the other men's luck, puffed up in a dirty orange one-piece bodysuit he'd got from his time on the gas rigs. Lying there, on the stones, it made him look like a seal. With that one rod of his, Billy liked to cast in, reel a few times, then pack up and move down the beach. Sometimes he even cast as he walked, reeling in without even waiting, then would stop and for some reason fish a particular spot for an hour or so. And he'd make a catch, always, he was that good. He was a natural fisherman, born to it; he could sense the fish as they worried their way offshore, hunting in packs and creeping into the sea holes.

'Jonny got a flounder,' Billy said.

'How far out?'

'Fifty yards? He's fishing that gully where it broadens.'

'It's a good spot.'

'One pounder,' Billy said, dismissively. 'He won't get nothin' bigger. You gonna hit the defence?'

'Yeah,' Owen said, slightly apologetically, because fishing over the sunken pillbox was the obvious thing to do at this part of the beach. 'Should get a good solid lie on it cause there's so little swell.'

'Could be right,' Billy said, reaching into Owen's bag. 'Could be wrong, too.' He winked mischievously and passed over a grip weight. 'Just to be sure,' he said, kindly. Owen had lost a lot of tackle in his time.

'She up this weekend?' Billy asked. 'Usually come Friday night don't she. She up?'

Owen nodded.

'Knew it.' Billy started grinning, showing a row of dirty wet teeth in the glare of the storm lantern, their little edges and sharp points not unlike those of the fish he caught. Owen might mention it to him at some point, when Billy needed bringing down a peg or two. 'So that's why you set up so early. She's driving you crazy, my friend. He come too?'

'Yep,' Owen replied, thinking of the way his living room had lit up when the weekenders' Mercedes had drawn up opposite his house, how the husband had left the car running, its cooling fan as loud as a hair dryer, while she got out her side and tried to open the door to their holiday cottage. He'd seen her, in fragments, through his own front window, and then through the metal framework of the car, her long hair being swept up by her free hand while she worked the key into the lock, smiling back at her husband with a show of triumph when the key turned. That flash of a smile – with teeth set better than you get round here, and a glimpse of the tip of her tongue, sticking out in a teasing manner, as if they'd had a bet about whether she could work that lock or not.

‘Keep your mind on them fish,’ Billy said, smirking, before getting up to wander off along the beach.

Owen looked at his watch. Eleven. The couple would be going to bed. She’d be putting moisturiser on her face because the wind was forecast cold and had a wintry bite to it this weekend and she got worried about such things. She’d be sitting on the edge of the bed with her legs to one side, on a white duvet that would smell of fresh air. That husband of hers would’ve chucked his padded jacket over the back of the sofa, kicked his office shoes off, and now he’d be in the en suite, brushing his teeth and gobbing in the sink, the lucky bastard. With her, waiting on the bed, all smelling nice. Owen shook the thought from his head and returned to the business at hand, watching how the sea was changing. A gulley ran offshore at this spot, going parallel with the beach, slightly deepening. He saw the flatness of the surface and knew there was a hollow of deeper water beneath it. The seabed was sand, and there were more holes toward the second set of surf where the bigger fish hunted. He’d worked all that out and didn’t want to share it with anyone.

He fished with two rods; the first cast a good forty-five yards, the other, tighter rigged, cast nearer. Slowly he would work these rods together, bringing the further one in closer and recasting the other one further till he found the fishing channels. You’d begin to get hits, little stabs at the bait and false runs of the line, twitches of the rod which meant the fish were there and were sniffing the hooks. Tonight he’d gone straight for the long cast and with that flounder caught at fifty yards he thought it best to bring the line in a bit.

But the real trick here was to find the submerged war defence. Several tons of twisted reinforced concrete – the sea scorpions gathered there, and so did the scavenger cod. Big ones at that. Easy to think you'd hit it, but it might just be a groyne stump, and that would only be a waste of time, unless all you were after was crabs. Thinking this way, he cast out the close rod, giving it a high swing to let the weight drop as vertical as possible, before he reeled it back, slowly, to lodge against the rear of the defence. *That's got you*, he said, before tightening the line to part-snag on the rough concrete. He tried a dummy pull to see the movement. The mussels would be dangling there, pushed onto his hooks, pungent and appetising, hanging in the dark shadow off the back wall of the defence. Them – nestled in the weed and shadow – and the hungry cod weighing up their options.

Along the beach the men had entered that numb-like state of the overnighters, each slumped into their bivvies or crouched near their bait boxes, in thick padded jackets and oilskins. Tiny pools of light went on from the torches, then off, as hooks were dressed, rigs changed, and drinks poured. Billy used to go for cod but lately he'd been after John Dory, a fish that had a lazy, stealthy pounce, which suited his way of laying the bait, and suited Billy in general – it being a fellow lone spirit. Sometimes Owen wondered whether Billy had a particular affinity with a single fish out there, and they set about playing this game each night, trying to outwit each other. Some of the lads were still fishing whiting, for the sport, but most of them had moved over to cod and flounder now, out of greed. Cod snagged their lines too often, losing their rigs and costing them money. They were a new breed of fishermen, into their gear and not really into the fish. Yet all these men, whom Owen knew from The Bull or the Rushcutters, tended to behave like the fish they aimed for, whether they knew it or not: the whiting fishers were loud and mean and impatient at the bar, the plaice catchers were more languid and humorous, and Billy, old John Dory himself, there like a sniper on his stool near the wood burner.

As his mind wandered he thought again about the holiday cottage opposite his house, in particular how glowing it seemed inside, each weekend, what with the low voltage spots they'd put up, and the deep rich paint on the walls. It was the kind of place that had an instant heat and warmth the moment they switched the power on, unlike his own cottage, which seemed stubbornly damp all year round. What's their secret? he wondered. Money, probably, that's all it is. A couple of weekends ago he'd decided to do something about it by changing the lampshade in his front room. The old one had been a dusty paper thing with several rips – but even with the new shade fitted the room kept its dull quality. Even the bulb seemed dimmer than the ones they had over there, and he saw it in their eyes too, when they wrapped themselves up in padded coats and set off for a walk on a Saturday morning; he saw how the husband sized up Owen's house with a simultaneous expression of how much he reckoned it was worth, and how much needed spending on it. These weekenders, they have a price on your head, always. And they're oddly ashamed of you, too, for affecting their own property's value, like they're some kind of disapproving relative.

He could see Billy making his way back along the shoreline, crunching loudly on the shingle, eating a peanut butter sandwich. As he reached Owen's bivvie he reached into his bag and cut a two inch peeler crab in half with a pair of secateurs. The claws contracted, then didn't move again.

'What else you got?' Billy asked.

Owen checked the bait wrap. 'Mussel, sand eel, lug and rag worm, some cuts of white mackerel.'

Billy nodded, listening to the list. 'I ent staying longer than 3am,' he said. 'I'm going to wait for the last run, see if the calmer water bring in the individuals, then I'm packing. Ent no point staying out longer.'

'I'm staying for the *feathers*,' Owen said.

'Yeah?'

'Gonna try it.'

'Why you doing that?'

'Just am.'

Billy shook his head, mystified. 'I don't know, that's bad water for at least an hour. What, low tide's 4:15am – then the feathers come, I don't know. Ent no one going to stay for the feathers.'

'Well, that's just superstition.'

'Could be, could be,' Billy said. 'But there again...'

'I'm surprised you believe in all that.'

Billy stood up. He shrugged. 'I don't believe in nothing. But I don't want to find out either way.'

The low ebb feathers was the half hour after low tide, and it was the local myth, nothing more than that. If you were unlucky enough to be out here on the beach after the low tide, you saw things, you were visited, something like that. No one agreed on any one story, but there were plenty of versions – of sounds coming from the sea, or of men who'd had running fights with shadows that slipped out of the shingle. A trick of the stones. Whatever. Some of these stories were pretty badly made up, when he thought about it – these fishermen had a limited imagination. But the feathers had become the stuff of gossip, and although no one really believed it, no one stayed out past the low tide either.

Billy walked off, chuckling to himself. 'That posh lass has got you driven out all night. You got the bite, you have!'

Owen watched Billy wandering off down the dark beach. He'd probably tell the other fishermen that Owen was staying for the feathers. So what. Most of them considered him odd, anyway. At the pub they were a group of sorts, but he wasn't part of it, not really. He'd always had that air about him that singled him out. A social awkwardness that made people keep their distance. Strange that Billy was so marginal himself, so much a loser in so many ways, yet so popular with everyone.

Owen knocked back one of the miniatures he had in his bait box, then shone his torch on the label to see what he'd drunk. Grand Marnier. It gave him some warmth. He looked at the flattening currents directly out to sea. He'd chosen his spot well, where the water had the tendency to go flat and lifeless. Most of the other men couldn't see the point in it, thinking the hunting fish liked a bit more vitality to the flow, but he was working on the assumption that the largest cod must be unusual – they'd only reached to being their size because they'd done the unexpected.

He tended to his lines, freshened his bait, bit into a cold chicken and mushroom pie and, as it approached low tide, drank some more miniature bottles of liqueur. One by one he watched the fishermen packing up. Each one left, removing his little smudge of colourful tent from the view, until the beach was empty. Owen liked it like this. He liked being the only one of them to stick it out, the only one of them that was man enough for a cold November beach in all its middle-of-the-night emptiness. It might give him an extra something when he was next down the Rushcutters. Either that, or it might single him out as being more strange than they'd previously thought. He'd made that kind of miscalculation before.

He checked his watch with his keyring torch: 4:45am. This was the feathers, then. Billy was right, the water was dead. Owen wondered whether the fish were asleep in their holes and gullies – if they ever in fact slept. The sea became thick and oily, with an oddly dark sucking noise, like the slap of a swell against the side of a boat. He didn't like the look of it, changing like that – the tide had sapped every last bit of vigour from it, leaving the water lifeless and vague, and he began to think any fish he might catch now would be unhealthy and malignant. He looked at his lines. Pointless. He could try the paternoster, or freshen the bait, maybe try a blow worm – Billy had left him some good ones – but he knew it was the fiddling nature of a fisherman who'd run out of ideas. Some fishermen do nothing but fiddle, changing their lines, rigs and baits every few minutes. No, he'll see this through.

The water made a quiet soft roll, rhythmically, along the shore, as it sucked back gently on the shingle, pausing, rising, falling again. He listened to it and watched the drifting currents, like ripples in fabric, moving, rolling forward, falling back, fading into the darkness of the night. A long slow lick of waves on the stones. In front of him, the flow was settling, becoming even thicker as the wreck of the war defence began to push up though the sea. A stiffening of water there, stilled by its own shallowness, the mark of a scar beneath the surface, making it look waxy and untrustworthy.

His head lolled with tiredness and, briefly snapping awake, he saw the beach had begun to look confusing. The rising slopes of shingle were so poorly lit they seemed like they were layers of gauze. Some of the ridges seemed impossibly close and abstract, others more distant and vague, as if they were theatre drapes being slid among one another. The beach in this light seemed like the sea itself, with moving surfaces and gaps, through which he glimpsed other shapes, mistakes of the darkness, strange solidities where he knew there was nothing but shingle. There were rising banks, slopes, dips, stones piled up like the dense grey dots of newspaper print, and he felt his eyes becoming heavy again – just a small concession to it, he thought, just an acceptance of how tired he was, coming to him like a further darkness more deep and real than the one that hung over the sea.

Sleep filled him, calmly, and this time he allowed himself to go with it, slumping his head onto his chest, listening to the thin hiss of the storm lantern by his side. Instantly he saw a glimpsed dream of the village. A view down the streets of the small fishermen's cottages with their narrow front gardens. A sound of his boots, echoing down an alleyway as the tip of his fishing rod trembled in front of him. He recognised his street, then his house, but his approach to it was strange: instead of going to his gate he turned towards the other side of the road, to the holiday cottage, the house where the couple arrived every Friday night, without fail, after their journey from

London. Surprisingly, the door to the new cottage seemed to be open, and he stepped inside. Standing in their kitchen he was struck by the warm air rising from the underfloor heating. Small precise lights set into the ceilings cast a clean, brilliant shine across the room. Everything was wooden, polished, there were fresh flowers in a vase on the table, clean mirrors on the walls, and in them he saw himself, wet and dirty and still in his beach gear, as Amelia came downstairs and joined him. She was sleepy from the journey, but happy to be there. Her hair was long and dark like a horse's mane, and each strand seemed to have been cut precisely, as if a ruler had been used by the hairdresser. It shone under the lights in a girdle round her head, like an angel, he thought, and a similar shine flashed down her calf, reflecting off her tights, as she walked confidently to the other side of the room. She leant against an old wooden Welsh dresser and looked at him, smiling, intrigued, and he felt he belonged there, with her, that some part of that smile was for him.

'Will you cut the fish?' she said, humorously, and he looked towards a table where a dark cod was draped awkwardly across a metal serving plate. The fish was ancient and huge, with a sickly greenish colour, and as he looked at it he saw its gills panting – their white frayed edges like deep knife wounds in the flesh.

'I need to eat,' she said, more impatiently, and he obediently approached the ill fish. Its eye looked glassily at him, mistrustfully, and as he touched the table the cod flapped heavily in panic, trying to wriggle off the plate.

'It's still alive,' he muttered, pathetically.

Amelia merely replied: 'I know, you must kill it. Kill it for me.'

In his hand was a long carving knife and he rested it across the broad back of the fish. He looked at the cold metal of the blade, and doubted himself.

'I – I can't do it,' he said, quietly ashamed.

For a second she ignored him, then her face darkened, and she whispered, coarsely:

'Then, get out, you loser.'

Immediately he was gripped by a huge sense of alarm and he woke, on the beach, staring into the face of an unkempt man who was close, way too close, crouching into the light of the gas lantern. Owen gasped in shock and seemed to take in a series of details at the same time: the man's rough jacket lapel with strangely shaped metal hooks pinned through the fabric, a lattice of black creases across the man's cheeks, the long strands of a sparse grey beard, the piercing depth of his eyes, flickering in the glare of the lamp.

'Nodded off, hin't you!' the man said, aggressively. 'You nodded off.'

'Get away!' Owen said. 'You – you crept up on...'

'You was asleep, fella.'

'Was I?'

'So I comes up, like.' The man stared unpleasantly at Owen, his eyes thick as lead. There was a terrible smell too, a gagging smell of his breath, like the rotten mulch and seaweed smell of the high tide line.

'You fishing?' Owen asked, trying to calm himself.

The man continued to stare, very close, like he was searching for something in Owen's expression. It was deeply unnerving. Owen leant back, away from the stranger. The man had a hard thin face, with deep dirty lines that could be age or could be scars across his cheeks. There was a hint of a smile there, too, the beginnings of a malevolent grin that Owen didn't want to see.

Then suddenly his fishing line started to fly out with a high mechanical whiz, and Owen looked instinctively beyond the man to see his rod tipping in a series of trembling jerks.

Relieved, Owen pushed past the man to tend his rod, which was tipping so low it was approaching the line's breaking point. He slid it off the tripod, managed the tension on the reel, and immediately felt the pressure of the pull stretching through his arms. *My God!* he said, staggering under the effort. As Owen began to slip in the shingle towards the sea he heard the man behind him.

'What you doing fishin' the low ebb?' the man growled. 'Ent no one do that. They all pack up 'fore the feathers.'

Owen didn't answer. The stranger came to his side, watching the bend of the rod as Owen tried to fight it to gain control. 'You live down Willow Lane, dontcha?' he said.

Owen tried to ignore him, alarmed.

'She's a firecracker ent she, that one opposite you. She's a prize.'

'I don't know what you're talking...'

'Yeah you do. She's a beaut.'

Own stumbled in the shingle, trying to control the pressure on the line.

'Don't worry, I ent startin' nothin'.' The man reached over Owen's arms and gave a great tug on the rod. 'Pull it, boy, you ent pullin'!'

Owen elbowed the man away and tried to raise the angle of the rod. Again the reel whizzed, Owen slipped further, buckling at the knees, as he was pulled towards the water.

'What is she?' The man asked.

'Eh?'

'Your hook, boy, what is she?'

'She's a... it's a two hook Mustad pennel.'

'Size?'

'Four.'

'Then you got no chance.' The man looked gleeful. 'You need you one of these,' he said, unhooking a twist of darkly shining metal from his jacket sleeve. It had a cruelly filed tip like a spear at the end. 'See, that's a hook.' He turned it in front of Owen, then pulled up his own sleeve and swiftly dug the hook through the skin of his forearm. 'Oh yeah,' he uttered, 'Look at me. Could hang me wi' that.'

Owen backed away from the man, revolted and afraid, yet pinned to his own struggle with the rod.

'Ah, you ent gonna land it,' the man said. 'You ent got the nerve.'

The rod pitched lower and Owen slipped further in the loose shingle. 'Give us a hand will you,' he said, desperately.

'I'll fight you for her.'

'You *what*?'

'Fight, over that gal live opposite you.'

'You're crazy – get away from me.'

'Scared of a little scrap eh? You ent worth nothin' boy, you ent worth me pushin' you over. Hant got no fight in yer so whass you out here for, fishin' the feathers? That ent for boys.'

The man leered at Owen, then climbed back up the bank to the bivvie, saying: 'You's out hair cause you ent got nothin' else, *fisher-man*.'

And with it the man suddenly lashed out at the storm

lantern, kicking it over with his boot. It smashed on the stones and the flame flickered briefly, then died. Owen tensed for whatever would come next, expecting more violence, not knowing how it would start, or what he should do. Would a fist come at him through the dark? He heard boots scuffling through the stones coming towards him, he tried to brace himself, gripping the butt of the rod like a weapon as the impenetrable shadow of the stranger approached. He couldn't even gauge how close the man was anymore. Owen gripped the rod and stared into the dark, his breaths rising in short, hurried intakes. The pull on the line was immense, and bit by bit he realised he was being dragged further, incrementally, towards the water. Looking for the man, he could only see liquid black shapes among the shingle, as the stones moved and realigned themselves.

Strangely, as the icy seawater flooded over the tops of Owen's boots, the pressure on the line vanished. The rod sprang up straight in his hands. He looked out over the swell at the grey first light of day that was spreading across the sky. Then he reeled in, slowly, not knowing what to expect. His line pulled out of the sea like it was a tiny thread of water, just as grey, and at the end of it there was his hook and his bait, untouched.

Owen walked fast, shaken, with his head down, returning to the village on the path that went through the reed beds. Most of the buildings were still dark and unlit, and the village appeared sparse and uninhabited as he walked through it. At Willow Lane he walked past his house, without glancing at it, turning instead to the smartly renovated cottage opposite. He rang the bell before he could think twice, and only then realised he should check the time. It was 6:45am.

He stood on the cold step for quite a while, suddenly nervous. Eventually he saw the slim figure of the woman approaching through the door glass.

She opened the door and stared at him, confused. She looked tired. Maybe she didn't sleep too well, he thought – it was something new about her he hadn't known.

'Hello,' he said.

She looked totally confused: 'It's – do you know how early it is?'

'Yeah, I'm sorry, I've – lost track. Been out all night.' He held up his fishing gear, stupidly, like a clumsy explanation. 'I live over there. I'm your neighbour.'

'OK.'

'That house.' He pointed with the tip of the rod and saw his house in the same way that she must view it: a damp and depressing place, with broken gutters and a gate half-off its hinges. 'Owen,' he added.

'Right.'

'You're Amelia. I mean – I've heard your husband say it, in the street.'

'He's Stephen.'

Owen wondered whether the conversation was now over. Amelia looked at him warily, and he assumed she was angry in some way. 'I've been fishing,' he said, 'at the beach.' That was a dumb thing to say, he thought – where else was there? And he was carrying a rod. 'I was there for the feathers – that's this time, right, it come after the low tide, but no one stay out for the feathers – they say it's haunted.'

She looked at him strangely, working him out. 'And was it?' she said, after a while.

Owen shrugged.

'Is there something I can do for you?' she asked.

'Well, it just seemed odd, you know, that we ain't never said hello. Us being neighbours and all that.'

'Well, hello. Again.'

'...I mean, I can do things. I've seen you have trouble with that lock on your door. I could have a go at that if you want, I've got all the tools.'

'I don't really think you need to. It's really not that much trouble.'

'Yeah? Well we put these things off, don't we? Are you French?'

'No.'

'You just seem it, you know, with the way you look.'

The woman frowned. She really wasn't that pretty, at this time of the morning, he thought. She took a step back, and began to shut the door: 'Well, it's early, I think I'll go back in now.'

'Amelia,' he said, stopping her, 'I had this dream about you, last night. I dreamt you had a fish in your kitchen – laid out on a plate. This big – a big dark cod it was. It wasn't a very healthy fish. You wanted me to kill it for you.'

He stared at her, trying to reassure her with a smile, but it felt wrong. He could tell it looked more like a grimace and it would be alarming for her.

'Oh, well, it's really early, Owen,' she said. 'I'd better...' she trailed off, beginning to close the door more forcefully this time. He stuck his hand out, and before she could think twice, she shook it. He felt how thin her fingers were, how long and bony they were, how they could easily be crushed by his own large coarse grip. And he saw the scales of mackerel on his skin, the juice from the rag worms, the salt and dirt from the beach.

He crossed the road to his cottage and sat in the living room, still in his fishing gear, resting his rod across his lap. A few minutes passed, then Amelia's husband came out pretending he had something to fetch from the car. He stood in his bright puffer jacket, but still with pyjama trousers, and looked with hostility at Owen's door before going back to the holiday cottage empty-handed. *You lucky bastard*, Owen muttered, but his voice seemed disembodied from himself, and he wasn't entirely sure that he'd said anything at all. He was exhausted, ragged from the night at the beach, and still with a sense of fear that some proximity of violence was nearby, stealthy and malevolent. Tiredness had made him bleary, but he was also afraid to go to sleep, because he knew his dreams would be an open doorway for something to emerge, coming for him. He thought about going to the Ruschcutters later, and knew the others would keep their distance, knowing he'd fished the low ebb feathers, it had singled him out as an oddball. Perhaps he'd return to the beach and look for signs of the rough man, but he knew his nerves couldn't take it. If he went back to the beach he'd stick his rod in the shingle like a fence post and he wouldn't bother pulling it out when he left. Across the road he noticed all the lights had been switched on, but each of the windows had curtains tightly drawn. He held the rod across his lap, pressing it down on both sides, until his arms shook with effort. It bent, as it was designed to do, then with a loud splintery crack it snapped in half. When he looked at his hands he saw the nylon fishing line was taut and painful, leading to an evil looking hook that had pierced through the skin on his forearm. He sat there, hooked, immobile, watching the blood beading from the wound and dripping to the floor.

Serpentine

With her backpack slung off one shoulder, Cara walked to the door and gave it a shove. The daylight was almost gone, and the static caravan was filled with shadows and unpleasant air. She dumped the backpack onto the floor and wiped some of the condensation off the window with her elbow. Through a small patch of clear glass she saw a grassy slope leading to a bank of trees and the miles of flat saltmarshes beyond. What a place, she thought. She searched for a light switch and flicked it on. The caravan was a mess. It stank of cigarettes and socks and there were beer cans and take out containers on the table, an electric guitar propped up in a corner, and a bowl of underwear soaking in the sink. She dipped a finger into the soapy water and found it was still hot. From somewhere beyond one of the doors she could hear a shower running.

She unzipped her bag and tried her mobile. No reception. But she texted her mum, regardless, thinking it would get sent at some point, then sat on one of the sofas, thinking of the long torturous drive to get to north Norfolk, the roads getting smaller and smaller until they were hardly wide enough to get the van through, and the trees getting more twisted, bent double from a salt breath the closer they got to the coast. It felt like the end of the world.

An internal door opened and a girl, about eighteen, stepped out, totally naked apart from a towel wrapped round her head.

'Who the fuck are you?' the girl said, although she didn't look surprised.

'Cara. Kitchen staff,' she replied.

'You Irish?'

'Yeah. Something like that.'

'Right.' The girl seemed unfazed by her nakedness. She was pale and thin, and looked sad. She crossed into a room at the back of the caravan. 'I'm Toni. You've got the room through there.'

'Any reception here?' Cara called out.

'Nah. I'll get you the Wi-Fi.'

Cara took a deep breath, the sense of journey and movement still settling. She was in no hurry to see her room, because she guessed it would be cramped and disappointing. A fine drizzle was falling against the window. She watched the droplets moving into each other, collecting into small runs of water threading down the glass. The moment seemed incredibly familiar, and it was suddenly apparent that all this was known to her and she was in the middle of something she'd experienced before. The thin curtains with their banded blue and white design, the cupboard doors made from some sort of laminated material, the central light with its plastic chandelier moulding, a cigarette ground into the carpet near her feet. She'd known these things and she'd known this room, though she'd never been here before.

The kitchen was noisy and sweaty and didn't need to be as hectic as it was. She spent the entire shift doing the pre-wash, loading the dishwashers, stacking the crockery and replacing the cutlery, then re-stocking the sauces in the fridge and helping to plate up when several covers had to go out at once. The chefs were barking out the orders and it was clear they didn't have much respect from the others in the kitchen. Cara made herself look busy, even when she wasn't, and didn't chat, knowing she'd be a target for any blame or stress that might flare up. Several times she was sent to a walk-in freezer in the yard to fetch boxes of labelled Tupperware, and when she went out there she marvelled at the high dark sky and the sharp smell of salt in the air.

At midnight, after the surfaces had been washed down, the waste bagged up and the cookers wiped, she walked back towards her caravan, exhausted. Her legs were heavy with all the standing. The hotel was an old manor house built on a slight rise, among fir trees and surrounded by fields where fruit was grown in the summer. There were five static caravans housing the seasonal staff, all in a row under a line of holly trees, partially shielding them. Some of the staff were sitting around a fire pit, where tall flames were licking through a pile of broken agricultural pallets. She found a fold-up chair in the grass and dragged it alongside, nodding to the others. Someone handed her a can of beer. On the other side of the fire she saw her co-sharer, Toni, dressed in a fleece over her hotel uniform, leaning against the shoulder of one of the waiters, a man called Blake. Cara drank her beer, thankful that no one was expecting her to talk. But Blake kept looking across the fire at her. He was thick set, manly, full of swaggy confidence. He gave her a wink, then pretended it was just smoke that had got in his eye.

Cara decided she wasn't going to react. She knew the drill at these kinds of places. Casual work and casual sex, expected to go hand in hand. She knocked back her beer and zipped up her jacket before walking to her caravan. Approaching the steps she again had the uneasy sense that she was living a moment she'd known before. This row of caravans, the holly trees pressing darkly over their roofs, the spill of light fading across the long grass until it was met by a wall of blank night. She felt a shiver spread across her shoulders, and a sense that she'd come a long way to get away from something that, unwanted, had followed her here.

She got into bed still wearing the sweatshirt and trackies she'd worn in the kitchen, because the duvet was damp cold. Her mind was restless and unsettled. After a while she propped herself up on one arm and pulled the curtain aside. She looked down the slope towards the featureless blank flats of the saltmarshes, and the pale glimmer of the sea beyond. She looked closer, gripped by an uncanny sense that there was something vital and demanding out there. Gradually, the definition of pools and creeks began to emerge among the darkness, between deeply feathered reed beds. She noticed a long shingle bank which was slightly paler than the sky and, in front of the bank, an area of the marsh which – as she stared – seemed almost to be brighter, a glow that seemed to pulse softly, like a heart beat, there in the dark.

She drew the curtain and slid the bolt on her door.

In the middle of the night she knocked hurriedly on Toni's door and, when there was no answer, she entered. In the dark, she waited until she could make out the twin shapes of Toni and Blake, in bed. She crouched by Toni and shook her gently by the shoulder.

'Toni. You've got to come and look at this,' she said. 'Quick.'

Toni woke and pulled herself upright.

'What's up?'

'Through here.'

Cara walked swiftly into the main room of the caravan, where she'd pulled the curtain aside. Outside, the moon was up and low bright clouds were moving in slowly over the sea. The marsh was black, apart from one or two creeks glinting in the moonlight. She heard Toni approaching behind her.

'Look – out there, on the marsh,' she said.

'Shit Cara, it's like three o'clock?'

'Can't you see it?'

Toni stood with a fleecy blanket wrapped round her shoulders.

'See what?'

'Over there, near the bank. Can't you see it? The light?'

Toni sat on the sofa, pissed off. 'I can't believe you woke me up.'

'Just have a look, will you?'

'I'll need my glasses.' She pointed to the counter and Cara fetched them for her. Cara knew Toni was deeply pissed off. She'd have to apologise in the morning. Toni rubbed her eyes, put her glasses on, and reluctantly stood by the window.

'So, what am I looking at?' she asked.

'See the bank?'

'Suppose so.'

'Yeah, and in front of it. That glow.'

'What glow?'

'Like a mist, shining. It's near that pool.'
'I'm so knackered, Cara.'
'You can't see it?'
'No.'

Woken by her alarm, and stumbling from her bedroom still in last night's clothes, Cara discovered Toni had already left. On the dining table was an A4 sheet with all the shifts marked out, and she saw her own name written next to a shift beginning at 10:30am. The caravan looked drab and the air was damp and fungal. She went through the cupboards and made herself two rounds of toast, adding strawberry jam from a collection of mini-jars that looked like they'd come from the hotel. She had the tea black, because the milk smelt off, and a cloud of steam rose off the liquid in the chilly air. She dragged a heater across the room and plugged it in, then sat by it at a small dining table while she ate. Her mum had texted a reply, saying she was worried and wanted to speak.

She remembered waking up a second time in the night, sometime before dawn, with a pressing sense of urgency. Pulling the curtain away from the window she'd seen the dismal saltmarshes stretching away in the gloom, with reed beds dotted among the mudflats, and the glint of water like darkly gleaming metal in the creeks and pools. She saw it again. Only this time it had sudden clarity. A figure, in distress. A woman. Cara had watched, holding her breath, while the woman waved her arm in panic, facing the caravan, then immediately vanished.

At 10:30am she met the hotel manager: a stout bossy woman who clearly enjoyed wielding undeserved power in a place like this, but who would be easily ignored in many other places. Cara was shown the various linen cupboards and storerooms. It was straightforward, but the manager insisted that Cara should team up with Toni to clean the rooms, to make sure standards were kept consistent. Toni shrugged, acquiescent, but then looked sullen and churlish as they changed the beds, making unhelpful gestures to show Cara where to hold the sheets and how to fold the valance down.

'Sorry about last night,' Cara said.

'No worries.'

'I just got a bit freaked out, yeah?'

Toni looked indifferent. She pointed at the finished bed: 'You got it, right? Coz I got other stuff to do.'

'Sure. You go ahead.'

Left in the room, Cara ran the hoover round and straightened the curtains. She refreshed the bathroom, changed the towels and refilled the soap and moisturiser dispensers, then wiped down the shower stall, sink and toilet. She sat on the loo and took a pee, flushed, then decided she wouldn't bother cleaning it again.

In the next bedroom she found luggage belonging to a young couple. He'd left his boxers on the floor of the en suite, and the remains of a room service breakfast were on a tray in the centre of the bed. She helped herself to a croissant while she looked round the room. There was a half-drunk bottle of Cointreau on the windowsill, next to several cigarette butts on a hotel plate, even though all the rooms were non-smoking. She looked through a bag of makeup, checked the lipstick and eyeliner, smelt the perfume. Floral. A bit young and obvious, without depth. His wash bag had indigestion tablets and – in a small grip-seal bag – a quarter-ounce of weed. Cara began to clear the room, then switched the hoover on to make it sound like she was busy. She went to the window and looked out towards the sea. The view was unremarkable – dull green saltmarshes, threaded with the complex pattern of creeks and pools. There was no sign of the things she'd seen during the night. She switched off the hoover, then quietly got into bed, lying down and pulling the duvet up to her neck before turning onto her side. She sniffed the pillow and smelt a male aftershave. She looked at the emptiness of the mattress next to her and wondered whether – tonight – there would be some residual presence of her in this same bed. A tricky complication, intangible and yet there, a thorn within the couple's relationship.

On the way out, she took a pinch of his marijuana, folding it into an empty biscuit wrapper to put in her pocket.

When all the rooms were done, she loaded the dirty laundry into the service trolleys and returned her cleaning materials to the store cupboard. She signed the time sheet in the reception and, while she waited for the manager's counter-signature, she wandered over to a large historic map of the area hanging in a frame over the fireplace. The hotel was clearly marked, although without the modern extension that had been built on one side. But what struck her was the extent of the saltmarshes stretching along the coast in both directions. The intricate maze of brown creeks and pools between the land and sea; a barrier of mud and marsh like a thick rim of fat on the land. She tried to work out where she'd seen the apparition of the woman and – among the names written on the map – decided it must be a strangely twisting pool labelled *Serpentine*.

Back at her caravan she quickly dressed in a thick jumper and coat, then set out towards the marsh. At the edge of the hotel's grounds there were thick hedges of brambles and gorse, so it took her a while to find a small track that led her through. There, she was stopped by a deep drainage ditch, bordered with tall reeds. Following a path alongside the ditch, she was eventually led to a raised walkway that led directly towards the sea. It was a firm footpath with grazing fields on one side, and the saltmarsh on the other. Several birdwatchers were heading out along the path, with telescopes slung on tripods over their shoulders, and every so often they peeled off to enter bird hides set among the reeds. It was an exposed path, and a biting wind blew across the marsh, stirring the reed beds in sudden gusts and making her eyes sting. She turned her collar up and bent forward, one hand against an ear to stop it aching. What was she doing, she wondered, heading into this wildness of air and salt, following some draw of instinct but, realistically, with nothing to find. The marshes stretched away, barren and empty, there was nothing out there apart from birds in small flocks huddled on the mud, or as scattered bright flecks on the open stretches of water. Last night's apparition felt like a surreal overlay; a darkly remembered dream. A woman in danger, desperate for help.

It began to drizzle, then quickly became dense rain, so she hurried off the path to seek shelter in one of the bird hides. Inside, it was muffled and dark, with a row of four bird watchers, all men, sitting on a long bench looking out through a slit in the wood. None of them reacted to her. The men looked depressed, wrapped in thick coats, watching nothing, passing time. Cara stood at the back, listening to the rain shower hammering on the roof, looking through the letterbox window at a slot of bright watery marsh, with birds getting drenched in the downpour. What had she done, Cara thought, coming to this dreary place? Outside, a group of ducks stood huddled by the edge of the water, with heads turned and buried into the back of their necks. Their feathers blew up in the draughts. She stared at one of them in particular and saw its flimsy eyelid beginning to lift. The duck looked back at her with a lazy, incoherent gaze.

It wasn't just déjà vu that she felt. It was the belief that, on days like these, a great revelation seemed tantalisingly near – as if she was able to see her life unreeling both ways, past and future, and know the directions and pulls that held her in place, finely balanced, waiting for a nudge this way or that. Recent events lined up, demanding her attention: the drop out of college, the long journey to get to the hotel, the necessity of a cash in hand job, prompted by an online advert. These things seemed stages in a journey she knew the answer to, an inevitable catastrophe, or face the pull towards Stansted airport and the defeat of a single flight back to Cork, followed by the need to start again, trying not to make a similar set of mistakes next time. Set out with belief; return with disappointment. But just how many times would she have to do this?

As soon as the rain eased she left the bird hide and set out on the path towards the sea. Almost immediately she recognised Blake walking towards her. The path was narrow, there was no way to avoid him, so she bent her head down and kept walking, hoping he wouldn't notice her. He slowed down, partially blocking her way as she approached.

'Had enough?' he asked.

She shrugged, nodding in the direction beyond him. 'Where does it go?'

'Well – I'd say to the arse end of nowhere.' He put his hands in the pockets of his jeans, in no hurry.

'A beach?'

'Nah. A pile of shingle.'

He pulled out a packet of fags and gave her one, without asking if she smoked.

'Cheers,' she said. He cupped his hand around the end of the cigarette as he struck the lighter, and she smelt the warm dry smell of his fingers. As she took her first drag, he looked at her, amused.

'Toni says you came in last night.' She met his gaze, blew the smoke towards him and didn't answer. 'Only, if you wanna threesome, you should ask, right?'

She gave an unimpressed look, but it bounced straight off him. 'I thought I saw something,' she said.

'Out here? Don't think so.'

A line of geese flew towards them over the marsh, making a low honking sound. Their ragged formation twisted like a wet rope, pulling taut at either end then growing slack in the middle. When they passed above, she heard the surging movement of their wings and their rhythmic, laboured breathing. She watched them drift into the distance, and soon they were lost in the line between land and sky. They didn't seem to be flying anywhere in particular.

'What you saw,' Blake continued, 'is what a shit-hole this place is. Probably realised it was a mistake coming here.'

'You reckon?'

'For sure.' He smiled, casual and enigmatic. He was annoyingly handsome. Strong, with dark messy hair and deep brown eyes. Each day he'd start off with a base level attraction others worked hard to reach.

'You here for a while?' he asked.

'Save it,' she replied. 'It's not gonna work with me.'

He laughed, quietly, then handed her a couple more cigarettes and his lighter. It was a cheap disposable one, with a Playboy bunny logo and a slogan *OMG it's HOT in here!* written below it.

'See ya later,' he said, easing past her.

At the end of the path she clawed her way up the steep shingle. The sea was dull grey and choppy, with half-formed waves breaking quickly. The wind whipped across the backs of the breakers, picking up wisps of foam and blowing them onto the shore, where they shivered in clumps on the stones. There was no horizon. Turning back inland, she looked across the flat miles of saltmarshes and the rise of land leading up to the hotel. Blake had passed the row of static caravans and was approaching the kitchens, one hand in his pocket. There's a guy like him in every outfit of hotel staff, she thought. Playing the numbers, taking his chances, getting a few notches on the bedpost. But perhaps he had something else that others didn't have. He was a mixture of things, not all of them bad. She spotted her caravan, nestled under the row of hollies, and again thought there was an aspect about it that was overfamiliar, although the significance felt frustrating and beyond her grasp. What is it, she wondered, that had made this subtle resonance? Déjà vu, premonition, these things were not entirely unknown within her family. Cara's mother, back in Cork, regularly stopped what she was doing, whether it was walking down an unfamiliar street or catching a reflection in a shop window, just to acknowledge a moment she had lived before in a life that was not her own. It was normal behaviour, so accepted that it hardly registered. And Cara's grandmother, now in an old people's home overlooking a bleak stretch of Lough Mahon, had been a lifelong mystic and seer of the future. In her youth she'd been invited to funeral wakes, to perform a vigil in the corner and tell the mourners whether the soul was restless and agitated, or at peace. She would ask for personal artefacts belonging to the recently departed, then turn them carefully in her fingers, picking up disturbance and vibrations that no one else noticed, as well as making sure the windows were open and the mirrors covered. She read futures from the wax left behind on guttering candles.

Cara began to walk back along the path, wondering what these women would say to her, now. Old wisdoms, passed down, and a family riddled with superstitions, but each generation seeming to dilute what was passed from the previous one, and Cara wondered whether she was in fact the last of a line. Perhaps she held something fragile and unknowable within her, but so deep in her consciousness that it was now almost a memory, a half-remembered voice, a forgotten and unreachable skill.

That evening, a large wedding party celebrated at the hotel. The bride and groom were in their early twenties, and they brought with them a loud and boisterous crowd that were up for a big night. The kitchen quickly became overwhelmed and toxic with stress, so Cara was relieved when she was enlisted into the waiting staff. Hurriedly she donned a hotel uniform to weave between the wedding tables, serving guests with plates stacked up on her arms. The guests were rude and dismissive to be attended by someone their own age. Leaning in to serve a main course at one of the tables, she picked up the bright floral scent she'd smelt earlier that day, cleaning the bedroom. Cara glanced at the person she was serving, and saw a girl with fake blond straightened hair and a mean face with small, pinched features.

'I didn't order that,' the girl said, not looking at Cara.

'Not chicken?' Cara replied.

'I'm veggie, babe.'

'Right, I can sort it for you.' Cara backed away from the table as the girl got out her mobile and started scrolling through posts. She had thin fingers and badly bitten nails. I've been in your bed, Cara thought. I lay in your bed and I smelt your boyfriend's trashy aftershave. She looked across the table and saw a man pouring himself a large glass of red wine. He was wearing a white shirt that was a size too small for him, because he probably worked out and wanted to show off his pecs. He looked like he worked in finance.

Trying to get through a crowd of men who were jostling each other while a photo was being taken, someone lurched back and trod on her foot, knocking over a glass of red wine across her uniform.

'Ahh – you bastard!' she cried out, before she could stop herself. The man looked at her with a sneer of curiosity, waiting for her to say sorry. The red wine had made a long stain down the front of her dress, like a wound across her belly. She stared at it, spooked by a sense of unfelt injury, deep and troubling.

The man put his arm around another man's shoulder and staggered off in a half-dance. And before she could return to get the wine refilled, she realised the hotel manager had taken her by the elbow, and was guiding her towards the kitchen.

'Get in there and sort yourself out,' the manager urged, nastily.

It was 1:30am before the shift finished. Exhausted from being on her feet for so long, run ragged by the chaos and noise of the event, Cara stumbled back towards her caravan through the long wet grass and – at the doorway – kicked off the pair of painful dress shoes she'd borrowed for the evening. The night felt undone and disastrous and she just wanted her bed. But before she switched the light on she noticed someone was sitting on the couch. Shutting the door behind her she realised it was Blake.

'Where's Toni?' she asked.

The tip of his cigarette glowed brightly in the dark, as he took a drag. 'Don't know.'

'You had a row?'

'Every day.'

She flicked the light on and saw him wince. She decided to ignore him, so went to the sink and gulped down a large glass of water. He was lounging on the couch, one foot up on the cushions and the other on the floor. It looked like he'd been there a while, and from the corner of her eye she could see he was privately amused. She tied her hair up, unfolded the biscuit wrapper and began to roll a spliff with the weed she'd stolen.

'In fact, we've split,' he said.

Cara didn't react. She finished rolling, then slumped onto the couch next to him. But not close. She lit the spliff and took a couple of deep drags, then realised she'd used the lighter he'd given her. She toyed with it between her fingers, looking at the Playboy bunny and the corny slogan.

'That wedding party was carnage,' she said.

Blake nodded, and she passed him the joint.

'You wore Toni's shoes tonight?' he asked.

'Yep. Too small.' She looked at the cheap dress shoes she'd kicked off in the doorway, and the sight of them, empty, mid stride, made her uneasy.

'Here,' Blake said, 'put your feet up.' He shifted to one side, letting her raise her feet onto the sofa's cushion. As soon as she did it, he reached for a foot and took it in his hands, starting to massage it. She thought about pulling away, but he'd done it with so little fuss, such natural confidence, that it would appear like an overreaction. He rubbed his fingers deeply between her toes and then worked his way into the arches. It felt good. 'Any better?' he asked.

'It's OK.'

He brought her other foot towards him. While he continued the massage, she kept turning his lighter between her fingers, all the while noticing a peculiar vibration emanating deeply within it. Was it a tingling sensation, arriving from her feet into her fingers, or was it something more inexplicable, like her own grandmother holding personal possessions, picking up the agitations that no one else could find?

'When I got here,' she said, 'I had this awareness – like I'd been here before, that this caravan was something I'd known.' He listened, calmly waiting for her to continue. 'And then today, out on the marshes, looking back at the hotel –'

'Yeah. I saw you'

'It scared me.' She paused, wondering how much to share with someone like him. She watched his fingers, kneading the tops of her feet, stroking up towards her ankles. 'It's not like a memory. It's not like that at all. It's like a – a warning.'

'About what?'

'I don't know. Look, I saw someone last night, out there on the marsh. I really did.'

He glanced up at her, giving her a curious smile, like he was expecting a punch line.

'Is that it?' he asked.

'Yeah.'

She didn't like being mocked. It was a familiar sensation, because men often did it to her, thinking it was their duty to point out a quirk they'd noticed: that she was not to be taken seriously. There were variations to the way they did it, but most men ended up giving her the same look in the end: *you're just a bit too off-kilter*. The only difference, now, was it had come soon with Blake. Sooner than most.

'You think I'm weird?' she asked.

He took it as flirtation. 'In a good way.'

'Where *is* Toni?'

'Passed out, somewhere. She's off her trolley.'

She studied his face. The strength of his jaw, set in an expression halfway between a smile and something more judgemental, and the lamp-like directness of his gaze, which was difficult to look away from. There was a quality that was unknowable about this man, and it troubled her. It felt as though he had a significance that she was yet to understand, that would be needed one day.

'What is it?' he asked, amused.

She shook her head, unable to grasp why she thought this way – what purpose he was going to have when called upon. Impulsively, she leant forward, held his face with both hands and gave him a long kiss. He tensed, surprised, but it was only brief. He quickly moved closer to her, responding, sliding his hand up the side of her body. And just as quickly she pulled away, holding his gaze for a revelatory second, trying to glean the leaks of insight about him that was eluding her. But all she recognised was lust in his eyes. Lust, and an assumption of imminent conquest.

'Go back to your caravan,' she said, flatly. He remained in the same posture, half-reaching towards her, looking startled. But he held his gaze, covering any embarrassment, before breaking into an easy smile. 'Whatever,' he said.

'Here, it's yours.' She held out his lighter with its Playboy logo, and as he took it she understood what the vibration deep within it was. It was because it belonged to a liar.

She walked steadily to her room, exhausted, conflicted, knowing she would somehow need this man, but also that she couldn't rely on him. Her room was cold, spartan, belonging to no one. Her bed looked miserable. She slid the bolt on the door and went straight to the window, pulling the curtain to one side.

Distantly, among the vague grey expanses of saltmarsh, the woman instantly reacted – an arm raised, waving rapidly, trying to get her attention. And in the next moment, just as last night, the apparition vanished.

She woke up suddenly, as if a shock of electricity had passed through her. Instead of being in bed she was standing at the open door of the caravan. In front of her, the grey metal steps faded into complete darkness. The curtain that hung on the back of the door moved softly in a draught, like seaweed in a deep, calm pool. She felt her skin tightening with fear. The caravan's living room was dreamy around her, tomb-like, with empty seats and unknown shadows, but she couldn't take her eyes away from what was in front of her. The hollow emptiness. Then, with gradual certainty, her body went rigid; something was out there. Right outside.

Just beyond reach, where the galvanised steps disappeared into an unlit darkness, a greater and more solid patch of night faced her, standing as tall as she was. Cara knew it wasn't human. It stooped towards her, filled with menace, and she knew that whatever it was, it was something that had sensed her; it had arrived because it had been summoned.

Cara held her nerve, facing the darkness, hoping that some form of insight might be found, coming down through the bloodline from grandmother, to mother, to her. Women who lived and walked with the spirits, and had no fear of them. But any sort of meaning felt illusive. Carefully, she reached down and grabbed hold of a plastic broom handle. The darkness faced her, unmoving, as she lifted the broom and pushed it, cautiously, towards whatever it was. Nothing. Then, incrementally, she pushed the broom further, and with horror she watched the bristles beginning to flatten as they met a solid resistance.

It was cold and bright when she woke up, alone in her bedroom. She checked her mobile and instantly realised she'd slept in late and had missed her shift. That manager, who'd grabbed her arm meanly at the wedding function, would be gearing up for a row. Damn this place, Cara thought, thinking every part of the decision to come here had been a mistake. Wrong to have dropped out of college; wrong to end up in a spiral of worry and unease. She felt nauseous from being in the fungal air of the caravan. There were spots of mould across the ceiling and threads of bright green moss along the windowsills. This place would make her ill.

Her mobile pinged and a message from her mother popped up: CALL ME. RIGHT THIS MINUTE. CALL ME.

Cara chucked the phone on the floor and lay back on her pillow, weary. She thought, abstractly, of the trees along this part of the coast, all bending away from the salt breath of the sea. They looked as if they were in some kind of agony. She picked up the mobile and called her mum.

'Cara, sweetheart,' her mother said, slightly breathlessly. 'Where are you?'

'Norfolk.'

'What are you doing there? I've been worried sick.'

Her mother's voice – the sheer familiarity of it – calmed her, and hearing its presence in this cold damp room managed to push some of the oddness away. She needed her mother, now. But she also knew the signs, too well, that her mother was locked into her own series of anxious thoughts. These kinds of conversations could quickly become tricky.

'Mum – I'm just earning some cash at a hotel. Kitchen porter.'

'For how long?'

'Couple of weeks, perhaps more.'

'But I can send you money, love. I'll send it to you.'

'I don't need it. Soon as I've got enough, I'm coming back.'

Her mother fell silent, which was often her way. Cara imagined where her mum was sitting, probably in the armchair in the conservatory, near her plants, where she liked to make calls. There was an easel set up there, because the light was good for her mother's watercolours. Painting was part of her therapy. Cara thought she could hear the sound of the fan heater, in the background, and one of the wind chimes that hung in the tree.

'What is it?' Cara asked. She imagined the view over the garden at home. The vivid green of the lawn. The bushes stirring in a breeze.

'So – I had bad dreams all night,' her mother replied, serious and urgent. 'There's a dark shadow settling over the family. I can't quite grasp it but I know what it means – I know it's close.'

Cara's spine began to tingle. 'There's nothing to worry about, Mum.'

'No – no – you're not listening to what I'm saying. I had these dreams.'

'And that's all they are, Mum. Just bad dreams.'

She heard her mother sigh with impatience. 'Cara – you mustn't go near it. You hear me? Whatever it is, you mustn't approach it.'

Cara took a moment, trying not to react. She pictured the darkness outside the door in the middle of the night, the bristles of the broom silently flattening as they touched something solid and mysterious. And the apparition on the marsh. The plea of a woman, calling for help. There was a connection between these things, growing in importance, but still eluding her.

Cara heard the front door of the caravan banging open. A couple of seconds later Toni appeared, framed in her bedroom doorway. Arms crossed, glaring.

'Mum – I've got to go,' Cara said.

'Don't.'

'I've got a shift starting.'

'But you heard me, didn't you, Cara?'

'Yeah. I heard you. Don't worry. I'll call you soon.'

'You do that. Call me very soon.'

Cara hung up.

Toni continued to glare at Cara, unflinching. Toni's eyes were slightly misaligned, Cara thought.

'What d'you want?' Cara asked.

'Bit of a bitch, aren't you.'

'You what?'

Toni pursed her lips. Her cheeks were flushed, but the rest of her skin was bluish pale. She looked anaemic. 'You're moving out.'

'Why?'

'One of the other caravans. They're all the same.'

'What's this about, Toni?'

Toni shook her head, in disbelief. She looked furious and just about holding it in. 'Blake's told me everything. Said you came on pretty strong. You total cow.'

Cara felt a burst of laughter, rising unstoppably, the situation was so unjust and ludicrous.

'You got nothing to say? Toni added, bitter.

Cara stared back, wondering what to say, then decided none of this was worth the bother. She got off her bed, blanking Toni as she started to shove clothes into her holdall. The room was small and claustrophobic, the walls paper thin, as if everything might collapse and fold in on herself. Toni stood her ground, full of spite, contemptuous and nasty. It didn't take long for Cara to gather her stuff, because she'd not really unpacked in the first place.

She went to the next caravan, which seemed empty. It had no curtains against the windows and one of the panes was blocked in with a sheet of hardboard. She chucked her bag into the bedroom, slammed the door shut, then went outside and stood in the wet grass. She took a deep breath, filling her lungs with the cold salt air, as she tried to let her anger subside. Stung by the lack of friendship, the sheer unpleasantness around her, she considered her options. Perhaps beg a lift, somehow, to Stansted airport. Ask that tyrant hotel manager to pay for the shifts already done, and call it quits. Or get her mum to buy her a plane ticket, although that came with its own pocketful of trouble. Her mum had the knack of counting all the times when she was proved right.

A rising breeze brought a stench of damp vegetation from the marsh. November, she thought. The month of the dead. The sun was already going down. It must be mid-afternoon. In the distance, she could hear the waves booming onto the shingle bank. Again, she was struck by the austere, simple geometry of land and sky. Low dark clouds were scuttling in over the sea, and she wondered whether a storm was coming. She grabbed her coat and hurried towards the marsh.

The path she found was little more than a cattle track, and it soon petered out. The ground felt leathery and strangely hollow, as if the mud was stretched tight as a drum. Initially she found herself walking over short-cropped pasture, with tufts of wiry grass where the land was dryer. But soon the marsh changed, as the plants became sparser, and the mud became more dominant. In patches, it was oily black and slippery. Remnants of samphire grew in low crabby twists, dark and glassy with the November cold. Vivid threads of seaweed clung to the tips of the plants, like some sort of algal cobweb. Where the mud became thicker, sucking her boots into deep hollows, she tried walking with her heels dug in first, as this gave the best chance of staying upright. It was bitterly cold. Occasionally, she caught glimpses of the pool, distantly, through the maze of creeks, but she tried not to think about what she might or might not find there. Instead, she kept her head bowed, concentrating on each foothold, each tuft of grass, each brackish pool that shivered on the mud.

Half-concealed by the dense foliage of the holly trees, Blake had watched Toni marching into the caravan to confront Cara. He'd heard a lot of slamming doors coming from inside, and thought he'd keep his distance while it all kicked off. Toni was a daily nightmare, and the new Irish girl was feisty; there was a chance both of them could turn against him. But there wasn't much point in hiding among the trees, either, so he slipped off to the hotel and helped himself to a coffee, before ambling back towards the row of caravans, wondering how he'd play it. Perhaps don't plan it too much, he thought. The answers usually declared themselves, if he played it cool. He reminded himself that Toni was like a spitting firework, and it might take most of the day to calm her down. He didn't want to talk that particular one off the ledge, so he decided at the last moment to let himself into the next caravan, where he saw Cara's bag dumped in the main bedroom. It was cold in there. He lit the paraffin heater, and for a while crouched on his haunches gazing at the grills of the ceramic plates, until they began to glow orange hot. But his back stayed cold, so he decided to sit on the sofa by the end window, pulling a loose cover across his legs to keep himself warm. He'd explain himself to Cara when she turned up, he guessed, one way or the other.

Cara was nearing the pool now, and had been following a wide creek filled with deep, stiffly flowing water. The passage across the saltmarsh had been frustrating. She'd been forced into a meandering zigzag, avoiding creeks and pools that snaked through the mud. Several times she'd thought she was getting near, only to be thwarted. The creek next to her seemed to take a wholly irrational course, like a partly coiled rope that had been thrown there, and each time she nearly arrived at the pool she realised the creek had twisted in front of her to bar the way. There was no question of crossing it. The water looked deep, untrustworthy, and very cold, and the banks pitched down steeply into it.

Some of the smaller creeks, however, could be jumped, and after crossing a series of these she suddenly found herself standing right by the edge of the pool. She'd reached it unexpectedly, and for a minute she couldn't be sure that it was the same one she'd looked at from the caravan. But slowly its orientation and shape made sense. It *was* her pool. The one known as Serpentine. She stood on a narrow strand of gravel and broken white shells, and the water in front of her seemed clearer and deeper than in the creeks she'd been following. The sea was louder here, possibly because the sound of the waves hitting the shingle bank reverberated off the pool itself. The surface of the water was pewter dark, stiffening into silvery wind shadows as the gusts dipped onto it. There was nothing to see. This was exactly where the woman had stood, but there were no footprints, no scuff marks, no sign that anyone had been here. She turned to look back at the hotel, nestled among the trees, and the row of caravans beneath the line of hollies. She was shocked by how dark it had become, and could see where the lights had been put on inside the rooms. The wind was biting, so she turned away from it. Already, purplish, brooding clouds above the horizon made the sky indistinguishable from the gloomy mass of the land, and for a brief moment she imagined the marsh was sloping up in a vast curve into the sky. Among the dull depths of the clouds she seemed to make out patterns of grass and mud and a labyrinth of creeks, deeply veined and misleading.

Cara's grandmother was pushing her walking frame along the corridor, heading to the day room, when the sensation of dread stopped her. She took a deep breath, let go of the handles, and took a step towards the window. It was getting dark outside, but there was still enough light to see the care home lawn, the rough broken shoreline beyond the fence, and the expanse of dull grey water of Lough Mahon. She muttered a prayer, a partial protection, as she felt the onrush of something terrible. Across the water, she tried to focus on the patterns of wind as they swept in polishing flurries, revealing glimpses of shapes and omens that could be deciphered. But her eyes struggled to see in the dusk, and the insight that she knew was out there, unveiled in fleeting outlines as they dipped and fell across the water, were tantalisingly beyond interpretation. But she knew, instinctively, that something awful was happening. Her body started to tremble, a sign that meant the spirits were gathering around her.

Cara walked with her head bowed. Her eyes were streaming in the bitter cold wind and she'd turned her head to one side because one ear was aching. Staring down, the plants had grown so dark it was difficult to distinguish them from the mud, causing her to slip, and once to step ankle deep in an unseen puddle. When she looked inland – wiping the blur from her eyes – she was surprised to see how dark the coast had become in a matter of minutes. She could no longer make out individual houses, and could only see fragments of lights glowing in the windows. She zipped up her coat and walked quicker, avoiding the creeks, leaping puddles. In front of her a large pool of water appeared; one she'd not seen before. She looked back towards the hotel to orientate herself, but was confused. She hadn't come this way. Walking slowly around its edge, slightly unnerved to have strayed this far, she suddenly realised she was standing on the same little shore of gravel and crushed white shells again. A few paces away were her own footprints.

She backed away, apprehensive, before stopping and forcing herself to be rational. This time she'd concentrate, count the creeks she needed to jump and the ones she needed to follow. But after a few minutes she came to a point where her route was obstructed by two deep cracks filled with water. She didn't know which one to cross. Both directions seemed familiar and yet also indistinguishable. She went for the easiest, deciding she could always return to this point. But when she did turn back, to follow the other direction, it proved to be equally unyielding. It seemed to lead her further from the hotel. Again, she had the sensation that the marsh was sweeping up into the sky, on all sides, catching her in a vast grey hollow. The thought made her dizzy, and she tried to focus on the smaller, more immediate sounds around her and the wind buffeting the grass, until she came to a dark, ominously wide creek that was rapidly flooding with seawater. She stared down at the web of cracks in the mud, numb with indecision.

Cara's mother was applying a wash to the sky in one of her watercolours when the feeling struck her. A kind of foreboding, as if a lurking presence was nearby, watching her. She looked through the conservatory windows. The garden was still and the light was fading. Shadows were growing thickly between the bushes. Looking back at her painting she watched the bleed of pigment spreading down the paper, like a cloudscape growing of its own accord, a magical animation within the stillness of the picture. She wondered what it meant – these patterns of grey and blue spreading like a tide, threading its way across a parched landscape. She was breathless, poised, waiting to understand it.

Then suddenly she knew: there was an urgent need to speak to her daughter. She grabbed her phone and dialled the number.

In the caravan, Blake listened to Cara's mobile ringing from the other room. He got off the couch and opened the bedroom door, he saw the phone where it had been left next to her holdall. The screen was brightly lit, with MUM identified as the caller.

He let it ring out. As he returned to the sofa he was struck by how dark it now was. But he didn't want to switch the lights on, in case Toni saw him, waiting in there for another girl. Instead, he searched among the kitchen cupboards and found himself a half-drunk bottle of sherry. He poured away the dregs of his coffee and filled the mug from the bottle, gulping down most of that before filling it up again and sitting back on the sofa with the cover pulled up, as before. He was beginning to feel stupid for messing around with Cara, who seemed worthy of a more sophisticated approach than he'd given last night. Perhaps he'd get a second chance, after all, when she returned? He listened to the wind stirring the trees, outside.

Jumping over three small creeks in succession, Cara thought she was on a route she remembered. Yes, a deeper creek here, then an area with shallow, kidney shaped pools. But the marsh was getting dark, losing its definition, and although she could see the lights of the hotel in the distance, the cracks and hollows were getting harder to spot. She came to a wide creek, unexpectedly, where the water had risen almost to the top of the marsh itself. She noticed strands of vegetation floating on the surface, and in both directions it seemed there was no way to cross it. Reluctantly, hoping it would speed her route out of this place, she decided the best option would be to wade through it. The water would be freezing, but it would save her all the haphazard changes of direction she was doing. She took off her boots and held them over her head, then stepped gingerly onto the thick mud of the creek and into the water. The chill of the water was agonising, gripping her feet like a vice. But before she could step back she slipped, as the mud gave way beneath her, pitching her down and shooting her forward into the water. She gulped as her head went under, then thrashed forward, reaching the other bank in a couple of strokes. It was only as she clambered out on the mud, coughing with shock, that she realised she'd dropped her boots, but at that moment it didn't seem to matter – all she wanted was to keep going, towards the lights of the hotel. Shivering, and fighting against the numbness of her legs and feet, she stumbled forward into a run to keep warm. But she didn't see the deep crack in the mud before it was too late. She fell in awkwardly, up to her thigh, one knee knocking back as if it had been hit with a plank of wood, and she cried out in pain. She knew it was a bad injury. Gingerly, carefully, she pulled her leg free, and was relieved to find she could still put weight on it. But the pain rose up towards her as she hobbled onwards. She tried to ignore the sight of the pool opening out in front of her once more, but her mouth went dry with fear. Again, she arrived at the beach of gravel and crushed shells, and stood in her own footprints. She nodded to herself, grimly, trying to usher in a kind of rationality, and for a brief moment she thought the marsh grew calm around her. A single breath of mist, rising magically. She stared, transfixed. But then with growing horror she noticed the thickening shadow that emerged, standing like a cracked wooden mast, leaning towards her. It faced her, unearthly, a few steps away. With a rush of blind panic she began to scream for help. She turned away from the darkness and waved both arms, furiously, in the direction of the caravan in the hope that someone might see her. She immediately knew it was hopeless, but she kept waving, as the cold gripped her body. Shaking uncontrollably, her voice faded. Then the darkness appeared once more, standing watchfully, just beyond reach. It seemed to be brimming with a strange energy, a counterpoint to her own life, a void that was urging her to step towards it. And she realised it's been her, her on the marsh all along, waving in the hope that someone will save her.

Blake brought his feet up and hugged his knees, struck by a sudden chill. The caravan was soundless but the trees were dragging spiked leaves across the roof. Outside, the marsh and sky were as dull as flint, gloomy and forbidding. He looked towards the reeds, and saw they were being hit by regular gusts, jostling like a sea. In the distance he heard the waves against the shingle, and then thought he saw something out there, out on the marsh, near one of the pools. A flicker of unexpected movement that he'd never noticed before, and didn't belong there. He cupped his hands to the window, waiting for his eyes to adjust, before deciding it was nothing. Nothing at all.

Lee Cooper

Standing among the removal boxes and plastic crates, Warren realised his bedroom had quickly become an echoing, dusty place smelling of him and the sixty years he'd spent in there. A few hours packing, and he left almost no trace at all. He shifted his weight from one leg to the other, and the floorboard creaked where it had always creaked. He pressed his foot down again, wondering now it was too late whether he could have, after all, fixed it. An hour before dawn. In front of him a poor grey light was already seeping through the curtains. He would have to do it today. There was no more time left.

He pulled one of the curtains aside and took a sly look across the dark earthy fields. Long furrows of wet, clumpy soil rose gently towards a small copse of trees. Crows were already beginning to stir in the branches. The view had changed little over the decades. There were no other buildings in sight, nothing to look at but this great mound of earth like a dirty brown wave slowly bearing down on him. Three fields, his life spent tending them, every last stone and clump of soil turned and re-turned in the seasonal battle and, in the middle of the largest field, the solitary shape of a man, standing perfectly still, facing his window.

It always surprised Warren that the scarecrow looked so lifelike. After so long looking through the bedroom window he was still momentarily caught off guard. Today was no different from all the other occasions; he'd looked across the field and seen a man looking back at him, arms outstretched as if carrying a gun across his shoulders.

After a meagre breakfast of bread and tinned sardines he began the slow walk out to the centre of the field. The soil was soft and dewy, and his boots grew heavy as the clay stuck on the soles. Ahead, the scarecrow stood rigid, facing directly at him, hardly moving as the air stirred across the field. It was dressed in a faded yellow anorak, a wide-brimmed rain hat and a pair of dark muddy jeans. Warren had made it to keep the birds away, but also – he now understood – to have a sense of companionship. It wasn't easy being a tenant farmer, all by yourself. And this field was a large space, with an emptiness that had always felt challenging. He'd built the scarecrow many years ago and repaired it several times since, adding a jacket now and then, a new pair of trousers when the others had rotted. Little by little the scarecrow had been entirely dressed in Warren's old clothes. When the wooden cross-piece of the shoulders had worked loose, it had been repaired. When the jacket had ripped in winter, a new one had been found. Warren had grown old, but his scarecrow had been kept continually young.

Each time, dressing and undressing the figure, Warren had felt a curious sense of intimacy that was difficult to overcome. Perhaps this was the reason that, recently, he'd begun to talk to the scarecrow. He'd named it Lee Cooper, after the pair of jeans he'd dressed him in. At first, Warren had been self-conscious. Talking to the scarecrow only seemed to underline his own sense of loneliness. But he made himself do it, starting with the day-to-day of farm business: what he'd planted, how the crops were doing, new fertilisers and their yields, government grants and the ever-present threat of disease. He often talked about the weather, gazing towards the sea, watching the clouds gather, as if he was side by side with an old friend. He talked about the environment, the climate that never used to sound like a crisis, and the death of soil itself, although these were topics he didn't feel he knew enough about. Over the months he'd begun to rely on these talks, and at Christmas he'd even taken a mince pie out to the scarecrow and left it on the soil. He'd stared at the mince pie, there on the earth, and said: 'Well, happy Christmas, fella,' before turning his back.

Lee Cooper had become a silent confessor to the old man's worries and to some of his hopes but, recently, the scarecrow had only heard complaints. Complaints about Warren's growing health problems and, latterly, about the financial trouble of the tenancy agreement he'd been fighting. But now it was all over. The boxes were packed and the last thing he had to do was tell his scarecrow.

A few paces away, Warren stopped. Lee Cooper faced him across the silent field. There was an asymmetry to the figure's shoulders, giving it a slouching, arrogant stance and, as Warren waited, he watched the ragged cloth of the scarecrow's chest filling out with air and then gently deflating. Lee Cooper had lost a lot of weight this year, was long overdue a repair, but with all the business about getting evicted from the farm the old man had decided to let it fall apart naturally. Clearly, the scarecrow was suffering. After one of the spring gales the head had slumped forward, taking on a sad and pensive posture, totally unlike how Lee Cooper used to be. Back in the day, Warren had taken pride in his land and pride in the scarecrow, hanging flowers round its neck in spring and giving it gloves and a scarf for the winter. It had been amusing, listening to the weather forecast on the radio, then deciding the scarecrow might need an extra coat for the night. Once, after half a bottle of Lamb's Navy, Warren had even drawn a face on the figure with a black marker pen. But that had been a mistake. He'd been unsettled for weeks, seeing a man's face grinning malevolently at his house. Now, the outline was almost completely faded and looked little more than the stuffed pillowcase it actually was. Only at brief times of the day – namely sunrise and sunset – when the light was weak, the old man thought he could see that face again.

'Well, I ent going to mess about because I've been up all night worrying,' Warren said. 'Truth is, I'm sorry. It's all over. I'm old and tired and I can't do this no more.'

Warren dug his stick into the soil and stared long and hard at Lee Cooper. He looked at the tiny rips in the yellow jacket, how the air continued to stir the fabric, giving the chest a sigh of life. At the hat brim pulled low and the face partially hidden beneath it.

'I come out here to tell you the truth cause you got a right to know. It's hard for us both but that's the way of things and that's the way of land. The tenancy's up, see,' he continued. 'The tenancy's up and I'm packed and off. Simple as that. If you want me to say it, yes I ent got no more fight in me. It's time to move on. Sixty years, my whole life's in this field and them ones over there. You might understand but they don't and that's that.'

His voice sounded frail against the awful size of the field and suddenly there seemed little point in saying anything more. Warren turned to look at the small house that had been his home for so long, and the solitary trail of his footprints in a line across the soil. The house looked neglected and damp. A chimney without smoke, a kitchen without the smell of cooking. Outbuildings gone to ruin. It was all in decay, he thought. Yet the soil was good. It was good earth here, fertile, some of the best in the area.

He looked along the line of his driveway, following the hedge to where it met the road, and the three ex-council houses that were built there. The last one, with all the broken down furniture chucked out in the back garden and the big satellite dishes screwed to the wall. That's something he wouldn't miss. That's for sure. The woman was called Caitlin and she'd had a bunch of kids with a bunch of men, but for some reason had always directed her anger towards him. He'd never judged her, he was sure of it, at least not to her face, but she'd had a ten year war with him, regardless, just because she needed to fight with *someone*.

He started to retrace his steps, thinking about the day ahead and the list of jobs he still had to complete. But after only a few paces he stopped, uneasy, as he thought again about Lee Cooper standing behind him. Perhaps he hadn't quite said enough. The hairs on his neck begin to stand on end. He believed that if he turned quickly enough he'd see the scarecrow looking straight at him, head upright, with that face newly drawn once more.

Back at the house he continued packing and labelling the removal boxes, shifting them gradually towards the front door.

He'd been doing this for days. He tried not to think about how the farm had once been, twenty or thirty years ago, and all its vanished vitality. That day when the harvest was so large they'd had to stack the barley in sacks in the living room. Or the time he'd lifted the ram over the gate, even though it was twisting like a mad thing in his arms. The strength he'd once mustered, day after long day, always taken for granted. Driving fence posts into the earth from sunrise to sunset, or that time he'd pulled the trailer from the ditch because the weather was closing in and he had no choice. The cider press, standing in the yard, with neighbours standing around grimacing with the sour cloudy taste, but getting pissed, nonetheless. And now his hip grinding in its socket, playing up in wet weather, his back bent and aching, and his hands covered in liver spots. Unresponsive fingers, like his bones had turned to wood.

The phone rang in the hall and it took seven rings till he got there, limping on his sore hip.

'Good morning Mr Colby,' the voice said, bright and annoyingly upbeat, like a cheap door chime. 'It's Mandy from Bramwells. I'm going to be your moving facilitator.'

'Right.' Warren knew exactly who she was. She always seemed to pretend they'd never spoken before. Or maybe it was just a technique of hers; her way of ignoring the arguments they'd been having.

'And how are you feeling today, Mr Colby?'

He rubbed his chin, contemplating the question. He should've shaved, he thought. The stubble was sharp and dry. He tried to look at his reflection, but the mirror had been packed away. Then he realised he hadn't answered. 'All right, I s'pose.'

'That's great. Now you haven't forgotten the van will be with you at 1:30pm tomorrow?'

'I got it written down.'

'Fantastic. We'll be transferring the facilities and council tax starting from tomorrow and we've arranged for a thorough clean to take place. So that's good, isn't it?' He didn't reply. She continued: 'So that's 1:30pm tomorrow!' She sounded like he'd won a prize, which he hadn't.

'It's writ down.'

'That's really great news, Mr Colby. Is there anything else I can help with, today? I know how difficult some of these moves can be.'

He wondered. She was – what – twenty, twenty-two? Would she really know much about what he was thinking, about moving after all these years? Maybe she did. Twenty's old enough to have a few kicks and set backs, here and there. But he also remembered how she reacted when she first came to the farm, taking off a pair of neat office shoes and putting on the cleanest pair of wellies he'd ever seen, just to go in the house. She'd priced up the outbuildings, looked sadly at the cracked gable end, then told him off for taking up the flagstones and replacing them with lino. She'd looked really upset about that.

'You still there, Mr Colby?'

'For the time being.'

'Right, well you have a great day, and I'll see you tomorrow,' she replied, hanging up before he could say goodbye.

At noon he ate tinned fish and cheese, then fired a shotgun towards the woods to try and make the crows take flight. But the shot fell way short of them, they stayed oblivious among the canopy, hopping between the branches, involved in their own noisy battles. He looked out at the vast span of the field with the lonesome figure of the scarecrow in the centre. The new owners would almost certainly cut it down. A scarecrow was never passed from person to person. A shame, he thought, because it had been a strong scarecrow, and for the first time Warren wondered about the birds and tried to recollect ever seeing *any* in that particular field. When he'd hung strips of tin foil over the kitchen garden the starlings had razed his seedlings in an hour, hardly noticing his efforts to keep them away. But this field was different. He'd never seen a bird land in it.

With most of the jobs finally ticked off at the house, Warren walked down to the pub that evening for the last time. As soon as he went in he noticed a couple of Caitlin's kids perched on the stools at the end of the bar. They saw him enter, and the oldest one looked at him, dead-eyed, with sallow cheeks and a mean expression. He always looked like he'd been awake for days. Warren ignored them, ordered a pint of stout and took it to a low table in the corner. He sipped his drink, keeping his eyes away from the kids. The oldest one had grown tall and strong. He could be a good farmer, except he was lazy; leaning there, with a hard bony skull like an anvil, and razor cut hair. And the younger one, sharp and twisted as barbed wire, hunched over his mobile. The light in his bedroom was always on throughout the night because he played computer games. Their mother had, over the years, grudgingly come to accept Warren, but it was her kids that now felt like they had to carry the fight onwards. They frequently looked at him, trying to make him uncomfortable, but neither could be bothered to take him on tonight. Warren drank his pint, then stood under the awning in the car park to smoke the cigar he'd kept for this occasion. It tasted bitter. He hadn't wanted to be alone for his last night in the house, but after the cigar he sat in the pub by himself, nonetheless, and stared at the fire in the grate and at the empty glass on his table. No one talked to him, and after an hour he left.

Early next morning, again before dawn, Warren got dressed in his work clothes, pulled his boots on and began climbing downstairs, taking one step at a time because his hip hadn't yet warmed up. He tried not to think about the fact he'd be leaving the house today, but each action had a sense of finality about it. He felt distracted and bothered. But when he turned into the front room he reeled back with shock because there, leaning against the front window, was Lee Cooper. Its long bony arms were outstretched as if it was trying to peer into the darkened room. For the first time in years the scarecrow's head was upright and the face was flat to the pane, a tiny cloud of condensation spreading away from the damp material, like breath.

Warren lowered himself carefully into his armchair as the blood rushed in his ears. He stared at the grotesque figure leaning against the glass. It must have been Caitlin's lads, he thought. The same lads who watched him walk out to the field every day and who occasionally whistled at him as he stood talking to Lee Cooper. It wasn't the first time the kids had messed around with the scarecrow, but to do this and to do it on his last day seemed too cruel, even for them. He thought about being at the pub, with that young one hunched over his mobile, a malicious smile at the corner of his mouth. Had they been hatching a plan?

Warren went out into the yard and stood behind the scarecrow. Seeing Lee Cooper from this angle – leant against the glass looking in – made Warren shudder with fear. He saw his own reflection in the window as he approached, and it made him hesitate with an irrational thought that Lee Cooper's head might turn to greet his outstretched hand. Gradually, Warren leant forward and touched the old jacket collar, and with his other hand began to reach round Lee Cooper's waist. He cautiously lifted the scarecrow away from the window. The wet jacket flapped open against his face and the trousers twisted fleshless around the wooden post. The head lolled sleepily against Warren's neck. The scarecrow was ice cold and dirty, it stank of the field, and he was suddenly amazed by how light and fragile it was. Just a bag of bones. He began to think about the sunny day in June when he'd first made it, and how it'd been a considerable weight to carry out to the field. The wind must have eaten away at the body over the years.

Suspecting the kids might return to play more tricks, Warren decided to bring Lee Cooper into the house. He lifted it into the front room and propped it against the fireplace, straightening the jacket and trousers as he did so. Then he went upstairs to finish packing. Immediately, he became unsettled. He'd made a mistake. It was wrong to let the scarecrow in the house. They belonged outside, in the fields, with the wind and rain, the hot summer sun and the frozen winter dawns. A scarecrow was wild, he thought. They are mysterious and unearthly, belonging to a different set of rules and orders.

Gradually, he calmed himself and listened to the total silence of the house. He crept out onto the landing, holding his breath, and peered down the stairs at the living room door. No sounds, but there was a sense of presence – or even anticipation – that was unpleasant and alarming. He was probably in shock, he thought. He went to his bedroom window and looked out over the field. The light was stronger now, and in the soft earth he could clearly make out a single line coming from the centre of the field to where he was, as if the pole of the scarecrow had made a ploughed furrow through the soil.

With a sudden determination that surprised him, he rushed downstairs and pushed open the living room door. Inside, the scarecrow leant where he'd left it, stark and huge against the fireplace. The arms seemed wider and more expressive than he remembered, and the head was hanging to one side in a sly, deceiving manner. The whole room smelt of wet earth and old clothes and, as Warren took a step towards it, he heard a faint crack of wood from deep inside the scarecrow's chest. He stopped – frozen to the spot – then gently pressed his foot on the bare floorboards to see if he'd somehow caused the sound. It was silent. His mouth was dry with fear, and he felt a worrying tightness spreading across his chest.

Lee Cooper faced him, huge and menacing, as Warren battled with indecision.

'I don't want you,' he said, even though his voice sounded full of fear in the empty room. 'You ent my friend!'

Feeling a surge of resentment – some well of anger that had been building up, Warren marched across the room, grabbed the scarecrow, and dragged it outside. Gathering newspaper and kindling from the wood store, he built a rough pile in the yard and hurled the scarecrow on top of it. When he lit the fire, he remained by its side until he saw the smoke beginning to rise and curl through the jacket. The head of the scarecrow darkened as the smoke built up behind the fabric, and for an instant Warren thought he saw the face he'd drawn on it so many years before, grimly smiling back. This was betrayal and now it was murder, he thought. He'd set fire to all the work he'd done and all the belief he'd once felt for this part of the land. He was cursing himself. Panicked, he pulled the still damp scarecrow out from the fire, dragging the flaming kindling and paper across the yard in a whorl of sparks and embers, and then stamped on the figure, stamping and stamping until all the flames were out.

An hour later he was filling in the shallow trench in the field where he'd buried Lee Cooper's charred body. The field was now a grave, he thought. After all these years, the scarecrow deserved this place. And as he walked back from the grave, weary with the effort, he saw his own footprints from the day before and the thin furrow where the pole of the scarecrow had been pulled through the soil. That's odd, he thought. There were no other footprints.

Soon after lunch the removal van turned up and the men started loading his stuff. Warren stood in the yard, watching them carry the boxes, then climbed into the cab and refused to look back in the side mirror as the truck bumped its way down the drive. He knew he would never come back here. Waiting by the side of the main road, Mandy from Bramwells was leaning against her car, eating a packed lunch from a Tupperware box. She was wearing her smart office shoes, and nodded at the removal guy at the wheel, but didn't notice Warren sitting next to him. That's fine, Warren thought. Better that way. Twenty minutes later the van had stopped again and the men were unloading the boxes and carrying them into the bungalow. Sixty years of life, and all it amounted to had hardly filled the long-based transit they were in. Warren was told to wait in the warmth of the cab until the heating was put on in the little house. He'd never had central heating anyway, but he didn't argue with the men.

He waited in the van, looking at the neat square of lawn, the low shrubs along the front path, and the estate agents' sign hammered into the corner of the flowerbed. The sign had a large yellow emoji of a smiling face on it, with the slogan *Welcome to your new home!* written beneath.

When the van had been emptied, Warren offered the men some tea without knowing whether he had a kettle inside, but they shared a quick look between them and told him they had things to do. He was glad. They handed him the key and he walked up the path and let himself in, going from room to room pulling the curtains shut.

He left the curtains drawn all day, knowing that beyond them there was only the thinnest of hedgerows before the endless sight of a flat brown field which he didn't want to look at. He sat in an armchair that must have been left behind by the previous owners, and looked at his boxes. Above him, he listened as crows scampered across the tiles.

In the morning he stood in the porch and looked out. A crow was hopping up and down on the lawn, and another one had settled on top of the estate agents' sign. The neon bright emoji face smiled at him, slightly rocking as the crow shifted its weight, and Warren shuddered with how much it resembled a demonic scarecrow, limbless and insanely grinning. He banged on the window and the crow flapped off lazily, making the sign tremble with life. He turned his back on it, thinking about the disastrous sequence of events from the day before. The business with Lee Cooper had been stupid and unnecessary, he thought. He'd been anxious about leaving the farm. That's all. That's why he'd got into such a state.

He was determined today would be different. He was in a new bungalow – with heating – and the farm and his painful battle with the landlord could all be put behind him now. He could pull the agents' signpost down. He could snap the post in half and lie the two pieces of wood along the edge of the drive. 'Cut the grass,' he said out loud, cultivate the land like he'd done all his life. That's the only way to live, he thought.

But he stayed where he was, in the porch, turning back to look at the sign. Another crow landed on the lawn. He checked that the door was locked, then returned to the kitchen. Sitting at a brand new glossy pine table, he began to stare at the wood. He'd made a series of mistakes, he considered. It was a mistake to have brought the scarecrow into the house, a mistake to lose his temper and try to kill it. Wrong, even, to pull it from the flames and bury it in the field. He was wrong to have ever left the land. He thought of Lee Cooper pressed into a grave of wet, dark soil. He thought of the worms that would slide into the yellow jacket while, above, the builders would renovate the house, converting the outbuildings and pulling down the asbestos shed roof, repair that cracked gable end and paint the window frames with posh colours. The new owners were going to re-wild the land, he'd heard, but he didn't quite know what that meant, other than a lot of weeds in that good soil. And he wondered whether anything would grow over Lee Cooper's grave, or whether it would be a permanent, inexplicable scar.

Let it all go, he thought. He was probably hanging on to a sense of the farm's glory days that were never, in fact, there in the first place. He'd struggled his whole life, companionless, more weary with each year, and all it amounted to was this: a bungalow of five rooms, with nothing left to do. He found a mug and a box of tea bags, but couldn't find the kettle and knew he had no milk, so he gave up on that and had some crackers with meat paste, instead. Sitting at the table, he grew unsettled by the noise of the crackers as he chewed them, and had the sense that he wasn't entirely alone. The house's silence felt joined together and complete, unlike the creaking, draughty house he'd always known. He watched his fingers beginning to tap nervously on the tabletop, and knew that the day was beginning to spiral downwards if he didn't do anything about it. So he forced himself to get up, resolved to go outside and start things off with pulling that signpost down. But in the hallway he stopped. There, by the font door, he saw his jacket hanging from the clothes pegs, and the old hat that the removals men had hung there, too. His jacket looked thin and neglected, hollowed out, and the hat hung above it, lopsided and downcast, with a brim that seemed to conceal something he couldn't quite make out. His own jacket and hat, now lifeless and emptied. And he realised, with horror, that there'd be no escape this time. He'd let it in.

The River Man

Mr Jelf raised his mug of instant coffee, blew a breath onto the surface, looked across the living room and winced. It was either a wince or a wink, John couldn't quite decide; these old men combined their expressions to save energy. From the kitchen, John could hear his wife, Liv, opening and shutting cupboard doors.

'Excuse me a minute, Mr Jelf,' he said.

He went into the kitchen and saw her leaning against the counter, her arms tightly crossed. Not a stance he was particularly fond of – it usually meant trouble. By her side was an empty plate and a pack of chocolate digestives.

John whispered: 'What do you reckon?'

She looked disbelieving. 'Difficult to tell. I mean, it's crazy, right?'

'Yep.'

'And – well – what's your take on it?'

'I think he's confused and – well – maybe there's some other issue going on there. Something we don't know about.'

'He's never said this kind of thing before?'

'Not to me.' John looked carefully at his wife, noticing he'd instinctively adopted her stance, crossing his arms and leaning against the new counter. 'What about you?'

'No. Never. I mean, he and I don't really chat much, anyway.'

He began to arrange the digestives on the plate. 'Alright, so we just go along with it?' She nodded, but looked unconvinced. 'We should probably go back in. I mean, I can deal with him – if you don't want to?'

'I'm fine,' Liv replied. 'You're the one I'm worried about.'

'Yeah? Why?'

'Overactive imagination.' She gave a half-smile, like she'd been putting up with him for years.

John returned to the living room and placed the biscuits in front of Mr Jelf. The old man looked up, grey-eyed, as if he'd just woken. He was holding his mug of coffee with both hands, and John could see traces of dirt from the veg patch etched into the skin. The guy smelt of soil and roots, even though John had asked him to wash his hands in the kitchen sink. Trying to spot confusion in the old man's eyes, John saw nothing out of the ordinary. He sat on the sofa, leaning back to make himself look relaxed.

'So, I'm curious,' he began. 'How long has this…' he trailed off. 'What do we call it, Mr Jelf?'

'An apparition, I s'pose.'

'Right.' John shifted the cushions behind him. 'Let's call it that.' He waited, encouraging the old man to continue.

'Seen it maybe five – maybe ten years,' Mr Jelf added.

He noticed Liv had come from the kitchen, and was resting quietly against the door frame, not quite committing herself to be part of the conversation.

'OK. And can you describe this thing?'

'A young man. In his twenties, I'd say. Walks around barefoot.'

'And you've seen him for five or ten years?'

'On and off.'

'At night?'

'He live in the small room, upstairs.'

From the corner of his eye John saw his wife react: suddenly alarmed, with a frown of worry as if she hadn't quite heard correctly.

'You mean the small room next to the bathroom?' he asked.

'That's the one.'

Liv stepped forward. 'Mr Jelf,' she said, kindly, 'what do you mean this apparition lives in the small room?'

'It's where he usually is, when I see him.'

A flush of anxiety was already colouring her cheek. She shook her head, slowly: 'I'm not quite understanding what you're saying, Mr Jelf. When you say there's an apparition in the room, what's he...'

'...Sits in the corner, mostly. Near the window. Sometimes paces back and forth. You know, barefoot.'

She looked at John. 'He's talking about Nancy's room.'

'I know,' John replied, calmly, trying to offer up a rational voice. He quietly studied Mr Jelf, taking his measure of the old man. He must have been large in his prime, tall and big boned, but was now stiff in his walk, always slow as he toiled in the garden, always hesitant when he talked. Perhaps he'd never been any different. Jelf was a curious man and pretty much kept himself to himself, like any oddball. But the thing that bothered John most was Mr Jelf's mouth. Or, rather, the expression it formed. It had an upward curl at the corners, as if the old man was permanently half-smiling, enjoying some sort of private joke.

'It's a lot to take in,' John said. 'Can you describe this man a little more for us?'

Mr Jelf reached for a biscuit and took an investigatory bite, and John watched those oddly shaped lips as he chewed. Jelf swallowed loudly, then shifted his weight in the chair.

'When I lived here, I never used that small room upstairs. Kept a few boxes in there, but I never went in. Not often.'

'It's our daughter's room.'

Mr Jelf rubbed his brow with a dirty finger, and seemed to grow a little vague. 'I'm aware of that,' he said. His eyes half-closed, then he let his chin drop, as if he was about to take a nap.

Liv stepped forward. 'Thanks for all the work in the garden, Mr Jelf. I think it's looking great out there.'

'Apples need picking soon,' he replied. 'Used to make cider, here. Think there's still a press in one of the sheds…' he trailed off, abruptly, then jutted his chin forward, and cleared his throat. 'He's come in,' he said.

John felt an unpleasant sensation rising up his spine. 'Mr Jelf? What do you mean?'

'He's come in, just now.'

John looked around them at the empty living room, and then at his wife. 'In here?'

'Yep.'

Liv crouched down, resting her hand tenderly on Mr Jelf's wrist. 'What can you see?'

The old man raised a finger and pointed towards an empty armchair near the wood burner. 'He's sat right there.'

'The same man?' she asked.

He nodded. 'Came in just now. Walked past you and sat down.'

Liv took her time. 'And what's he doing, now?' she asked.

'He's looking at you.'

'Me?'

Jelf nodded. John saw the clear unease on his wife's expression that often led to something more upsetting. 'Mr Jelf, there's no one sitting in the chair. Look – it's empty. He walked over to the armchair, thinking he'd pat the cushions to prove it. But he stopped, close, looking at the empty space, feeling uncomfortable. 'The chair's empty,' he repeated.

'If you say so.' Mr Jelf continued to look at the armchair, grimly. John moved away from it, struck with the absurdity of staring at the bare cushions, but unable to stop himself being spooked by it.

'Shall we phone Michelle?' Liv said.

'Michelle?' Mr Jelf asked.

'From Heron Court? Michelle with the car?'

'If you want.'

'I'll go and do it, John,' she said. She returned to the kitchen to make the call from her mobile. She spoke in hushed tones to Michelle, who was always there to help out when Mr Jelf needed it.

Left in the living room with the old man, John quickly felt awkward. 'She'll be right over to collect you, I'm sure,' he said, hoping that was going to be the case. Mr Jelf didn't react. He kept looking at the empty armchair, with that curious half-smile playing at the corners of his mouth.

Mr Jelf had lived in their cottage for at least thirty years, as far as they knew. When they bought it from him, he'd given a tour of the garden, proud of all the planting, so it'd been a natural decision to let him stay on as a gardener. He helped with the veg patch and orchard, and would do so at least long enough to see the crops he'd planted come to harvest. It would allow a kindly transition from living in the cottage for so many years, to his new and possibly disorientating life at Heron Court care home on the outskirts of town, near the bypass. So far, the arrangement had worked well. It had been useful while John was getting to grips with the cottage and all its idiosyncrasies, its bizarre plumbing, antiquated wiring and even to explain some of the strange noises he'd heard in the night. All a matter of the building settling, he'd been told, the house made noises from late summer onwards, into autumn and then to winter, with the beams expanding in the damp air, the floorboards pulling against the nails, the doors subtly warping in their frames. It was built by the river, and had some of the river's seasonal flow, too. Mr Jelf described the house much like a person getting ready for winter, breathing in a different way, slowing down and huddling tight to itself. But today's talk had been alarming. It was the first time Mr Jelf had ever said anything about a presence in the house. He'd never mentioned an apparition of a barefooted man living in the small room upstairs.

Just before setting out to fetch Nancy from preschool, he and Liv discussed the situation while they sat on her newly flagged kitchen patio; her favourite place among the renovations of the house, so far. Liv was sympathetic towards Mr Jelf but also insistent that he shouldn't be allowed in the house. 'It's only going to confuse him more. And I won't have him upsetting Nancy,' she said. John agreed, knowing decisions concerning their daughter's welfare were always best coming from her.

'How old do you think he is?' he asked.

'Eighty, eighty-five?'

'We can probably assume there may be some dementia issues. He was confused about some other things last week – didn't he forget which way to come into the house? You remember?'

'And he didn't seem to know who Michelle was, this morning.'

'Right. I mean – he seemed fine when she turned up, but, yeah. Perhaps he's on some sort of medication and has forgotten to take it?'

Liv leant back on the bench, facing the winter sun with her eyes shut. It was good to see her taking stock, being still. She looked pretty, John thought. Relaxed. Relocating to the cottage had been his idea, and it was largely about giving them this kind of space.

'We could ask at the housing office, if they've got some sort of check on that,' he said.

'Check on what?'

'Whether he's been taking his medicines.'

'Yeah. Sure,' she said, sounding like the subject was closed.

'If he doesn't come into the house, that might help him,' he added. 'He lived here for thirty years – it can't be easy for him seeing us make all the changes around the place.'

He thought about the small river, passing by silently at the end of the garden. It encouraged a sense of tranquillity. Green light shining among the willow trees. A quietly moving reflection of the sky, never stopping. There was much to learn about it.

He looked at his watch. 'I'll go and get Nancy,' he said.

She smiled, more at ease than he'd seen her for weeks, but as he got up she reached out to stop him.

'John, let's swap rooms with Nancy.'

He paused, curious. Liv was usually utterly dismissive when it came to anything that could be deemed supernatural. 'Why?' he asked.

'Just because.'

'That's not an answer.'

'Well, it's a good room, bigger than you think. You could have a desk in there.'

'Liv – we've just agreed Mr Jelf's only saying these things because he's a confused old man.'

'I know.'

'And can I remind you that you're an out-and-out sceptic. In case you've forgotten, Nancy doesn't even have a tooth fairy.'

'I know. And Nancy told all the other kids that Santa wasn't a thing.'

'Which didn't help settling her into the new school.'

Liv smiled, but held his gaze, insistent: 'But let's swap, OK?'

'I don't particularly like that room,' he tried, knowing he was losing ground.

'Oh, I get it – actually it's you that doesn't want to go in there.'

'Maybe.'

'Scared of the barefooted man in the corner?'

'Stop.' He checked his watch again, showing her the time. 'Better go.' But he knew she wasn't going to change her mind.

He decided to break the news to Nancy on their way back from preschool. She could be tricky when it came to making changes, so he adopted the tone that usually worked with her. 'Mum and I have decided to swap rooms with you,' he announced, making it sound like he had no say in the matter himself, as if parents also had to answer to higher sets of rules. Changing bedrooms was merely a fact they'd all have to get on with.

'But – I like my room,' she answered.

'Of course, but your new room's gonna be bigger. And it's got a great view from the window. It's even got a fireplace.'

'So if it's so great, why don't *you* want it?'

He suspected she was just trying it on with the objection. The move was clearly an upgrade. She was always telling them how small her room was. So he answered with a similar tease, leaning across the front seat to touch the tip of her nose with a finger: 'You deserve it because you're so special. That's why you should have it.' He gave her a wink, letting her know there may be other reasons he was concealing but he certainly wasn't going to say what they were. She's outmanoeuvred, he thought, satisfied with himself. Nancy was an amateur when it came to negotiations, unlike her mother, who was a pro, and a far more impressive adversary. Nonetheless, Nancy could spin her decisions several times a minute, so he was glad that – back at the cottage – she immediately ran upstairs to see the new room that would be hers.

'OK. How'd you manage that?' Liv whispered.

'Simple bribery,' he answered.

They spent the evening moving furniture, emptying Nancy's room of its toys and clothes, then returning to their room to dismantle the double divan, which they then dragged onto the landing. As they hauled it into the new room, John paused at the doorway, disquieted by the empty floor space and the bare walls. The plaster, quickly painted when they'd first bought the house, was now distinctly off-colour again. The bedroom looked lonely and confined, as if he was walking into some form of trap. He wondered how they could've let Nancy spend the last few months in here, in such a depressing space. Pushing these thoughts away he assembled the bed, before dragging more furniture in. They tried putting the wardrobe in the corner. It was the same corner Mr Jelf had mentioned, where the barefooted man was meant to appear. John looked at the wardrobe and said he wasn't keen on it there. It was as if he'd created a doorway for something to emerge from.

In the end, they left the wardrobe on the landing. He made a rough space for his work desk. It was cramped and far from ideal. But it was at least a change made for good reasons. It might, John considered, even be a good thing. He'd hoped that the move to the cottage would restore certain elements in his relationship with Liv, but so far their marital distance, their quickness to fall into brittle, pointless arguments and the lack of attention they gave to each other had followed them – wholesale and unaffected – from their previous house. He'd spent many nights lying awake wondering whether their relationship would ever return to how it had once been, before Nancy, or whether it even had that possibility anymore.

It was all false hope, John realised, as he got ready for bed a few hours later. Liv had just told him that – now they were in a much smaller room – he'd have to make an effort not to leave his clothes on the floor, and that, actually, he shouldn't do it at all. He reacted as though he'd been told off, which was the case, but told off by someone who was better organised than himself, which was certainly not the case. He didn't point it out, because he still hoped a new night in a new room was what they needed. To camp out together, like the students they'd once been, building a relationship in makeshift spaces. But these particular hopes evaporated, too. Liv sat on the edge of the bed applying moisturiser to her face from a little tub, usually a sign that she intended to go straight to sleep, and tucked the bottoms of her pyjama trousers into a pair of night socks, because she said the new room was cold and damp. He watched her, silently, thinking anything he might say would probably only add to the night's problems, rather than solve them. She was lit by the glow of a lampshade she'd propped up on the floor, next to her side of the bed, and the play of shadows it cast on the opposite wall were unsettling. A flickering movement, being cast towards the specific corner Mr Jelf had talked about. He briefly imagined Mr Jelf standing in the doorway, locking eyes with a barefooted apparition which was glaring back at him, and decided to push the image from his mind.

Liv got into bed, adjusted her elasticated eye-mask till it was comfy, then quickly slid it up across her forehead and sat up against her pillows.

'This is no good,' she said, with a loud sigh. 'Are you cold?'

'A bit.'

'It's freezing in here.'

She threw the covers aside and went to the landing to fetch a thermal vest from the wardrobe. She threw it on the bed and in quick, practical movements, unbuttoned her pyjama top and slipped it off. John averted his eyes, suddenly shy that his wife was now naked from the waist up, sadly realising it was a sight he'd not seen for many weeks, if not months. The sidelight was still on, and in its glow he watched Liv sit at the foot of the bed, examining her armpit for ingrowing hairs before she put the vest on. He saw the side of her breast and, in that instant, felt an odd sense of warning, as though he needed to tell her to cover herself. She was being watched. The thought was fleeting, but convincing, and instinctively his gaze went to the empty corner of the room, wondering what he and Liv had let themselves in for.

Sometime in the middle of the night John woke, disturbed by an awareness of changes around him. He took a moment to realise where he was, in Nancy's old room, but something else demanded his attention, harder to comprehend. The air was thick and overly still, not cold as it had been when they went to bed, but now stuffy and humid. He stared at the wall near his side of the bed, the plaster looked mistrustful and pliable, as if it had grown a thick pale rind of skin. Gradually, he raised his head from the pillow to look at the corner. In the dimly lit room he saw a wallowing shadow there, crouched and menacing. He traced the outlines of a man's arm, held out towards him, and the side of a rough face, indistinct and angled in his direction. The figure was perfectly still, trying not to give itself away. John felt sweat breaking out across his forehead as the fear took hold, but he continued to stare at the corner, transfixed. Quietly, he slipped a hand free of the duvet, and reached for his mobile. He swiped the screen and activated the torch, shining its stark white light towards the man. Immediately, he saw the shape was nothing other than his own jacket, clumsily fallen from where he'd left it.

Liv stirred, next to him. 'What's going on?' she asked, sleepily.

'Nothing. It's nothing,' he replied. He switched off his mobile and lay back on the pillow, thinking she was right: he should make more effort not to leave his clothes on the floor.

Over the next few days he spent most of his time in the bedroom, working at his desk. Occasionally, when his computer screen timed out, he'd see a ghostly reflection of himself leaning over the keyboard. He studied this reflection, watching the corner of the room beyond his shoulder, because ever since that first night he'd felt a degree of dread about it. But in the flat grey surface of the monitor's screen he could see nothing; no wisp of the flickering movement he half expected. Liv thought it was odd that he spent so much time in the bedroom, but to John it made complete sense. Fear is not overcome in a single triumphant moment; it's dismantled by long hard hours of mundane time spent next to it. And it was working. Gradually, the room was becoming his.

From the little window near his desk he had a view over the garden, and often saw Mr Jelf digging in the veg patch or raking up leaves. He's caused a ton of trouble, John thought, watching the old man walking stiffly past the plants. Sometimes Nancy would run up to Mr Jelf, little trippy steps in her big wellies, handing him slices of cake, or would return to the house carefully carrying his vegetables like it was the most important job in the world. Occasionally, he watched Mr Jelf talking to himself, gesturing impatiently at various things in front of him. There was a chance, John considered, that the old man was messing with them out of some sort of grievance over losing his house. He'd lived there for thirty years, after all, never realising he was sitting on a sought after piece of real estate. River frontage, un-renovated – it was inevitable the cottage would be snapped up. Ultimately it was basic economics: a couple with savings put aside, looking to downshift in a rural idyll, coinciding with an old man's dwindling resources. It happened to be Liv and himself, but it could have been anyone. There was nothing other than that. Nothing personal. But Mr Jelf might see it differently.

John made sure that he folded his clothes away each night, so he wouldn't be disturbed by any shapes in the dark, and he was beginning to sleep soundly. But gradually he became aware that Liv was becoming unsettled. When she was in bed she turned repeatedly from side to side, mumbling in her sleep or kicking her legs. On one occasion, waking up with a return of an unwanted disturbance somewhere in the room, he saw her by the window, statue still, her head angled to one side as if she was listening.

'Liv?' he whispered. She didn't react. He climbed out of bed and approached her, cautiously. She didn't move. Her shallow breaths came in regular intervals, and he realised she was fast asleep.

Every weekday morning, he took Nancy in the car to preschool. It was a journey he always looked forward to. They talked easily about her friends, about her day ahead, and they liked to make up stories about the people they saw, particularly the dog walkers. Getting a dog was Nancy's big unspoken wish. But it was during one of these mornings, nearly at the preschool gates, when Nancy turned to face him and asked: 'Daddy, have *you* seen the man in the corner?'

Instantly, he was on full alert. 'What man?' he replied.

'In my old room.'

He slowed the car and pulled over to the verge.

'Why've we stopped?' Nancy asked, in her singsong voice.

'Just for a while,' he replied.

'We'll be late.'

He looked at her, thinking how carefully he needed to approach this subject. 'What man in the corner?' he asked, trying to sound playful.

She became deliberately matter-of-fact: 'A man, who stands in the corner. With no socks or shoes.'

'Nancy – love – have you seen this man?'

His daughter returned his gaze, steadily, but he could tell she was getting worried. She knew that she might be saying something wrong, that would get her in trouble. She looked out her window and stuck a thumb in her mouth. It was a gesture she hadn't done for months, since announcing she wasn't going to do it anymore.

'Darling,' he continued, softer now, 'I'm not angry. But I need to know. Have you seen this man?'

She shook her head, fast.

'Then how do you know about him?'

'Mr Jelf told me,' she replied.

Back at the house, John went to his office space, determined to prioritise work rather than dwell on what Nancy had told him. Liv was out at a meeting with Aisha, from the architects, to discuss plans. He soon found himself leaning back on his desk chair, unfocused and frustrated. What is it about work, he thought, that makes it so continually maddening? Years ago he could work all day long, or at least that's the impression he remembered, whereas now he seemed to focus for meagre two-minute chunks. Brief flurries of typing, followed by staring at the wall or checking his mobile. It was disastrous. Each time it happened, when he allowed his mind to wander, he came to the same conclusion: he was inert because he was surrounded by unresolved issues. His job was going nowhere. His marriage was limping along, searching for a new start that never arrived because in fact neither of them truly wanted it. They were probably only staying together for Nancy's sake. And now Nancy was talking about Mr Jelf's bogeyman. Liv would spit nails when she heard that.

Outside the bedroom window, Mr Jelf had lit a fire in a pile of damp wood and leaves, and was standing next to it holding a rake, watching the smoke billowing across the lawn towards the trees. John shut his eyes and listened to the house. Even though Liv was out and Nancy was at preschool, the house didn't seem entirely silent. He heard tiny creaks inside the walls and faint sighs as if a door was moving in a draught. He turned his computer off, thinking the whir of its cooling fan might be masking something else. Again, he listened. Sounds, constantly, some of them very close by. His skin pricked with fear. Slowly getting out of his chair, and afraid to look towards the corner behind him, he was certain the room had altered. It felt oppressive and claustrophobic and not a place he wanted to be in.

A few seconds later he was outside, determined to have it out with Mr Jelf. The old man saw him coming and seemed to turn his head away, busying himself with raking the soil in the veg patch. John felt his anger rising. Who exactly was this old man who was still in their garden? It wasn't his anymore. Why were they being so charitable to him?

'Mr Jelf,' John called, 'if you've got a minute, there's something I want your opinion on.'

Jelf stopped raking the soil, and John noticed it had already been done, earlier.

'In the garden?' Jelf asked.

'No. The house.'

Jelf stood calmly, leaning on the rake. 'Liv says I shouldn't come in.' He looked at John with that disconcerting sneer at the corners of his mouth.

'I *know* what she said. It won't take a minute.'

He led Jelf through the kitchen and up the stairs to the landing. The old man seemed large in the small space, stooping under the parts of the ceiling that sloped down towards the eaves.

'In here,' John said, trying to sound offhand. He guided Jelf towards the small bedroom, and pointed out a patch of damp on the ceiling. 'I was wondering whether that's an old stain, or whether it's something that needs fixing?' In fact, he'd already investigated the stain and knew it was nothing to worry about.

'Think that's old,' Mr Jelf answered. John noticed he was refusing to step across the threshold.

'Thought so. Well – thanks for looking.' He studied Mr Jelf, and noticed he was trying not to face the far corner of the room.

'What is it?' he asked. Jelf frowned and hung his head. 'Is it the man? Can you see the man in here?'

Jelf nodded, slowly, not raising his eyes.

John thought about how the room had changed in the few minutes before he had gone to fetch Mr Jelf. 'Where is he?' he asked.

The old man raised his head and looked directly into the room, moving his gaze slowly across the space.

'He's standing right by you.'

John felt something odd, prickling his skin. 'Here?' he asked, moving his arm slightly to one side.

'Yep.'

'What's he doing?'

Mr Jelf didn't turn to look. He announced, firmly: 'He's looking at your wife's things. In the drawer.'

In shock, John looked next to where he was standing, at the open drawer of Liv's dressing table, where she kept her underwear. He slid the drawer shut, trying hard to remember whether the drawer had been open when he'd left the room.

As expected, Liv was furious when she heard what Nancy had said on the way to preschool. 'He's got absolutely no right bringing *her* into this,' she said. 'She's just a child! When did he even speak to her?'

'Probably when she was helping him with the veg patch,' he answered. John was fairly sure Liv was searching for someone to blame.

'Have you *seen* Mr Jelf talking to her?' she asked. The architect's sketches were spread out on the kitchen table. It looked as though he'd interrupted something that was frustrating her.

'I think so.'

'When?'

'From our bedroom window. I've seen them chatting in the garden.'

Liv shook her head in disbelief. Nothing made her more angry than anything that might upset Nancy. Her only daughter. Her chief project. He was certain, now, that she'd moved him into the blame position: a man idly sitting at his desk while his daughter was told horror stories in the garden.

'So what do we do?' he asked.

'He's not coming here anymore.'

'OK. And how do we tell him?'

She turned back to look at the architect's plans. 'You'll find a way.'

A typical exchange, he thought, as he returned upstairs. He'd tried to share something they should both be concerned about, and should work together to fix, but within a couple of minutes the balance had shifted, his role now cast as someone who'd let the team down. *Jelf, you total shit*, he muttered, imagining the old man sitting in an armchair in the sheltered housing scheme by the bypass, effectively driving a wedge between him and Liv with his quixotic little half-smile.

John tried to work but his heart wasn't in it, so he decided to sort this situation out with Jelf once and for all. It took him ten minutes to drive to Heron Court, where he parked in one of the dedicated bays for visitors. Walking into the reception he tapped on the office door and pushed it open to see Michelle, the care manager, sitting in front of a computer. 'May I have a word,' he asked.

Michelle closed down a spreadsheet and turned to him, kindly and professional. 'Of course, John, how can I help you?'

'Just a casual question, really. About Mr Jelf.'

She didn't seem surprised. 'Fire away.'

‘Well – as you know, he’s been doing some work in our garden. But we think it might be confusing him, spending so much time at the house. We don’t think it’s a good idea anymore.’

Michelle nodded slowly, neither agreeing not disagreeing. Born to placate, John thought, unsure as to whether Michelle was an ally or not.

‘Perhaps – you know – he might be skipping his medication?’ he asked.

‘For his confusion?’

‘Yes.’

‘He’s not on any medication.’

‘Right.’

She turned to face her computer, again.

‘And if I could just ask,’ John continued, sounding foolish now, ‘does he sometimes – well – see things? In his room, perhaps?’

Michelle smiled, but he could see her patience would soon run thin. ‘We listen to all sorts of things in here, as you might imagine.’

Mr Jelf took the news calmly, or knew it was better all round if he didn’t react. He was sitting in a high-backed chair in the corner of the day room, and kept his eye on birds feeding from a plastic bowl stuck to the outside of the window while John told him what had been decided. ‘It’s just – well – Liv’s very certain of this,’ John said, cowardly. ‘She says it’s not right that Nancy could get upset. We can’t have her thinking the cottage is haunted.’ Mr Jelf looked back at him, slightly frowning, but with that oddly shaped mouth that seemed to suggest mockery. John knew he was already losing ground here, so he repeated the successful tone his wife had used: 'She's just a child,' he said. 'You shouldn't have told her.'

Mr Jelf shook his head: 'I didn't tell her anything.'

'You didn't?'

'No.'

John rubbed his face, weary with it all, unsure how to proceed. The old man seemed unruffled. They waited in silence as a caterer wheeled a noisy trolley of crockery through the room.

'Why would I tell her?' Mr Jelf asked.

'I don't know,' John replied, tersely. The only other people in the day room were a young woman sitting on a windowsill, and her father beside her. The woman had just shoved a framed photo of a sunset away from her, dismissively, and was leaning forward earnestly towards her father. John could hear the old man sucking on a boiled sweet.

He lent forward so his conversation wouldn't be overheard: 'You've got to understand, Mr Jelf. This is a new start for my family. I want it all to be OK. I don't want them getting scared about the cottage being, well, having *a presence*. It's a lovely place.' He stood up to leave, wanting to get out of there as quick as possible. 'I want it to feel like a home.'

He handed over the apples he'd picked up at the supermarket, which he'd put in a plain brown paper bag.

'From the orchard?' Mr Jelf asked.

John looked at the shiny, neat apples, and knew he couldn't lie. 'Not really,' he said. He put them on the table and turned to go. But he quickly knew he'd regret it if he did. He slowly sat down on the chair again.

'But while I'm here, Mr Jelf, perhaps it's best if you tell me a little more about – about the apparition?'

He saw a flicker of interest in the old man's eyes. 'You've seen him?'

'No. Not as such.'

'You will.'

John noticed his palms were clammy, so wiped them on his trousers. He couldn't quite believe he was having this surreal conversation. 'I want you to know I don't believe in things like this.'

'So why are you asking?' Mr Jelf replied, with a touch of impatience.

Unable to answer, John just nodded his head, dumbly. 'I guess – because I want to know if it's – why it's so interested in my wife? You said it was looking at her. Then looking at her things. Her personal items.'

'That's right.'

'So, why?'

Mr Jelf leant forward for emphasis. 'He's called the River Man.' He lifted a hand and waved it back and forth, pointing through the window at the fields. 'And he's been known in several places along the river, and I've heard some people reckon it's the soul of a man that drowned. He's been in several of the houses.'

'Which houses?'

'That I don't know.'

'But now he seems to be at the cottage.'

Mr Jelf nodded. 'Five or ten years, yes.'

'Like he's taken up residence? But why?'

Mr Jelf chuckled, unpleasantly. 'Often wondered that myself. Some of the old timers think he latches onto something. He senses what you want, and sets out to ruin it.'

'You're an old timer yourself, Mr Jelf.'

'I'm talking about them that's older than me – most of 'em dead by now.'

John ran a hand through his hair, exasperated. 'Do you actually believe *any* of this?'

Mr Jelf looked back at him with a steely calmness: 'My sister used to live in that room. Ten years ago, she got ill in there. Started to sleep walk. Found her out in the garden a few times, making no sense of where she was. She told me about the man just a few days before she went.'

'Went?'

'Sleepwalking I suppose. They found her body in the river, trapped in the reeds.'

Returning to the cottage, John stopped by the road bridge to gaze along the river. On one side was an overgrown millpond where the water was deep and thick with weeds. In the other direction, leading to their cottage, the river narrowed beneath a line of willows. During the summer, reeds had grown in deep green swathes along the banks, and dust and seeds had settled on the calm water. Now, the banks were thick with mud and brambles and the trees were bare and dark. He could see the cottage in the distance and – from this angle – realised it was undeniably part of the river's ecosystem. Its air was the air of the river; damp and ancient and green. The river's breath swept across the garden, rose up against the cottage's windows, flowed through its rooms, bringing a sense of abundant, verdant life in summer, then a marshy decay in winter.

You can look at this winter landscape two ways, he reminded himself. Either see it full of potential, of endless renewal and regeneration: roots buried, waiting to sprout when the warmth reaches them, buds on the trees, bullet-hard, but with fresh green leaves waiting to emerge. Either that, or see it as continual struggle and menace: thorns out to scratch you, branches withering then falling from the trees, mud and stench and leaf rot piling up in layers of decay.

John considered the sight of their cottage and wondered whether it would be the fresh start the family needed, or just an acceleration into an unhappy stage in life, where more and more he saw himself and Liv living separately. The stresses of bringing up a young daughter, the unspoken refusal to have a second child, the emergence of a new way of behaving which seemed transactional and a daily negotiation just to avoid resentment and bitterness.

As soon as he walked back in, Liv asked how it had gone with Mr Jelf.

'He took it well,' John answered. 'I told him Nancy was too young to be hearing this kind of stuff, and that we wanted a period of cooling down.'

'You said that?'

'More or less. I think he understood the gist. I suggested it might be good for him to distance himself from here, the cottage was bound to confuse him. And I explained we had his best interests at heart, because he needed to be given time and space.' He was casting himself as a capable moderator, sensitive when he had to be, then tough and direct when it was required. 'I said he shouldn't come round anymore, and we could look after the veg patch ourselves.'

'Can we?'

'I offered to drop some of the kale and spinach round to him when they're ready. And if the slugs get them, then I can always get some veg from the supermarket and pass it off as ours.'

'He'll know.'

He thought about the bag of shiny apples he'd given to Mr Jelf. 'Maybe. Maybe not.'

Liv looked at him closely, unimpressed with his breeziness. He didn't like the scrutiny. 'Did he mention the apparition?'

'Not really.'

'But something?'

'No.' John continued in his offhand way. 'Nothing more than he said before.' He couldn't lie in front of Liv. She always knew. He rapidly changed tack: 'You know – I have this suspicion that the whole thing's just something he's made up.'

'Why?'

'Because this is his house, and we've taken it from him.'

'He doesn't seem like that kind of man.'

'But in fact, we know nothing about him, do we? He could be a real vindictive bastard.'

He woke suddenly in the middle of the night. The air was stuffy, damp, and smelling of the river. He listened to the house and heard faint cracks from the floorboards outside the room. Going to find out what it was, he discovered Liv standing halfway down the stairs, paused by the small window that overlooked the river. She was very still and seemed to be listening to something but – as he approached – he realised she was fast asleep, her head turned to one side, her eyes half-closed. He hesitated, thinking how strange and otherworldly she looked. Her expression was anxious. It was cold on the stairs, much colder than in their room. He gently touched her shoulder, and tried to guide her back. She resisted. Her body felt heavy and solid, her bare feet planted firmly on the steps. 'Come on,' he whispered, but knew it wasn't right to wake her in this state. He put his arm around her waist and encouraged her to return to their bedroom. She came, compliant, but still with a sense of unwillingness, and as they reached the doorway she spoke, quiet but determined:

'I don't want to go in.'

The room was shadowy and quiet in front of them. He held her for reassurance, but saw from her face that she was still asleep.

'The man is here,' she said.

He made no mention of it in the morning. Liv seemed distracted, with heavy shadows beneath her eyes, and at breakfast showed no sign of wanting to eat. She made a pot of coffee out of habit, but left it on the side while she stared through the window, towards the river. Rain was falling steadily, and the garden looked subdued and oppressive.

'What's up?' he asked, quietly.

She pushed the pot of coffee away, as if not liking the smell. 'Do you think we've made the right choices?' she asked. 'I'm not talking about the renovation. I'm talking about the entire project. Moving here. You think it's a mistake?'

She deserved honesty, he thought. 'I'm not sure. I'm really not.'

She faced him, weary. 'Is it going to rain all day?'

'I think so.'

'So we're trapped. In here.'

Her expression scared him. A simple plea, for something to be done. He wanted to ask her about her dreams from the night, whether there was anything they might learn from them, but was scared to ask in case it unlocked something neither of them would understand.

'Liv – let's get in the car and go for a drive,' he suggested.

'And go where?'

'Dunno – let's just see where we end up. Just – get away from here.'

She looked as though it was the best option among poor choices. 'I'll get my coat.'

They drove for an hour, avoiding main roads, going down narrow lanes between the hedgerows, passing gaps where the wintry fields looked bleak and misty with rain. The windscreen wipers were on constantly. At each junction he paused the car, idly deciding which direction to go. Stopping at a farm shop they walked numbly around the aisles, while the rain drummed on the roof above them. They ate lunch there, then decided to spend a lot of money on food for the evening. They hardly talked, they'd wasted the day, the whole trip felt like a farewell of sorts, but as they drove back there was a feeling that, strangely, they'd done something right.

Nancy was excited that both her parents had come to pick her up from preschool, and as they drove back to the cottage the mood seemed to be lifting, filled with Nancy's busy chatting. There's nothing to dread, John thought, as he parked the car outside the cottage. Unease can grow in calm spaces, but you move and it quickly falls apart. It's more fragile than you think.

He spent the evening cooking, which always relaxed him. While he cooked he saw glimpses through the open doorway of

Liv and Nancy, their feet up on the sofa, a blanket across them, watching children's TV. He paused, humbled and amazed by the glimpse of family, took a step to one side, removing them from view, then stepped back to frame them again, seeing all that he had once more.

Sitting up in bed that night, he watched Liv brushing her hair in front of her dressing table. She was letting it grow, and had gathered it to one side to run the brush through it with long, downward strokes. It had been a good day. Nothing exceptional. Nothing to remember. But a step in the right direction. This was a place they could live in, after all, and if they put their mind to it, they knew how to reinvent themselves.

Liv brushed her hair in rhythmic strokes, and he grew slowly uneasy about it. There was something too regular about the way she was doing it, too sensual, almost hypnotic. Gradually she lowered the brush and let it dangle from her hand, as if she was going to drop it. He cast his eye to the corner of the room, instinctively, and sensed the air becoming humid and unpleasant. And when he glanced back at Liv, he noticed she had angled her head to one side, trying to listen to something. He was about to speak when he noticed some of her hairs, on that side of her head, beginning to rise with static. Not daring to move, he watched the hairs lift together, then move, caught in the glow of her side lamp towards a focal point an inch or two away from her, as if attracted to an unseen object.

'Liv,' he whispered, fearful. 'Liv!'

She startled, as if a jolt of energy had woken her up. She turned towards him, disorientated, her eyes struggling to focus.

'Did you fall asleep?'

She shook her head. 'Oh – I'm so tired. I think so.'

He quickly got out of bed and sat with her, putting his arm round her shoulders. Her skin felt cold and clammy.

'What just happened?' he asked, worried.

'I don't know.'

He nodded, resting his forehead against her shoulder.

'Why don't you sleep in with Nancy, tonight?'

She took her time to answer. 'Why?'

'It would make me feel better. This room's damp. I want to sort it out. Get a de-humidifier.'

'You're not making much sense.'

'I know. But perhaps – just tonight?'

'The room's damp?' she mumbled, and he wondered whether she was drifting back to sleep. She didn't sound entirely coherent.

'There's that damp patch on the ceiling. It's rained all day and I think it's going to drip on the bed. You're best off in with Nancy.'

'What about you?'

'I'll take the sofa, downstairs.'

She stroked his wrist. 'John, we had a good day, today.'

'Yeah. Yeah we did.'

'OK. I'll go and share with Nancy.'

'Promise?'

'John – you're sounding weird.'

'Sorry – it's just – it's going to rain all night. We shouldn't sleep in here.'

'Right. I get it.'

He vowed to himself, the following day, that they'd never sleep in the small room again. But convincing Liv would be tricky. He prided himself on being rational, and was going to have to persuade her without admitting that he now believed that room was haunted. He didn't want to tell her that the presence seemed to have singled her out, latching on to her, and that several times he'd found her sleepwalking. Last night, the image of her brushing her hair in a sensual trancelike state – it had deeply unsettled him.

Deciding it might be best to discuss it over a bottle of wine, he drove to the local supermarket. He almost didn't see Mr Jelf until he was nearly too late. The old man was standing by a row of tins and cereals, and was clearly agitated. John held back, retreating behind the end of the aisle to conceal himself, as Mr Jelf lumbered towards him. Jelf was talking out loud and, just a few feet away, John listened as the old man remonstrated with someone nearby. The words weren't clear but it seemed like he was telling someone to go away. Carefully, John edged forward to look down the aisle, wondering who else was involved. Mr Jelf was in the middle of the aisle, arguing with himself.

As he paid for the wine, he told the cashier there was an old man in a distressed state. They could both hear Mr Jelf's voice, now raised to a series of tight angry shouts, from behind the aisles.

'It's OK,' the cashier answered, sympathetically. 'He's often in here. We're used to him.'

As he drove up to the cottage, John was suddenly clear about what he had to do. So far, he'd been on the receiving end: afraid of an old man's stories, afraid of a strange masculine presence in his own home. It had made him, in turn, afraid of his family's reactions, and exposed how precarious his relationship was. Now, seeing the tormented state Mr Jelf had been in, he knew the answer was to fight, actively, for what he had. Nancy would be integral to his quickly forming plan. He went straight to her and asked what she wanted most in the world. He already knew the answer and she delivered it as predicted: a dog. 'Right,' he answered. 'Well – guess what – we're going to get you a dog next week, and you can choose it.' She clutched her hands together in simple delight. 'And Nancy,' he continued, making it sound like another gift, 'I was thinking, why don't you make your bedroom in the play room, next to the lounge? That room upstairs is too big and empty, and if the dog sleeps downstairs, then you can be near the dog at night?' It was a plan that was craftily suggested, but he knew it also made total sense, and he congratulated himself in the discovery of yet another reinvention of the cottage's limited choice of spaces. 'What do you think,' he asked? The whole negotiation was achieved within five minutes, and John happily listened as Nancy ran to tell her mother what was going to happen, in the simple steps he'd outlined.

Liv listened, clearly suspecting John was behind it, but struggling to understand his motives. They'd already agreed to get Nancy a dog, so she couldn't really object. 'Good,' John said, sealing the deal, marvelling at this new drive to take action. They spent the weekend moving furniture, once more. Nancy, excited to be claiming the play room, with a view into the lounge where they placed a brand new pet basket, and them moving back into their old bedroom. It was all done by Saturday evening. He slept soundly and deeply that night and knew, instinctively, that Liv was not going to sleepwalk anymore. Not in this room.

Over the following few days John took over the small bedroom, turning it into his study. Working there felt like being a sentry, monitoring the malignant force that he'd briefly but foolishly allowed to come too close to his family. Through the window he viewed the garden, now empty because Mr Jelf had also been dealt with. And the presence of the River Man, thwarted, stuck in there with him, but kept at bay, unable to influence his wife. Occasionally John noticed the room began to mutate around him, becoming damp and oppressive as the river scent rose, but as the days passed it seemed to be growing weaker, and happening less and less. He filled the room with his files and papers and worked continually through the day, productive, resilient, writing with his heart and soul and enjoying every last word of it, and once in a while turning in his desk chair to face the mysterious corner, where he would give a broad, undefeated smile, towards whatever might be there.

As expected, Liv began to sleep soundly, as if an unknown burden had been lifted. John never told her how he'd tackled the presence. He left her to sleep late each morning, while he established a routine of going into the small room and working before the others were up. The glorious hour or two when he was awake and his family were asleep. This is how you dismantle the superstitions that swirl around these old places, he thought. You listen to the stories, you get scared, then you realise how stupid you're being. By holding up the multifaceted light of family life, or the endeavour of focused work, you can defeat this nonsense.

He leant back in his chair and shut down the computer. It was still early and the room felt truly empty. For the first time since he'd moved in to this cottage, he knew it had been purged of whatever it was that had once lingered here. Liv would be awake soon, so he went down to the kitchen and began cooking her favourite breakfast: slow cooked tomatoes. He used the punnet full of late season crop they'd grown in the garden, and enjoyed pushing the mixture of tomatoes around with the tip of the wooden spatula. The butter slowly became rich and glazed. As he slid the tomatoes onto the toast he realised the windows had steamed up. He gave the pane a quick wipe and, beyond the wintery green of the lawn and the stiff brown reeds by the river, he glimpsed a fragment of white that shouldn't be there.

The pan crashed onto the floor as he flung the door open and raced across the lawn, his lungs shocked by the cold air. He reached the riverbank and leapt into the broad mass of reeds, landing painfully among the stalks. A surge of water and foul mud swept up around him. He saw Liv, drifting in front of him, lying on her back still dressed in her nightwear, her face pale and without expression. As he pushed towards her she rolled dreamily onto her front, hanging face down in the green river water. He wallowed, agonisingly slow, forcing his way through the reeds, fighting to untangle the thicket of stalks, his feet sinking into deep icy mud. He stretched out an arm, shouting her name, and saw her hand floating in the ripples of water, just beyond reach.